On Sale
June 3, 2025

Paperback
ISBN: 979-8-88574-051-7
5.5 x 8.5, 280 pages
Tentative Price: $16.95

Also available in eBook

Hub City Press
186 West Main St.
Spartanburg, SC 29306
(864) 577-9349
www.hubcity.org

Distributed to the Trade By
Publishers Group West
1700 Fourth Street
Berkeley, CA 94718
(510) 809-3700

BOD

In 1994, the real fictitious town of Bodock in Claygardner County, Mississippi. In the wake of the storm, what is left unbroken, and what broken things can be rebuilt? Hailed by Maurice Carlos Ruffin as "leaving no feeling untouched," Robert Busby's debut balances grit with heart, violence with depth, and tragedy with humor.

Two siblings survey the damage to their family's orchard after the storm while their rich nephew circles in the hopes of buying up the property. A slacker divorcee drives his ex-father-in-law to his lung transplant surgery. A cop tries to piece his broken family back together in the wake of the loss of his son. In 1816, a farmer's wife plots with an enslaved woman to stop her husband from committing a terrible act. And in a town that is not quite Bodock, a population of ghosts reckon with their unsettled pasts. In the spirit of Brad Watson's *Last Days of the Dog-Men*, Bodock traverses time and dimensions to surface the struggles of the everyday.

Bodock: Stories is the winner of the 2024 C. Michael Curtis Short Story Book Prize.

ABOUT THE AUTHOR

Robert Busby writes, runs, and raises two humans with his wife in Memphis, Tennessee. Before that he grew up in a small dry town in the hill country of North Mississippi and got his MFA in fiction at Florida International University in Miami. His stories have appeared in various literary magazines and anthologies, including *Arkansas Review, Cold Mountain Review, Flash!: Writing the Very Short Story, Footnote, Mississippi Noir, PANK, Sou'wester,* and *Surreal South.*

ADVANCE READING COPY 6/3/25

BODOCK
STORIES

ROBERT BUSBY

HUB CITY PRESS
SPARTANBURG, SC

THIS IS AN UNCORRECTED PROOF COPY AND IS NOT FOR SALE.
BEFORE QUOTING FOR REVIEW, PLEASE CONSULT THE FINAL EDITION
OR CHECK WITH THE PUBLISHER.

Copyright © 2025 Library of Congress
Robert Busby Cataloging-in-Publication Data TK

All rights reserved. No part of this book may be reproduced in any form or by any electronic means, including information storage and retrieval systems, without permission in writing from the publisher, except by a reviewer, who may quote brief passages in a review.

Cover design: Kate McMullen
Cover image © NPL DeA Picture
   Library/Bridgeman Images
Interior layout: Kate McMullen
Author photograph ©
Proofreaders:

If you've read the galley, we'd love to hear what you think!
PUBLICITY CONTACT: KATE MCMULLEN / KATE@HUBCITY.ORG / 864.577.9349

PUB DATE: 6.3.25, 5.5x8.5 | $16.95 Paperback (979-8-88574-051-7)
This is an uncorrected proof copy and is not for sale. Before quoting for review, please consult the final edition or check with the publisher.

dedication TK

CONTENTS

Mistletoe — 00

Fraternal Twins — 00

Steer Away from That Darkness — 00

Seasonus Exodus — 00

Bodock, 1816–1834 — 00

The Parable of the Lung — 00

Stubborn as a Fence Post — 00

Heartworms — 00

Frison the Bison — 00

Twenty Mile — 00

Offerings — 00

MISTLETOE

Noon, and another dump truck drove by the farmhouse on County Road 336 between the Thaxton and Friendship communities in Claygardner County. It was the fifth one today. The truck hurled a volley of air through the kudzu along the far side of the road and some of the vines caught the draft and lifted, spreading out and shivering like the arms of primitive Baptists. The truck groaned as it pulled itself up the hill, hauling gravel from Eutuban Lumber & Quarry out to Highway 6. Raymond Vaught could tell it was gravel the trucks were carrying. Bits of it flew up and out of the dump bucket and skipped across the pavement instead of exploding like the clods of red dirt the trucks had been hauling the previous few days.

"Was this all you had for lunch, Raymond?" Faye asked from the kitchen.

From the front window, Raymond glanced back at the large bunch of mistletoe he had been contemplating in the bodock tree in his yard before the truck blew by. When he'd worked the wheelchair around, he propelled himself toward his sister in the kitchen. Carpet and linoleum flooring defined the two rooms. Faye's hair was in a bouffant, and she gestured at the bowl of English peas on the kitchen table. Next to the bowl was the respirator Raymond had taken breathing treatments on every morning since he was diagnosed with throat cancer two years ago and his larynx was removed.

Faye brought the bowl to the sink and poured its contents down the drain. "If I'd known you was eating cold canned vegetables again, I could of brought some more stew over."

She began rinsing the bowl under the faucet. Raymond maneuvered the chair over to the sink, slid his hand under the white kerchief tied around his neck, and placed his thumb over the tracheotomy hole. The square edge of the counter pressed against his under arm when he reached up with his other hand to turn off the water.

"Shit, Faye. You ain't come over here to wash dishes."

Faye set the bowl in the porcelain sink and dried her hands with the rag on the counter. She looked out the window above the sink at the land stretching behind the house for fifty acres before it eased in the direction of Highway 6 for another fifty, land that all three of them had grown up on. When their father, Ike, died fifteen years ago in 1979, agriculture had mostly ceased on the land already. The twenty-acre orchard at the back of the property had gone to Faye, along with the farmhouse and the handful of equities and stocks Ike had felt comfortable leaving in the Peoples Bank in Bodock even after the Crash.

"Phil came by my house a couple of days ago," she said. Phil was the only son of their late brother, Horace. "He asked me about selling some land."

Horace had been older than Raymond by two years and had inherited the first forty acres of land directly behind the farmhouse. But three days after their father's funeral, Horace lost his inheritance to Raymond in a game of Texas Hold 'Em. Raymond owned that land now along with the barn and the back forty the barn resided on, which had made up his own inheritance.

"Why's he bothering you about Horace's share?"

"He wants to buy mine," Faye said.

Raymond said, "You tell him no?"

"I didn't," Faye said.

"What about your orchard?"

Fayed looked down. Raymond noticed the gray hem of hair at her roots when he followed her eyes to his missing leg.

"I don't want to sell the orchard. Daddy left it to me. I just wasn't sure what to do. I wasn't sure if we was going to be able to keep it maintained. Especially now after the, um, ice storm. I mean," Faye said, still gripping the hand towel, tugging at the fabric. "I mean Jason ain't in no shape to do it, even if I knew where he was."

Faye's son, Jason, had been in and out of prison since he was in high school for a slew of drug-related offenses. He was thirty-two now. In the brief windows of sobriety Jason had enjoyed since he was a teenager, Raymond had hired him alongside the migrants and local high school boys looking for work during the peach harvest Raymond had overseen every summer. Since his amputation, Raymond hadn't figured out yet how he'd manage to stay on the hired help so they kept working instead of sneaking naps under the generous shade the orchard afforded or smoking marijuana at the top of a ladder, inconspicuous there amongst the branches.

"I ain't dead," Raymond said. "I just ain't got a leg. What'd you tell Phil?"

"I told him you handled that stuff," Faye said. "I told him the decision was up to you. He said he'd probably drop by this afternoon to talk to you."

The night Raymond won Horace's property, it was just the two of them playing poker and shooting the shit in a backroom of the Feed Mill Restaurant. Then Beauregard Eutuban approached the table to give his condolences before asking to sit in a few hands. Horace was shitfaced by then and obliged and, after he lost all his money to Eutuban, bet his share of the property on the next hand in an effort to get out of the hole. Raymond, who wasn't much more sober than his brother, tried to talk Horace out of it but Eutuban pointed out that the bet was already on the table. Eutuban called so Raymond bought in as well, too drunk to determine a more viable option for keeping the land in the family. Raymond lucked out and won with a three-of-a-kind when he landed a nine of clubs on the river.

The next morning, Raymond and Horace awoke in the cab of Horace's Chevrolet C10 pickup. They were parked in the middle of the backyard of the farmhouse. Raymond stepped out to have a smoke and stretch and realized he was still about half drunk when he had to support himself on the side of the truck until he found his legs.

"You believe that black sumbitch?" Horace said. "Pop'd roll over in his grave he knew how damn close we came to losing all this. Hah. That rich asshole had an agenda the minute he sat down, you know?"

Raymond had his arms over the bed of the truck, squinting out one eye from the smoke wafting from the Winston tucked in the corner of his mouth. He took the cigarette between his fingers, looked at Horace through the dusty back glass of the truck's rear window. "That," Raymond said, pointing just beyond them both, "that'd been Eutuban land." He jarred the pillar of ash off the end of the cigarette into the bed of the truck and motioned to his left. "My land was safe. I got the money to cover my ass if I'd lost."

His brother was mute on that point so Raymond pushed himself off the truck. Something underneath the passenger seat distracted him. He took a knee and pulled out the worn baseball mitt he'd used playing third base for Bodock High School. In the pocket of the glove was a baseball, stained copper with the red clay that covered the infield of every ball park in northeast Mississippi. He slipped his hand into the glove, punched the ball into it a couple of times, the sound of leather applauding in the early morning quiet.

"Mine?" Raymond asked, holding the glove up to Horace.

"Yeah," Horace said. "Phil's broke. Needed one to try out for junior varsity first base so I let him borrow yours. Must've left it in here after practice."

"This ain't a first baseman's mitt," Raymond said.

"Hell, know that," Horace said. "That one was just gonna get him by until I could get paid."

Raymond tossed the ball into the air. When he caught the ball, he made a slow move like he was throwing out a runner at first who'd forgotten to tag up. He took the glove off and walked it over to the truck and placed it on the dashboard. From behind the pack of Winstons in his shirt pocket, Raymond removed the wad of Horace's money that Raymond had won back from Eutuban—along with the Eutuban L&Q check Eutuban made out to cover the difference of the value of the land Horace had wagered—and fit the wad between the ball and the glove.

"What's that?" Horace asked.

"Money to buy Phil a decent glove," Raymond said. He said, "It's yours for the land."

A month later, Horace got drunk and ran the used Charger he purchased with part of the check off Rufus's Bridge, where he drowned in Dob's Creek below. No one was living in the farmhouse then—Faye was residing in the city limits of Bodock, married to a state trooper from the Delta—and so Raymond moved in there shortly afterwards.

After Faye left, Raymond adjusted the parking brake on the wheelchair and pulled up his khaki pants leg, removed the shoe from his left foot and slid off his sock. At the end of his big toe were the same signs of discoloration and dead skin his right foot had shown. Two months ago, Raymond's right leg was amputated at the knee, the arteries so clogged from the smoking habit he'd started when he was fifteen and managed for fifty years they couldn't pump down the antibiotics needed to heal the sore, keep that gangrene from taking root.

Now the left foot buzzed with the same faint tingling sensation. He opened a drawer next to the pantry and retrieved the box of silver nitrate sticks he'd nabbed from his nurse's medical bag yesterday while she was in the bathroom caking makeup on her face. He removed a stick from the box and ran some tap water over one end to activate it and set to work burning off the edges of dead skin so the nurse wouldn't notice. He had no intentions of losing both legs. Had the shotgun out in the utility room if no other solution presented itself. More than once the nitrate wandered off the nerveless areas and he winced at the pain.

Then Raymond worked himself into his waistcoat and retrieved a plastic bottle of Coke from the fridge. The Coke was flat. Raymond topped it off with a little bourbon, took a pack of Nabs from the pantry, and managed the wheelchair over the hump in the doorway and down the plywood ramp he built before the surgery. Raymond avoided scraping the Buick in the carport with the wheelchair and parked beneath the awning of the house. Tore open the Nabs with his teeth. He became thirsty after a few peanut butter crackers and pulled on the Coke as another truck roared by. MDOT was supposed to have broken ground on the road construction three weeks ago. But the ice storm had delayed the work until power was restored in the county this week and the streets and highways had been cleared of debris.

Raymond's gaze fell once more on the bodock stretched across the front yard. The tree had survived the storm mainly intact. At the base of one of the bodock's thick branches grew some mistletoe that had endured the storm as well. By itself the shrub could kill the limb it clung to. Raymond had seen mistletoe do that and worse. Had paid witness to the shrub's hurried reproduction, how three or four shrubs could rot out half a live oak a hundred feet tall. Raymond was considering his options for taking care of the mistletoe when a new Buick LeSabre pulled into the driveway and parked within a few feet of where Raymond was sitting. Gravel dust curled around the back end of the car that gleamed with a fresh coat of white paint. The shocks breathed a sigh of relief when Phil squeezed himself out. Gravel clicked beneath the scuffed leather soles of his loafers as he made his way to Raymond.

"Evening, Uncle," Phil said. Phil worked at a GM dealership over in Tupelo twenty miles east of Bodock. The white button-down Raymond's nephew wore had the dealership's logo stitched to the left breast pocket. His name tag was pinned to the right side of the shirt. His head was shaped like a gourd.

Raymond held the pack of crackers up at Phil. "Nab?" he said.

"Nah."

"Sure?"

Phil patted his gut. "I'm good."

Raymond shrugged and set the pack in his lap and rubbed his hands together to brush off the salt and crumbs. He drew a handkerchief from his shirt pocket, held it to his trach, and hocked into the cloth. Raymond nodded at the LeSabre. "What's with the Buick?"

Phil glanced at the car as if it were his first time seeing it as well. "This here's the '94 LeSabre. Clearance sale, making way for when the '95s come off the truck in a few months." Phil ran a finger along the crease between the hood and side panel. He picked some pine needles from the windshield wipers and released the needles to the ground. He nodded at Raymond's LeSabre in the carport. "GM's made some changes since they put out that model."

Phil started to rattle off the upgrades but Raymond told his nephew to quit treating him like one of his customers. Before the operation, to see if he wanted to trade in his own LeSabre, he'd done some research on the new models. So he knew, for instance, that the frame was longer than his model's year by four inches and wider by nearly a foot-and-a-half. He also knew the headlamps were replaced with streamlined ones, that the engine had been updated from a 3.8-liter V-6 to the new 3.8 Series I.

"Faye was by this morning." He eyed his nephew as he pulled from the Coke.

"Guessing you know why I'm here, then," Phil said.

Raymond nodded. "Even if they hadn't sawed off my driving foot, another discount on a new car ain't fixing to get me to sell you the orchard."

"I didn't bring the car over here to bribe you, Raymond," Phil said. "But go for a ride with me anyway. Hear me out. If I can't get you to reconsider this afternoon, I'll drop the business altogether."

Once Phil had helped Raymond in the passenger seat, they turned right out of the driveway onto County Road 336. The car didn't smell new so much as clean and he appreciated the added interior room the longer frame afforded his one leg. Raymond thought about telling Phil to give the car some gas, see exactly how the Series I engine was all that different from the regular V-6. He decided against it and took a another pull from the Coke.

"Know I ain't got to tell you," Phil said, "but be careful not to spill that in the demo."

In the console cup holder was a McDonald's cup. Raymond drew the straw from the plastic lid and stuck the straw into the bottle. "Better?" Raymond asked.

They came to Cane Creek Road and Phil hung a right and headed south, away from the orchard, toward where the road construction was beginning at the intersection of 15 and 6. Trees had fallen near the road during the storm and now lay collected in brush piles along the shoulders of the highway. Some of the openings the fallen trees had left in the woods flanking the old road held stretches of ground for hundreds of yards where at one time you couldn't see more than twenty feet into the thicket.

Raymond sipped from the straw. "You fixing to tell me where we're going?"

Phil went to drink from the McDonald's cup. He realized the straw was gone when his mouth got nothing but air. He removed the plastic lid and let it fly out the window. "You been out to check the damage in the orchard?"

"I'm sure it's minimal," Raymond said. "Besides, we don't prune em until March anyway. If we lost a scaffold branch, we still got enough shoots to choose its replacement from."

Phil waited a minute before saying, "I'm aware how much I'm

asking here for Faye to give up her peaches and all."

"So you ain't planning on getting into the preserves business?"

Phil chomped ice. "We both know I don't have any use for twenty acres of peach trees."

They'd driven two or three miles down the highway by then and were coming within view of the road construction. A bored heavyset traffic flagger wearing a yellow vest continued spinning the pole with a stop sign affixed at the top as she waved Phil and Raymond through. Phil pulled off onto the shoulder once they were past her. A hundred yards beyond the car, convicts in orange coveralls dismantled a brush pile and loaded the trees into a dump truck parked nearby, making way for the bulldozer spreading gravel over the dirt path that had been laid parallel to the original two lanes of the highway.

"Okay," Phil said. Once he'd shifted into park, he went into his spiel. There was a two-year timeframe for the road construction project, which was to convert Highway 6 into four-lane to better accommodate traffic between Oxford and Tupelo. But in those fifty miles, there wasn't a single fill-up station. The trucks were driving thirty or forty miles in either direction just to pump diesel. Phil wanted to remedy their problem by building a truck stop where Faye's orchard sat adjacent to Highway 6.

"And once construction's done," Phil said, "there'll still be a need for a truck stop on the highway, with the National Furniture factory and the county school bus system and all. With the income from the convenience store merchandise, I'll be able to about give away the damn diesel."

"All right," Raymond said and polished off the bourbon-and-Coke before returning the straw to the McDonald's cup. "But Faye ain't gonna sell you the orchard so you can build a Texaco there."

"She'll do it if you tell her to."

Raymond said, "But I ain't fixing to tell her to."

Phil stared at Raymond for a second. Raymond rested his head in his hand, his elbow propped up on the armrest of the door. Phil said okay and reached behind him. The steering wheel cut a crease in his gut when he leaned up and removed a pair of binoculars from the black leather case he had retrieved from the backseat. He concentrated on the convicts through the binoculars before handing the lenses to Raymond. "Look," he said when Raymond accepted the binoculars. "There, at the one to the far right."

Raymond furrowed his brow. He started to speak but instead of bringing his thumb to his trach, he took the binoculars in both hands and directed his attention to a convict wearing a blue toboggan and struggling to drag a branch from the brush pile to a dump truck parked nearby. When the convict reached the truck, he used his thigh for leverage and catapulted the limb into the dump bucket. The pile of timber in the truck quivered when the branch landed. The convict turned towards them and Raymond could tell by the hem of bare skin around the convict's toboggan that his head had been shaved. His pale, skeletal face was blue from the cold, his eyes dark and heavy and deeply set into their sockets. The rest of his body seemed as emaciated, his frame struggling to announce itself under the oversized coveralls. Raymond didn't immediately recognize him.

"Goddamn. That's Jason," Raymond said.

"Yep. Was driving through here yesterday on my way back from Tupelo. Thought I seen my cousin in this chain gang or whatever. Pulled a U-turn and confirmed it. Had Cal Albertson look into it. Jason was arrested over a week ago after his car was searched at a roadblock on Buford Pusser Highway just outside Selmer. Raymond, they found a damn Ziploc bag full of Percocet in the floorboard beneath his seat. He already had himself a outstanding warrant here in Mississippi so the great state of Tennessee got Jason off their hands and released his transfer back here. Bail's been set at $25,000. Hearing's gonna be next week."

"Faye know about this?" Raymond said.

"If she does, she ain't heard it from me. Obviously ain't made bail though. So I'm guessing she don't."

"And the hearing's next week?"

"Wednesday," Phil said. "Preliminary. Cal told me this was Jason's third offense. Or fourth. Looking at a maximum of six-to-ten in Parchman but said with the right lawyer he could probably get off with a two-year sentence suspended to probation. House arrest, at the worst."

Raymond didn't say anything. The binoculars rested in his lap and he watched Jason return to the pile and pull two branches, dragging one in each arm. A dump truck rushed by and the momentum caused the car to sway. The truck approached a large mound of dirt adjacent to the pile of gravel the bulldozers were feeding from. The dump truck climbed up one side of the dirt pile, inclined its bucket, and deposited its contents. Coughed exhaust into the gray air before driving away.

"Look," Phil said, "what Cal meant by 'right lawyer' is one other than some court-appointed attorney that ain't fixing to give two shits about how long some drug addict gets sentenced. And the kind of representation needed to keep Jason out of prison? Could run pretty high, you know. And I'm pretty sure I can convince Cal to go ahead and represent Jason himself, save Faye some time having to find a lawyer on her own. Might could probably even convince Cal to do it near pro bono."

"That's awful goddamn convenient for you," Raymond said. "Did you come up with your truck stop plan before or after you found out Jason'd been arrested?"

"You think whatever you want, Raymond," Phil said. "Not gonna change the fact Faye's son's going to the pen for a long damn time unless you convince Faye to sell me her land."

"Might be best thing for that boy to spend a few years picking cotton on a prison farm."

"Don't doubt you there. But Faye's gonna find out about this business sooner or later. Wouldn't be surprised if something about it ran in the *Bodock Post* this Wednesday. And what do you think Faye's fixing to do then? Share your sentiment about what's best for her son or go ahead and sell or mortgage the place and bail Jason out like she's always done and always gonna do? You know as well as I do which one of them it's fixing to be. And if that's the case, I don't see a reason why she don't sell that land to me as anyone else."

Raymond didn't say anything. It had become hot in the car and he tugged at the collar of his shirt. His forehead had broken out in a sweat. He pressed the power window button to get some air into the car but the engine was off so he unlocked the door.

"What're you doing?" Phil said.

Raymond swung both legs out. His left foot landed on the gravel shoulder. Raymond just wanted to talk to Jason, see if he could convince his nephew it was best if Jason told Faye he needed to go away awhile.

"Raymond," Phil said. "Shit, Raymond, what're you fixing to do?"

Raymond grabbed the frame of the door and started to pull himself up.

"Raymond, stop." Phil reached across the seat and grabbed the back of Raymond's shirt. Raymond swiped the hand away.

"Fuck off," Raymond mouthed inaudibly and made like to stand.

Once he'd found his balance, Raymond hopped forward, using the side of the car as a brace. When he reached the car's grill, Raymond kept his left hand on the hood for support and reached his right hand to his trach and started yelling Jason's name. He could barely hear his own voice for the construction. He tried again. Nothing doing. He took his handkerchief out of his pocket and waved it over his head. Behind him he heard Phil yelling. When he turned, he saw Phil coming after him. Raymond pushed himself off the car, used the momentum to start hopping toward Jason. Phil grabbed Raymond by the arm.

"Raymond, shit." Phil pointed to a deputy standing near the inmates. The deputy was wearing a brown jacket and khaki cargo pants. A rifle was slung over his shoulder. He was looking in Raymond and Phil's direction. "You trying to get us arrested?"

"That son of a bitch ain't fixin to arrest us."

Raymond made to pull away from Phil and lost his balance. On his way down, he was just able to reach an arm out and catch himself before he fell too hard. Gravel bit at his knee. Embedded in his palm like eager ticks.

"Raymond," Phil said. "Damn! You all right, Uncle?" Phil tried to help but Raymond pushed away, told his nephew again to go to hell. After a few failed attempts to stand, Raymond scooted over to the ditch and used its incline to get his footing. When he couldn't map out a way up the side of the ditch, he surrendered to Phil's hand. The cold ground had dampened the back of his khakis and the wind only provoked the chill. They reached the car and Raymond rested both hands on the warm hood for some time until he caught his breath. When he looked in the direction of the convicts, he caught Jason watching them before Jason quickly turned away.

"Come on," Phil said. "Let's get you home."

Late afternoon when they arrived back at the house. Phil returned to the car after helping Raymond back into the chair they had left parked in the driveway. Raymond steered himself over to the driver's side window. "What about I sell you my land?" Raymond said. "It's already got a barn you can convert into a store. Save you some time getting that station up and running."

Phil had already cranked the ignition and Raymond felt the warmth of the engine again breathing against the back of his arms and neck. Phil shook his head. "Won't work, Raymond. Wouldn't make much sense to build a truck stop where no trucks can get to."

"So we'll build an access road."

"Couldn't see the store from the highway."

"I could sell some of my land to someone else," Raymond said.

"What kinda deal you thinkin you gonna get this soon before the hearing?"

Raymond started to argue but knew Phil was about right. Phil shook his head. "Look, I ain't forgot how you tried to help out my old man all them years ago. But I got to look out for me and mine. Daddy pissed away any chance he might've had but that don't mean I got to. Talk to Faye, Raymond. Let me know something by morning." He shifted the car in reverse and backed down the highway.

Raymond sat in the driveway for some time after Phil drove off. Eutuban had always had an interest in Ike's acreage. But he was dead now. That option or any other to sell wasn't any different than just to sell his nephew the orchard and let Phil do with it as he pleased. Raymond could see where Phil was coming from. And the land would remain with the family at least. But the land would be purposed for a reason other than the family had intended, which seemed to Raymond an inadequate justification. His mind reached back then to that poker game nearly two decades ago when he decided to take a gamble and keep his and the land's wheels spinning in some past he wasn't going to be around much longer to remember now. How foolish he'd been to think he could've ever prevented the land from outlasting its purpose, any more than he could keep himself from outliving his own body.

Raymond finally moved. Instead of going inside to call Faye, he navigated his way around the Buick to the utility room at the back of the carport. In the corner next to the washer and dryer stood a canvas gun case. He unzipped the case to reveal the Browning twelve-gauge automatic, the smoky gray steel of its barrel slightly distorted with age and the silver-plated magazine and the rubber shock absorber that punctuated the wood stock. At the bottom of the case was the Plano shell box. Inside the box were ten rounds of buckshot. Raymond drew back the operating handle and deposited the first shell into the chamber. The bolt snapped closed and he fed four more shells into the magazine. Because it'd been a long while since he'd fired the weapon, he set the box of extra shells in his lap to account for any rust in his aim.

In the yard, the sun sat on the horizon like an orange slit in the gut of some purple beast. Raymond set the brake on the wheelchair and fit the butt of the shotgun in the nook of his shoulder and watched as the bodock tree began to expand into one dark mass of shadows in the fading light. He wrapped his finger around the trigger, anticipated the recoil against his fragile shoulder. Raymond still wasn't certain telling Faye about any of it was the best thing for her or Jason. Wasn't certain that he wouldn't just let it ride one more time and hope that this would all work itself out. Nothing ever worked itself out. Maybe he didn't have to say shit to Faye. In the morning maybe he could just call Phil, get him back over here and have a talk with Raymond and this old shotgun. Then turn the Browning on himself afterward and die knowing he'd done all he could until the very last to keep the land not just in the family but out of the hands of dumbass Horace or any of his descendants. So that was the real reason, huh? He stared down the length of the barrel and that revelation stared at him hard and he didn't know what to do with it. This thing before him though. He could handle this. He could rid this bodock of the thing slowly taking its life away.

FRATERNAL TWINS

THE AFTERNOON BEFORE THE ice storm snuck through Bodock, Mississippi, and flung woods to the earth by the acre, the older twin was drawing beads some proximate-but-safe distance from a mockingbird perched on the power line strung across the yard. No other reason for doing so but to yield a rise out of his too-trusting brother.

This was Wednesday afternoon, a few hours before the sky ripped open and five inches of ice poured out. Bodock Junior High had let out early amid the threat. There was concern of late bus routes, the only thing between the precious cargo and slick roads being drivers ill-accustomed to navigating such. The brothers had rushed home to use the extra time before dinner to continue wearing the new off a pair of pellet guns. Their X-Men and Batman backpacks nipped like terriers at their legs as they sprinted down Main Street and skated across a Piggly Wiggly parking lot already heaving with the vehicles of weather-panicked shoppers. Behind the grocery store, they ran along the train tracks until they took a narrow four-wheeler trail carved during the previous summer. The trail brought them to the point in their backyard where the emu pen brushed the woods.

Their father had referred to the lofty birds as the redneck cousins of ostriches and had invested much money in the fowl for their eggs and steaks. The pen was a chain-link skeleton now. Their father, intoxicated one night in the month after that brief market had collapsed, had freed the emu to fend for themselves.

Holstered in the older brother's back pocket was his own pellet gun, a gas-powered revolver instead of the pump-action air rifle he'd forcefully borrowed from his brother. The distance between them and the perched mockingbird was too great for the revolver to pose a legitimate threat. They were fraternal twins and so their resemblance seemed more distant than the jointly occupied womb. The older brother, Nathan, was taller and the more handsome of the two. Nicholas had a larger head and a more sentimental nature. Nathan had already fired twice at the mockingbird, one shot intentionally south of the power line and one impossibly to the left. The bird's song was unaffected by the pellets whispering safely by. Something inside Nicholas's towhead explained his brother's aim as purposefully wild. Further, the mockingbird's gray feathers made for a difficult target, barely decipherable against the clouded backdrop except for the flicking of its white-spotted tail feathers. Still, Nicholas could ignore neither caution nor the gullible thump in his chest.

"Nathan, don't," he said. "Don't shoot it, man."

"Shut up," Nathan said. "Let me concentrate."

"It's the state bird."

"What does Mississippi even need its own bird for?"

"You'll go to hell for it anyway."

"Says who?"

"Anyone," Nicholas said. "*To Kill a Mockingbird.*"

"You mean, 'How to Kill a Mockingbird.'"

Nicholas tried to edit the smile drawing across his face. When his efforts proved pointless, Nicholas directed his face elsewhere until he'd reclaimed his composure. They had just watched *To Kill a Mockingbird* at school. Nicholas recalled something about falling out of favor with God for harming a mockingbird or any other innocent bird. Otherwise, he'd been distracted for most of the movie by the lice hopscotching in the sable hair of Lacey Eutuban Judon draped in front of him. Nicholas had never before desired to examine the entire surface of someone's body, even and especially those parts covered by swimsuits. The ellipsis of her backbone imprinted in her neck had inspired in Nicholas the sudden impulse to invite Lacey to swim the creek with him so he could long over every square inch of light brown flesh she'd inherited from her black father and white mother. And then there was the guilt when—after Lacey was escorted from the class by the school nurse—he felt relieved he'd never once disclosed his infatuation with this half-Black girl to anyone.

Nathan pumped the lever on the gun several times to deposit power into the rifle before overstating the sight's distance above the bird. Both the rifle and the revolver were Christmas gifts. A month's worth of practice could be assessed in the remnants of plastic Coke bottles and sand castle molds blown up and scattered across the yard. But those had all been near targets, twenty feet at best. The gun's trajectory at this range was one unfamiliar to Nathan. He was as surprised as Nicholas when he pulled the trigger and the bird dropped in slow suspension from the power line.

"Holy shit," Nicholas said. "You killed it."

"No I didn't."

"You're going to hell."

"It ain't dead," Nathan insisted. But he was quite damn sure the bird had expired. Then a wing fluttered. Nathan's heart mimicked the gesture. Both brothers waited for the bird to take flight, to soar away in some miracle they had only ever read about in the Bible. Moses parting the Red Sea or the ascent of Elijah. Jesus raising first Lazarus and then Himself from the dead. Nathan mouthed a prayer for just such a miracle. But the bird's flight was restricted to some grotesque flopping, a one-legged ballerina pirouetting to the refuge of an oakleaf hydrangea in the middle of the yard.

When the boys reached the bush, the bird was cowering aggressively amongst the shadows of the lower branches. Nathan could feel his heart chipping away from itself like so many plastic Coke bottles. He was sure the bush was on the verge of ignition, that the ferocity of God's voice would transform Nathan into a pillar of ash more easily digested by the earth. Instead, Nathan only heard the bird. But perhaps that too was the voice of God. He realized then the most impressive miracle was not that Jesus had conquered death but that He had graduated from adolescence without ever having done anything terrible at all. Certainly not shooting a mockingbird. Or masturbating to fuzzy Cinemax sex.

Nicholas, too, recognized innocence in front of him and knew he no longer belonged to it. He could have knocked Nathan's dick in the dirt two seconds ago or any of the boys at school scratching like apes in front of Lacey in the cafeteria lunch line the week after the Martin Luther King holiday, before a lice inspection was conducted on the entire class. The other boys picked at each other's scalps and mock-ate what they found there as Lacey was escorted from Mrs. Dorsey's class an hour after the inspection. Nicholas made no move at any point to defend her. Now, his cowardice and vanity had brought to tears two of God's creatures. The mockingbird's pleas were synonymous with the appeal Lacey's eyes made as they searched for some savior in the cafeteria. Her lunch tray, held between the bent, skinny wings of her arms, had quivered noticeably.

Nicholas grabbed the revolver from Nathan's back pocket. "I should've stood up for Lacey," he said.

"Licey Lacey?"

"I'm fixing to shoot you in the fucking forehead if you say that again." Nicholas motioned the handle of the gun at his brother. "You have to put it out of its misery."

"Maybe the vet can come do it."

"You know Dr. Svenson's number?"

"Mom does."

"Exactly."

"I can't do it."

"Pussy," Nicholas said.

Dinner was pot roast and carrots slow-cooked the length of the afternoon in a Crock-Pot. Boxed mashed potatoes and Hormel gravy from a pouch. Nathan sat across from Nicholas at the oval table. Their father had just concluded blessing the meal and sat to Nicholas's left. Utensils tilled the everyday dinnerware and the aquarium behind them gargled lamplight and their mother forced questions about school and, as usual, had to coax answers from Nathan that seemed to satisfy her. Their father nodded occasionally. He still wore the navy coverall uniform of the Bellsouth telephone company where he was assistant supervisor. Except when telling his family that he'd probably be—in his exact words—worked like a slave these next few weeks on account of the storm already at siege against the county, the father contributed little to the supper banter and kept his head tilted in favor of the near-noiseless commentary of a college basketball game broadcasting from the living room television. Nicholas also proved uncharacteristically uncooperative of the mother's interrogations. Nathan feared their mother would register the change and know exactly the sin they'd committed, as if she possessed telepathic powers or had transported herself back in time or had all along been able to bargain the physics necessary to extend herself into two places at once and had done so that very afternoon.

"Is everything all right, Nicholas?"

Nicholas's concentration remained on delivering the gray meat on his fork to his mouth without dripping any gravy. "Sure."

Say something, Nathan wanted to blast. Say any damn thing. Be your usual corny stupid self. But their mother received her son's forced smile at face value. Only Nathan registered any change at all in Nicholas. Nicholas had been right: Nathan was too much of a wimp to hasten the bird's escape from the misery Nathan had condemned it to. But the ease in which Nicholas leaned down and fired half a clip into the mockingbird's head—and the nonchalance in which Nicholas handed Nathan the still-warm gun before digging a tiny grave with his bare hands and going about the rest of the day's business—was too much for Nathan to bear alone.

Later, Nathan lay in bed staring at the popcorn ceiling. Nicholas's back was to him. The sleet pattered on the roof like hooves and wrapped the house in a cocoon of white noise. Nathan allowed his worry to lessen to a concerned relief. Even after he awoke later from a dream where he was chased by a flock of flightless, lumbering mockingbirds tall as the emu that haunted the surrounding woods with their glowing green eyes, Nathan had been able to tell himself that his sentimental brother would come around. As insurance either way, he sweated out a prayer promising to give up anything, even masturbating, if God would just take back what had transpired that afternoon or otherwise grant Nathan the power, mutant or Biblical or otherwise, to redo it himself.

Overnight the world fell powerless and frigid. Nathan awoke with Nicholas at daybreak to the billows of their breathing suspended above their beds and a sound like M-80s exploding in the surrounding woods. Later that morning the brothers saw that the forest behind the house shimmered in a glaze of ice. Sections of drooping trees had been laid to rest overnight by the incredible weight that had accumulated and remained in the woven branches. As if the X-Man Cyclops had forgotten to wear the ruby-quartz lenses that corralled the destructive energy beams that otherwise grew from his unobstructed eyes before he too had greeted the world that morning.

Trees continued to hurl their limbs to the ground with increased frequency throughout the day. Midmorning, their neighborhood was disturbed by a barking car alarm when the hood of their neighbor's LeBaron folded beneath the weight of a tupelo gum. The brothers and their mother were roasting hotdogs for lunch in the garage over the blue flame of a propane camping stove when a cedar in their own backyard surrendered a limb. The branches scratched like fingernails on chalkboard against the roof above the garage. Things quieted down some but the lingering echoed whispers of distant falling timber arrested the brothers by their mother's orders to the house for the entirety of that Thursday afternoon.

After lunch the brothers holed up in matching blue-and-yellow parkas and double-layers of wool socks in their bedroom to will the afternoon away on their handheld Gameboys. Neither brought up what had happened the day before. The unacknowledged event seemed to expand like an agitated Bruce Banner until yesterday's truth assumed its own hulking space in the room. At some point Nicholas fumbled his Gameboy to the carpet and excused himself.

Something caught Nathan's eye in the window. He watched as his younger brother, hands shoved into his pockets, rocked on his heels facing the hydrangea where they had buried the mockingbird. In the corner of his eye, Nathan saw one of the longleaf pines that dominated the woods collapse to the forest floor like a palm branch on the Sunday of Jesus's Final Entry into Jerusalem. Nathan found himself concerned for the well-being of their father's emus out in that violent terrain. Last summer, Nathan would give impromptu chase to the flightless birds whenever they rode up on one in those woods. Nathan couldn't figure why God had let his reckless emu herding go unpunished but yesterday had allowed one of his pellets to find the mockingbird. Part of Nathan wanted to affirm the sin, the confession cleansing his conscience and Nicholas's.

A whole other part of Nathan grew bitter toward Nicholas's inability to let this or anything else go. Nathan trailed his resentment inward to an unenviable outcome: his brother buried alive alongside the mockingbird so that, should Nicholas rat them out, only the soil would collect their truth.

Nathan couldn't un-see the scenario.

That evening, the boys watched their father out on the back deck grilling in February. Buried in his down parka, an orange Thinsulate glove on one hand and a char-stained oven mitt on the other, the gas grill slinging its glowing warmth into the encroaching night as it seared the contents of a thawing deep-freeze. Their father brought news that the storm had arrested most of the Mid-South without electricity for at least a week or more. Flames lapped at the stew pot where two bags of purple hulls simmered around red onions and deer bacon. A loin of venison sizzled whispers at Nathan. The boys were still bundled up in their own parkas, their jeans tucked inside matching blue rubber boots. Nathan looked over at Nicholas, who was lulled by something in the woods.

The smorgasbord of venison and peas, stewed to a near paste, huffed greetings from the dining table on paper plates of Wolverine and other X-Men left over from the twins' most recent birthday. The flames on the table danced by their single wicks and a battery-powered radio spoke from the mouth of the den.

"Nicholas," their mother said. She glanced over her shoulder at the patio door that shared the wall with the aquarium. The wind panted and whistled through the cracking rubber trim of the sliding door. "What do you keep looking at?"

"Nothing, Mother."

She eyed Nicholas suspiciously before addressing the father across the table.

"Yeah?" the father asked.

"Ask the boys about school."

"The boys don't want to talk about school." The father cocked his head from the radio and glanced at either son. "They've got a few days' break from school. Y'all ain't wanting to discuss school, do y'all?"

The brothers shook their heads.

"Then ask them about anything," the mother said. "What they did all day not being in school."

The father curled his elbow onto the table and rubbed his buzz cut that merged seamlessly into sideburns and beard.

"What's she getting at, boys? Y'all staying out of trouble?"

Nathan stared at his plate of half-eaten food, wishing for a pair of Cyclops's glasses to prevent his eyes from breaking to Nicholas's.

"I shot a bird," Nathan blurted.

The mother said, "You did what?"

"I didn't mean to."

"Where?" the father asked through a mouthful of food.

Nathan kept his eyes on the plate of food before him. "It was on the powerline."

"In the backyard?" the mother asked.

The father added, "From the house?"

Nathan nodded.

"That's an impressive shot," the father said.

"Yes," the mother said. "Let's encourage our sons going around killing innocent animals. It's a shame we didn't get them the guns when you had those ludicrous emu for all the neighbors to see."

"A pellet gun wouldn't take down an emu, honey."

Nathan said, "You can take away my pistol. I shot the bird with Nicholas's rifle, but I took it without asking him."

"What kind of bird was it?" the mother asked.

"It was an accident."

"What kind of bird?"

"I'd rather be eating this than any old blackbird," Nicholas said. Nathan looked up from his plate as Nicholas turned from whatever held his attention on the wall. Nathan almost corrected Nicholas. Only a full admission of truth would save them, Nathan was certain. But Nathan was enchanted by the semblance of familiar, doe-eyed sentimentality in his brother's eyes. "Feels like we're pioneers in a log cabin before electricity. Not bad, Dad. Almost as good as Mom's pot roast the other night."

There was a short delay before Nathan realized his role in this familiar sibling performance. "Kiss-ass," Nathan said.

"Language," their mother said.

Later, the mother placed the candle on the aquarium while she cleared the table and discovered the scavenger fish floating on its side. Nicholas had named the fish Elvis because of the way it swam in a squiggly pattern up and down its plastic bag when "Hound Dog" came on the car radio on their way home from the Wal-Mart in Tupelo. The water was dark without the aquarium lamp. The mother announced that Elvis was dead. Their father looked up from a *Car & Mechanics* magazine, took the small Maglite from his mouth like a cigar, and said Elvis had been for like fifteen years now. Their mother replied that she was referring to the fish. Without speaking Nicholas felt his way around the dark corner of the supper table to scoop Elvis from the aquarium. Their father wondered aloud if it would be inappropriate to flush Elvis down the toilet but Nicholas was already moving to the backyard without a coat on, Elvis cradled in his palm.

Flashlight at his side, Nathan plotted behind the door until Nicholas retired to their bedroom after burying Elvis. Nicholas crossed the threshold and Nathan watched his brother lumber across the room and sit on the edge of the bed parallel to his own. His back was to Nathan, washed in the blue glow of the camping lamp on the nightstand.

Nathan eased the door shut. "This has gone on long enough."

Nicholas recoiled to gather his brother at the door. Nathan clicked on the flashlight. The illumination caved in his brother's face.

Nicholas said, "What were you doing behind the door?"

"Do you just enjoy executing animals?" Nathan said.

Nicholas shrugged.

"Look, I fucked up, aight. I didn't mean to shoot the damn bird. Quit rubbing it in my face I was too chickenshit to finish it off."

"It ain't your fault I didn't knock their dicks in the dirt when everyone was making fun of Lacey," Nicholas said. "Ain't your fault I didn't keep you from shooting at the bird. Your aim became suddenly true as punishment for my prideful nature."

"That's the dumbest shit I've ever heard."

When Nicholas didn't respond, Nathan grabbed his brother's shoulders. The flashlight in Nathan's left hand shone straight up against the popcorn ceiling. "Snap out of it, Nicholas. She's just a girl. She's a Black girl, for Christ's sake."

"She's mixed."

"She's still Black."

"I love her," Nicholas said. "I love her and I wouldn't even stand up for her."

"You don't love Licey Lacey."

Nicholas punched Nathan's cheekbone. Nathan tasted copper and tossed the flashlight on Nicholas's Batman comforter and shoved Nicholas into the nightstand dividing their beds. The camping lamp landed on its side on the blue carpet. Later, the lamp would reveal a gap the size of Nicholas's back in the drywall. Nathan would conceal the hole with the Wolverine poster that hung on the back of the door.

Their wrestling match came to a brief intermission in anticipation of one of their parents being beckoned by the disturbance. When the door didn't swing open after several long moments, when no one even called down the hall to see what the hell was going on down there, the match proceeded to the floor. Nathan's arm found its way around Nicholas's neck. Their nylon jackets hissed at each other. Nathan was heavier than his brother but Nicholas bore a cock-strong wiriness and eluded his brother's neck hold and swung to his brother's backside, where Nicholas leveraged his brother into a suplex. Nathan hit the ground holding Nicholas's forearm. The older brother's weight carried the younger one over with him. Carpet burned their ears and forehead. Nathan managed another hold in Nicholas's vulnerable state that Nicholas again broke. This went on until their bedroom door swung open, the threshold framing only the silhouette of a man. The brothers, winded and exhausted, hustled to their respective corners.

"I was told to come down here and tell y'all to pipe down," their father's voice said. "What was y'all doing?"

"Nothing," Nathan panted.

"We was just wrestling," Nicholas said.

A few moments went by before their father's voice responded. "Well, wait til tomorrow to decide a winner, aight?"

"Yessir," the brothers said.

When the closed door had erased their father's silhouette, Nicholas said, "I don't enjoy it."

"I know."

"I can hear em."

"Hear who?"

"Elvis tonight," Nicholas said. "Others. They plead to be relieved of their suffering and the humiliation of their slow death."

"You hear any now?" Nathan asked even though he didn't see how what his brother was saying could in any way hold truth.

Nicholas chewed on the question. "Yeah. One of Dad's old emus, I think."

The camping lamp spilled a bucket of blue light over the carpet. Nathan was glad his own flashlight remained where he had tossed it on the bed. He didn't want to see his brother, who had to have been possessed. There was no other explanation. In the semi-dark, Nathan recalled the story of Jesus herding a man's demons into a drove of pigs. Then the story of the person who fought to brush Jesus' ankle in a crowd, who was instantly healed of whatever affliction they suffered. Not unlike the female X-Man, Rogue, who had the mutant ability to assume another's power by direct contact. Nathan wanted to absorb Nicholas's suffering. But he couldn't. He didn't have this power. He didn't have any special power. By his own estimation, Nathan was especially powerless.

"Which one?"

"One we named George. I think. I heard him when Dad was grilling. Thought it was the mockingbird speaking to me from the grave." Nicholas barked a quick laugh. "Why not, right?"

"That why you was at the bush this afternoon?"

Nicholas nodded. "They all speak to me in Lacey's voice. Thought Elvis was the mockingbird too til Mother found him. George is injured out in the woods somewhere."

Nathan couldn't take it anymore and retrieved the camping lamp and directed it at Nicholas. Nicholas's face seemed reserved to the fact that life's potential for tragedy would always be a weight he'd carry too heavily. Maybe Nathan couldn't absorb his brother's suffering, but he could at least bear witness to it. Not unlike the disciples whom he had until right now comprehended not as real people who had to choose whether to watch their best friend die for reasons the disciples hadn't yet understood, but as near-superheroes in some story Nathan had been told so often he took for granted its meaning.

"Guess we'll have to take care of it in the morning," Nathan said.

The brothers took to the woods early. When they'd awoken, their bedroom window held the blue glow of dawn as if the spilled light from the camping lamp still burning its battery on the carpet had grown until it encompassed the whole waiting world. Nathan wasn't convinced they'd come up on an injured emu. He wasn't sure they wouldn't either. He preferred neither scenario.

After they bundled themselves in thermal underwear and matching parkas and toboggans, the brothers carried their rubber boots and wound their way out of their home, skiing along on socked feet at the edges of the linoleum floorboards. They waited until they had threaded themselves through the crack of the back door to slip on their boots. The branch-littered backyard crackled beneath them. Once inside the tree line, they found the woods creaked like the old Methodist sanctuary. A few minutes in, Nicholas broke from the four-wheeler path and Nathan followed him up the slope of a small ridge and down into the gully on the other side. Slung over Nicholas's shoulder was their father's shovel. The shovel's yellow, fiberglass handle punctuated Nicholas's winding movements through the trees in a way that reminded Nathan of a wind vane in a storm.

"Not much further," Nicholas said. Then, looking back, "Don't guess you hear it?"

Nathan shook his head no and continued after his brother. After selecting the shovel from the storage shed, Nathan had suggested sneaking the four-wheeler from the garage as well so they could more quickly get to where they were going, take care of this business soon as possible before whatever strength, biblical or mortal, mutant or otherwise, that had possessed Nathan last night betrayed him now. Nicholas had voiced concern over being able to hear the emu above the engine. A four-wheeler would've proven impossible back here now anyway.

They were making good time though even as they neared the heart of the woods, where Nicholas had to sew the shovel through the thick, lower brush. Skeletal curtains of thin limbs intertwined with ivy and Spanish moss snatched the toboggans from their very heads as they traipsed over the forest floor carpeted in some places by kudzu that disguised shin-eating logs and holes small enough to twist an ankle or—their mother often warned—large enough to hide their own fallen corpses. The trees and their branches that the storm had persuaded the woods to shuck like corn husks made their mission even more cumbersome.

Nathan became aware of the misshapen noise that had reeled them here as they emerged on a pine that had arched over like a ready catapult. Nicholas handed the shovel back to Nathan and duck-walked beneath the pine. Nathan passed the shovel over the trunk once Nicholas had made it and joined his brother in the half-acre clearing on the other side of the tree. They came up on the emu, a grotesque five-foot mound of brown dirty feathers blending into the evergreen needles of the spruce pine holding the bird to the ground. Caution had calmed the emu when they first walked up. Now the bird forgot its curiosity and resumed wrestling against the tree.

"Can't we just lift the tree off of it?" Nathan asked.

"Internal bleeding," Nicholas said.

Standing there now, Nathan couldn't imagine how he hadn't heard the creature's deep, drumming misery from the house. Nicholas suggested that Nathan might want to walk away until the burial, that perhaps he should at least turn his head, clamp his hands against his ears. Nathan removed his coat and walked it over to the emu where he placed it over the bird's bald head to calm both himself and the squirming creature. Nathan nodded at his brother to proceed.

Nicholas wielded the shovel above his too-large head and swung the still-sharp spade down at the bird's neck. The first two attempts were ill-managed swings that produced only divots and sprayed earth and the slow discovery that some force was propelling Nathan toward his brother. Unlike the disciples who were bound by prophecy and fear and their own sense of futility, Nathan did have a choice: He couldn't absorb his brother's suffering, but he didn't have to sit back and just be witness to it either. He could stand next to Nicholas, a relief to his brother's burden. Not only now, as Nathan broke the forward motion of the shovel and eased it from his brother's grip, wrapping both hands around the handle before he made dull contact with flesh, the emu's head rising beneath the blue-and-yellow parka and shrieking what life was left in the upper region of its throat before falling silent. He could also rub shoulders with Nicholas next week as well, when classes convened again and Licey Lacey returned to Bodock Junoir High with the stubble of a shaved scalp visibly free of lice, in clear view of every chickenshit sixth grader who dared have his dick knocked in the dirt.

STEER AWAY FROM
THAT DARKNESS

BRADLEY STEERED HIS CHEVY S-10 through the dark to the back of the Campbell property to drop off the deer. He saw Dewayne back there discussing something into a cordless phone, pacing across the open-aired shed where deer and other game were processed. In a past life the processing plant had been an abattoir where ancient Campbells of only a slightly better economic circumstance had possessed actual hogs to butcher. Now it was a front for a meth business that Peach Campbell had begun before Dewayne hijacked it. A single light shone off the back of the plant and elongated Dewayne's shadow up the front of the camper.

Bradley reversed toward the shed then killed the ignition and stepped out of the small pickup to unload the deer from the truck bed. "Sup, boss," he said.

Dewayne held up his hand. Bradley didn't know how long he'd be so he lit up a Newport and leaned against the back of the truck. Twenty-four and still acne prone, a blond chunk in his Atlanta Falcons Starter jacket, he'd done nothing but gain weight since he'd started the morning shift at Hardee's when he moved out of the house at seventeen. Before he took to running meth, the steady job barely covered Bradley's bills each month, which meant he would've been kneading biscuits another five years and fifty more after that before he could save up for community college.

He didn't know what he wanted to be yet. Just knew he didn't want to be here.

In the back of the truck was Bradley's climbing tree stand that had rattled across the bed the whole way here, banging its welded aluminum against the metal walls of the truck bed, occasionally thumping into the flesh of a buck that Bradley had scooped up off the side of the road. A car had busted the deer up something good but the deer had probably gotten in a few good punches. In the morning, someone would be getting their hood or windshield or bumper repaired. Bradley hadn't cut into the deer yet to see how bad the damage was. One of the antlers had broken off though. Would've been about a six-point otherwise, but the deer would still serve a purpose. Its meat would be broken down a few yards away in the plant, then wrapped around baggies of meth and stored in the old vertical freezer in the shed, all of it packaged in marked boxes on Wednesday, two days from now, and driven by Bradley to a Kosher butcher shop in Memphis, in the back of Peach's refrigerator truck parked up at the house.

Dewayne flicked a cigarette off into the dirt and searched the cordless for the talk button to end the call. Then he ducked in the camper and Bradley saw him saying something to Peach's sister Lori, who lived in the RV. Dewayne emerged with a store-brand Coke and bee-lined to the passenger side of the truck carrying what looked like about a ten-gallon white bucket by a thin metal handle.

"What's that?" Bradley said over the truck hood.

Dewayne grabbed at the passenger-side door handle. "Unlock the truck."

Bradley struggled across the bench seat to open the passenger door. Dewayne set the bucket in the middle on what they called the bitch seat and set his bony ass in shotgun and closed the door. It was obvious Dewayne wanted Bradley to take him somewhere, but Bradley had never been alone with Dewayne, had pretty much avoided their crank scientist like a boy dodging his drunk, abusive father. His head filled with thoughts and his chest got so heavy he believed his heart had stopped.

"Where we goin?" Bradley asked.

"Surgan on the phone. Said we got us a situation out at the lab."

Bradley sat still for what felt like a damn eternity. He had been happy enough to keep poaching for Dewayne same as he had for Peach. But unlike Peach and Surgan, who manned the lab when Dewayne wanted to dip his dick in Peach's sister, Bradley didn't cook. At all. So he'd never had a reason to go out to any of the labs and wondered what the reason was now. Bradley had been using their contact in Memphis to procure some Vicodin to deal for himself. Not even dealing really because he only had one customer. But now Dewayne had found out somehow. Bradley was sure of it.

"You gonna crank it up or run us out there like fucking Fred Flintstone?"

"Uh, should we unload the deer first?" Bradley thinking if he could just get Dewayne out of the truck, maybe get Dewayne's arms full of broke-gut deer, he could just take off running, his fat ass panting through the woods.

"No."

Bradley nodded. "Aight." He thought about just making a run for it anyway but he wouldn't get far. Peach had told him how Dewayne had snuck up on their previous mule and done him in. Dewayne wouldn't have much trouble doing the same to Bradley

ROBERT BUSBY · 39

with or without a head start. He realized now that it had taken him too long to recognize that. He was a sitting duck next to Dewayne. He finally caught a grip on the key and when the ignition turned over, he damned the dependability of his truck. The certainty that it would start and carry him to the gallows.

Dewayne sniffed then leaned toward Bradley, sniffed again. "Them damn Newports you smoking?"

"Uh, yeah."

Dewayne had already pulled one Winston from the pack in his shirt pocket and removed another now. The shirt was flannel and unbuttoned and the loose T-shirt underneath fell against a body deprived of all fat, just bone and muscle and tendon like spring-loaded traps. He tucked both cigarettes between his thin lips, cupped his hand around the lighter flame, touched it to each Winston. His arms were lean but the hand that offered Bradley one of the lit cigarettes was wide as a shovelhead.

"Can't smell that menthol shit all the way out there," Dewayne said.

Bradley accepted the Winston, trying not to think about those Looney Tunes where they gave Bugs Bunny a last cigarette as he faced a firing squad. At the least Dewayne wouldn't shoot while Bradley was driving. He pondered different plans of escape for when they arrived at the lab. Really just different versions of the same plan: hauling ass by foot or tire in the opposite direction of Dewayne. The radio quietly murmured something about a cold front coming through in a couple days. Bradley stole a glance at the label on the lid of the bucket: PHOSPHORUS, RED, 99%.

"It safe to smoke around that?" Bradley asked.

"I wouldn't use it as a ashtray."

Fifteen minutes later on the other side of the county, Dewayne told Bradley where to turn off County Road 211. Told Bradley to kill his headlights, and with only the red tinge of the running lights to see by, the dirt path got swallowed in the moonless dark. Bradley slowed to navigate the fire road which in its long disuse had grown a long tuft of grass like a mohawk between two worn lines of dirt that also sprouted patches of grass. The whole way Bradley had pondered a lot about how he could create a diversion using the red phosphorus. The big obstacle of course actually getting the bucket open without Dewayne noticing.

"I ain't never been out here before," Bradley said.

"Just follow the lines. Steer clear of the darkness."

"Aight." Then, trying to gauge what his own future looked like: "Y'all gonna be ready for me to run this batch up to Memphis on Wednesday?"

"You in a rush or something?"

"No."

Dewayne pulled on his Winston. "Stop at the gate."

Bradley wasn't looking and had to slam the brakes before he barreled through a wall of kudzu stretching across the path. Dust coughed into the vines. Dewayne got out. Bradley looked for a flathead screwdriver to pry open the lid like on a paint can. All he found was a bicentennial quarter. Through the windshield he saw Dewayne with his arms elbow-deep in the kudzu wall. He tried to open the red phosporus but as a lever and fulcrum the quarter and the bucket rim both sucked ass. From the vines, Dewayne pulled a chain. Bradley watched the wall of vines break from the bodock tree on the left side of the path and wobble toward the truck. He saw that the kudzu disguised a rectangular gate that had been fashioned out of two wood pallets nailed together. The hinges must have been affixed to another tree on the right side of the path. Bradley had the idea to use the keys in the ignition to pry open the phosphorus just as Dewayne waved Bradley through. Dewayne closed the gate behind the truck.

Only then did Bradley realize that he had missed the head start staring right at him: for a whole minute, Dewayne had not actually been sitting in the truck.

Another two hundred yards and they reached the lab, the outline of an abandoned doublewide stilted on cinderblocks and rotting away at the edge of a hollow. The path went out from under the truck, and Bradley parked in some flattened bluestem grass. In the dark, Bradley thought again about the fate of the drug mule who had preceded him. Ludicrously early one morning, Surgan, instead of Peach, had been shitfaced at the processing plant when Bradley dropped off a deer. Surgan had spilled all about it: Five months ago, Joe had died when the previous lab exploded, Joe had been the only one cooking that night, and they all would've considered it an accident except that when Peach got out there to relieve Joe the next morning, all he found was some dude taking a piss on the smoldering ashes, a semiautomatic M4 Bushmaster slung over his shoulder. Peach had told Surgan how this dude had his shirt pulled up over his nose and mouth and in the navy blue of early dawn he could only see those eyes devoid of any emotion, just some kind of depraved apathy watching Peach. He shook off and zipped up, walked towards Peach. Said his name was just-D-Wayne and that Memphis had sent him to shape up their little outfit. Started spouting all this chemistry that Peach didn't understand but he caught the gist of it: Dewayne was taking over. If Peach didn't like it, well. Look at Joe's crispy fried corpse there.

Now Bradley was sewn to the cloth seat with fear. He butchered the recitation of the only prayer he knew. Then a flash of bright light filled the cab and Bradley's whole shitty lonely life blurred before him, the half-siblings he didn't know because he hadn't stuck around after his mom got knocked up by someone in his own high school class and the singlewide where he slept now with the lights on so wood roaches wouldn't crawl across his face. The associate's degree he wouldn't earn in a field of study he hadn't chosen yet. Then he heard Dewayne stepping out of the truck, pulling the bucket of red phosphorus across the bench. Bradley opened his eyes, expelled an audible sigh of relief. A small circle warmed his boxers where he'd squirted some piss out. Not enough to dampen his jeans.

Outside the truck, Dewayne lit another smoke but didn't offer Bradley one this time. One whole side of the trailer was covered in kudzu that seemed to be digesting the prefab house back into the earth. Even during the day, Bradley imagined the trailer difficult to spot. Not that this neck of the woods got much traffic anyway.

Peach was still sitting. "Where's Surgan? Told him to fetch you after he got off the payphone."

Dewayne said, "Honestly don't give a shit what you told Surgan."

Peach shrugged apologetically at Bradley. He and Bradley went way back to middle school. Peach had landed this gig for Bradley, Dewayne needing a new runner after he barbecued the last one. But for his part Peach had tried to keep Bradley from this side of the operation. Dewayne the scientist, Peach and Surgan the sous chefs. Bradley just muling the product to, and its ingredients back from, Memphis. He stood at the hood of his truck, still coming down off his scare. Between Peach and the trailer was a bare area of earth where the bluestem had been cut and burned. A propane tank sat beneath a two-eye camp stove in the dirt. On each eye a large pot where acetone was extracting the ephedrine. Bradley fought against his jittery hands to pick a Newport from the pack and steady it between his quivering lips to greet the lighter flame. That menthol filling his nostrils instead of the lingering acrid sulfur that hung about the place, the stench of boiling alcohol and cold medicine.

"I was at the plant when Surgan called," Bradley said.

"What was you doing there?" Peach asked. From the flashlight Bradley watched him work his words up out of an underbite that gave the false impression of a strong chin.

"Dropping off a deer," Bradley said.

"Told y'all not to call til that ephedrine been reduced," Dewayne said.

"Huh? Nah, Dewayne. There something else."

Peach wore a nylon coverall used for crawling beneath houses that crinkled as he led them to the rear of his '83 Cavalier where a three-wheeler that Bradley was pretty sure didn't belong to Peach had been parked. In the tall grass next to the three-wheeler lay an old man tied up and gagged, his wrists and ankles bound with rope.

Dewayne said, "Well that's unfortunate."

"We heard him ridin this way on that three-wheeler so we ducked and hid. Surgan waited behind that tree over there and knocked his geezer ass off his three-wheeler as he rode up."

"He say anything?"

"He complained about us breaking his ribs or something. Said he owned this land."

Dewayne nodded and smirked. "Found yourself some trouble, didn't you, old timer?"

Dewayne kicked the man's Velcro shoes, which flopped lifeless in the grass. Bradley tasted a sick in his throat when he realized he was about to pay witness to whatever fate Dewayne had in store for the pathetic geezer bound and gagged in the tall wet grass.

Dewayne said, "He don't say much."

Peach popped the trunk on the Cavalier, pulled out a single-shot rifle where it lay atop the spare tire. "Here's his gun. We can pop him and bury him off somewhere."

"Nah. Last thing we need's something that look like a murder or missing persons. Cops swarming this place, county going on lockdown or some shit." Dewayne mulled over something. "Bring me that ether."

Peach returned with a plastic jug labeled starter fluid and a gas mask over his face.

"Give me your shirt."

"Ain't got another one, Dewayne."

"Not even at your house?"

Peach sighed and unzipped his coverall and pulled his arms out of the sleeves. Dewayne had pulled on a pair of rubber gloves, squatted and held the T-shirt over the mouth of the jug. He tipped the container so only a small section of the shirt soaked up the fluid. Then he turned the old man over and as the body rolled out from under the truck, Dewayne pressed the T-shirt against the man's swollen, veined nose before they saw why the body hadn't been making much noise.

"Hell. This sumbitch done croaked already."

Six hours later. Bradley pulled into Rob-a-Lot, a two-pump Amoco out on a stretch of Old Highway 6. The hour was still dark except for false dawn on the horizon and the fluorescent lamp in the awning above the pumps humming and flickering, barely strobing its light over an empty lot. No other light between the pumps and the store, which made it an easy target for hold-ups, burglars following the shadows making it inside the store before the Syrian cashier could push the alarm.

Bradley had left the lab about three hours ago after Dewayne had boiled up a plan for disposing of the Colonel's dead body. Bradley had only had a couple hours to sleep. But he had been too wired, his mind's eye playing on a loop the way the old man's body had flopped over lifeless in the tall wet grass when Peach had gone to loop a safety-orange hunting vest around the Colonel's dead arms, so when Bradley arrived home, he just kept on his black slacks and Nike hightops and the red Hardee's polo he had been wearing during his shift yesterday morning and brewed a cup of coffee, figuring he'd just make an all-nighter out of it. Now he parked on the dark side of the gas station, avoiding the lights until he reached the payphone in front of the store. He dropped in a quarter and dialed the number to the sheriff station, which he'd copied onto his arm in ballpoint ink from the phonebook the county had thrown against the door of his trailer a year ago. And while the line rang four times, Bradley inspected his hands where the blood had dried from when he carved the deer according to Peach's instructions so that the carcass looked less like roadkill and more like coyotes had gotten hold of it. Then Bradley helped Peach load the deer onto the back rack of the three-wheeler, as well as his own tree stand and the old man's rifle. Dewayne had been helping Peach set the Colonel on the seat, holding the limp body upright while Peach mounted the three-wheeler behind the old man, when Bradley pulled away from the scene.

The operator, a male voice, came on and stirred Bradley from the nightmare. For a moment, instead of calling in the report the way

Peach had told him to—that he'd been on his way to work and saw some old bastard slumped in a tree stand at the edge of a big field and got out to check on him and reckoned he was probably dead—Bradley contemplated telling the operator the truth and then just hightailing himself out of Bodock for good. But that was just a hope he latched on to in order to keep from sinking. Right now, looking off into the darkness as if on some quick stop on the moon, he felt that, even if he could make it all the way to Mars, where he could stare off in a direction opposite this strange planet he stood on now, straight off into the ever-growing abyss, it still wouldn't put him far enough away to escape the old man's dead face, his drooping flesh and stilled, still-open eyes looking off into another type of infinite distance, waiting on Bradley.

Two days later, Wednesday, the headlights of Bradley's S-10 pickup splattered against the front windows of Hardee's at three-thirty in the morning. He had a key and would have the restaurant to himself until the rest of the breakfast staff dragged in around four.

He brewed a pot on the Bunn and combined sugar, self-rising flour, baking powder, buttermilk, water, and solid vegetable shortening in a metal bowl and whisked the dry components together before cutting in the wet ingredients. Working in batches of twenty-four, he laid out the circles of dough on a sheet pan and stuck them in the fridge before kneading out another rectangle of dough and cutting two dozen more circles from it. Just keeping busy, trying to get his mind off whether their plan had worked. The weekly newspaper came out on Wednesdays, so he reckoned he could scan a copy at work once the issue got dropped off to see if anything had been reported. Bradley didn't figure he'd be long for this world in prison. The thought of going to the Farm at Parchman caused him great anxiety, so he'd pulled another all nighter spotlighting. But no deer stumbled through the ravine behind his trailer so he'd come on into work even earlier than normal.

At four o'clock, he poured more coffee and took a cigarette break in the last peace and quiet of the restaurant before he started baking each batch at four-thirty. Then, for nearly four hours, he struggled to keep up with the constant stream of customers swallowed into the restaurant and spit back out into the rain. Not until nine did the rush hour crowd die down. By then, Bradley could feel the cold front through the drive-thru window. Still he continued to sweat, the long blonde bangs of hair matted to his pimpled forehead.

At ten-thirty, his manager pulled him off of breakfast duty.

"Got a phone call, Brad."

"Who's it, Mr. Moorman?" Bradley asked, removing his visor, swiping his arm across his slick forehead. His gloves left a print of wet dough on the bill of the visor. Besides the one time his mother had tried to make contact with him, nobody had ever called up here.

Moorman seemed as surprised as Bradley by the call. "Said his name was Conlee. Anyway, make it quick. Ruthie called in, said she won't make the lunch rush cause she's gotta pick up her boys from their school out in the county. Says she don't trust the buses to get em home before this ice hits even though schools'll be out before that mess gets here. So when you're done, I need you to get started on lunch prep. You can take the call in my office. And tuck your shirt in."

Bradley tossed his latex gloves, thick and padded with raw biscuit dough, and tucked in the shirt that his gut had pulled from his pants again. Done-lap disease they'd called it in high school, his belly done lapped over his pecker.

He heard what Moorman was saying about helping with lunch, but he wondered if his manager remembered he had to take off early on Wednesdays to run crank up to Memphis. Not that he'd told Moorman that much a few months ago when he asked if he could skip his fifteen-minute morning break and his lunch break to take off right at noon on Wednesdays for some odd job he'd picked up to help ends meet. Moorman had been reluctant but ultimately all right with it. He'd allowed it, at least.

Bradley went on back to the rear corner of the restaurant. He could count on two hands the number of times he'd actually been inside Moorman's office during his six-year employment. It was a sort of controlled chaos, everything having a place or a tray but seemingly just thrown there. The phone was easy to find and Bradley held the receiver and pressed the first blinking light like Moorman had told him to.

"Need you to head up to Memphis now," the voice said.

"Peach?"

"Who's Peach?" the voice said. Then: "Don't say my name, dumbass. Already starting to ice in Memphis. Stan's afraid we won't get him the venison he needs to serve his customers. So he need you to go on and take off now."

"I'm at work, man."

"You want to tell that to Dewayne?" Peach asked.

Bradley did not.

"Aight. Surgan fixing to meet you at the plant in thirty."

Bradley wondered why Peach would use Surgan's name but not his own. He said okay because he didn't have much choice and hung up the phone.

Before heading out to the plant, Bradley made a quick stop at his place first to grab a coat and take care of a couple of things. It had been a muggy-ass seventy degrees when he went outside this morning but now the mercury had already dropped to thirty-eight. Weather would be even colder in Memphis and then back here in Bodock by the time he returned. He didn't have much time to change so he left on his black slacks and Nike hightops and just threw on his Falcons Starter jacket over his red Hardee's polo. He brewed a small pot for the road from the Mr. Coffee he'd taken with him when he moved out from his mom's six years ago. He would've just poured a cup before he left the restaurant but he was pretty sure Moorman would've denied the request to take off. So instead Bradley had just snuck out, abandoned his shift. Pretty sure he could just kiss that income goodbye now, which pretty much sucked. He'd had the job since the summer after eleventh grade. Instead of returning to Bodock High for his senior year, the Hardee's gig had allowed him to rent the singlewide so he wouldn't have to keep coming home and finding his mom on the couch and her bare legs in the lap of someone the exact same age as Bradley, her filling his old man's absence with a frequency of young bucks who took algebra and geography with Bradley but never said two words to him otherwise except to copy his work or steal a glance or three at his quizzes. Hardee's and spotlighting deer had helped him make rent and the utility bills, keep some beer and groceries in the fridge and the lights on. But not much else. He could've crashed out at Peach's, but he didn't want to be any more involved in that shit than he had to be. Without the Hardee's gig, he'd have to find another way to make ends meet so he wouldn't have to dip into his savings of drug-muling money, which he kept in an animal crackers tin duct-taped beneath the carpet in his bedroom where a hole to the crawl space had rotted through.

Mostly though he'd stopped to put some food out for his dog before he hit the road. While the coffee finished brewing, he scooped some Kibbles 'n Bits from under the sink and poured it into a plastic bowl outside, the rim of the bowl jagged and gnawed by Possum's teeth. A wood roach and some flies lay in her water bowl, so he slapped the bowl against his leg to knock out the exoskeletons and ran her some fresh water as well. She was a stray and he was afraid she wouldn't ever return if she found an empty bowl for dinner. He didn't get many visitors and she gave him something to look forward to. She had beechnut tan fur like George Jones's hair, why he'd named her Possum, and he kept a bed of old towels in the crawl space beneath the trailer in case she preferred a warm dry place to sleep. He even had the thought she might be coaxed into sleeping inside tonight because of the storm. He'd appreciate that company, the noise to distract from the way that old man's body had flopped over lifeless in the tall wet grass.

When the maker quit coughing, he poured the pot into a Hardee's to-go cup stained brown on the inside from several reuses. Then he locked up and headed out.

Bradley cut over to Highway 9 South and hauled ass in the S-10. The wipers in need of replacing, just stuttering across the windshield. Peach lived on Coopers Crossing off Pontocola Road near the southeast corner of Claygardner County. When he saw their mail box, Bradley swung into the driveway, following it past the white-brick shotgun on the left into the deep woods at the back of the property, the two-wheel-drive pickup slipping over the damp, sparse gravel that lay like broken teeth in the mud.

The refrigerator Ford truck had been backed in so it aimed down the trail, and Bradley parked on the right side of the truck, where the words CAMBELL BUCK PROCESSING had been stencil-painted on the side of the cooler. He threaded the key to his S-10 off the ring and hid it for Peach under the floorboard mat. Around eight tonight, after Bradley arrived back from Memphis, Peach would drive over to Bradley's trailer and exchange the S-10 back for the refrigerator truck loaded with the ingredients for next week's batch.

Just like they'd done the last seventeen times.

The keys to the Ford would be in the makeshift desk inside the processing plant. Bradley pulled his Starter jacket closed and ducked quickly from his truck to the open-aired shed that only had two walls and a tin roof that the cold rain tapped against. He found Surgan reclining on a fiberglass bench pulled from an old school bus, his boots propped up on the desk, mud dripping from the soles onto the splintering plywood stained with grease and blood.

"Sup," Bradley said.

"Nada," said Surgan, whose family was from somewhere in the Middle East. None of them knew for sure. Definitely wasn't Mexican. His father owned Rob-a-Lot where Bradley had called from the payphone two nights before. In high school, Bradley had bought smokes there whenever Surgan worked the counter. Surgan would pocket the money from any underage sales and had, at least on one occasion, been one of the burglars of his old man's store.

"You ain't bring us no biscuits?" Surgan asked.

Bradley shrugged. Surgan had a fat joint tucked behind his ear. On the desk in front of him was an opened Altoids can and a snorter the size of a masonry nail. Surgan hit the powdery substance, then offered the tin to Bradley. Bradley shook his head.

"Better not let Dewayne see you doing that, bro."

Surgan grinned, put the tin away, lit the joint from behind his ear. "Dewayne's preoccupied, amigo."

Surgan laughed and pointed at the camper showered with flecks of mud long ago. In front of the camper was a busted grill and some lawn chairs. Cigarettes and random debris dotting the dirt. Peach's sister, Lori, had been ostracized to the camper to contain her meth habit. Dewayne must have been thinking it foolish to have her shooting up at the farmhouse just off the road where folks dropped off their deer. Bradley figured Dewayne let her on the property so he could keep an eye on her and his dick never far from being inside her. Bradley thought he saw the camper bobbing some, its tires humping the cinderblocks bracing either side of the tires. Heard some low womanly moaning emitting from the camper.

Bradley said, "What's Peach doing?"

"He's getting some beer for us right now. Mostly riding around pouting. He'll come down here once he's given em enough time to finish. Of course that inbred fucker would probably know how long his sister takes."

Next to the deep-freeze against one of the walls where they kept cuts of meat and scraps was a whole sheet of plywood that had been fashioned into a butchery table. Beneath the table was a blue cooler. While Surgan rattled on about how dumb Peach was, Bradley took two store-brand Cokes from the cooler, one for each coat pocket for the haul to Memphis. Thought about breaking Surgan's nose with a third one for talking about Peach like that, but Bradley just popped open the can, chugged at it, got the extra pack of Newports out of his pockets that he'd grabbed on his way out of the trailer. Bradley thought he felt the air drop another couple degrees just in the time he'd been standing here. Nudging on closer to thirty-two, when the rain would become sleet and any precipitation that had already fallen would slick over into ice. Thought about that long drive up to Memphis he had to make in weather that just kept on getting worse. He wanted to get on the road.

When there was a lull in Surgan's rambling, Bradley said, "The truck already loaded?"

"Yeah. I done took care of it. Dewayne wanted to get started banging Lori, so I let him have at it. I mean, it makes sense that short-bus retard just let Dewayne come in and muscle him out you know? That shit wouldn't happen with me, though."

Bradley said yeah but was thinking what was Surgan doing if not waiting around for the chance to get in on Dewayne's sloppy seconds or something. He packed the Newports against his black Hardee's slacks, ripped off the cellophane, let it flutter to hard-packed dirt.

"Peach's keys behind there?"

Surgan pulled a set from one of the stacked milk crates that held up either end of the plywood desktop and tossed the keys to Bradley. Thought about that first drive he'd ever made and how, seventeen hauls later, he still hadn't gotten over the nerves of driving meth two hours up US-78 to Memphis. If he had known ahead of time what all Peach's offer would entail, Bradley liked to think he would've turned it down. But it was good money. Two thousand extra dollars a month for going on five months now had been a complete one-eighty for Bradley.

And he could leave Bodock. Not this second: If he left now, they'd immediately come looking for him. But he could buy himself a few days head start by completing this last haul. He hadn't saved up as much as he'd wanted. But he had enough. In the morning, five hundred dollars would be awaiting him in the glove compartment, which would round his savings out to the nice whole number of nine grand. That had to be enough to set him up in some community college town farther away where he could find a shitty job and a shitty place to stay and pass the GED so he could enroll in some classes. Maybe Possum would come with. Maybe even the pretty older woman he dealt Vicodin to. She flirted with him some and had kissed him twice. Once with her tongue when he had expressed some doubts about all the risk he was taking. That was in the parking lot of Flick's, in the dark beyond the utility lamp, after their first exchange. She'd offered to get in his cab and do more then, but he'd never gone any further than a handjob in high school after the girl who'd administered it told her friends she had a hard time finding a rhythm because his fat stomach kept swallowing up his small, flaccid dick.

The woman hadn't kissed him since that night she slipped her tongue between his reluctant lips. Bradley hadn't been turned on much by the gesture, and if he were being honest, he reckoned she'd probably sensed that too. Besides not trying to make out with him again, she hadn't made a big deal out of picking up on him not being into her.

One time, he'd told her he was heading to college soon, and she'd told him she wanted to get out of this shithole, too. The hope he latched onto now was that she seemed just sad enough at times that even a friend like Bradley might could make her happy.

Bradley dropped the Newport and drove it into the ground with his Nike hightop, slurped some coke and jingled the keys as the moaning from the camper grew louder and the humping tires picked up their pace.

The Jewish butcher shop was squeezed between a Laundromat and a Mexican restaurant on Summer Avenue. Behind the shop,

Bradley reversed the refrigerator truck within a few feet of the shop's back door. The precipitation already a wintry mix of rain and sleet. Throwaway meat that had soured in a dumpster in the recent heat still stunk up the lot. Stan opened the door, pulled a red dolly behind him. The wrists of a calico sweater and an insulated wind jacket staggered from beneath the cuffs of his off-white butcher's jacket. His apron covered in old pink bloodstains and fresh red ones. He wasn't fat but carried the double chin of someone who used to be.

"You're late."

Bradley pulled on the Newport. "Got caught up in this storm."

"You have to drive through Arkansas to get here?"

"Why would I be driving here from Arkansas, Mr. Kramer?"

"I dunno, Brad. How am I supposed to know these things?"

"I drove straight here from Bodock," Bradley said. "You know this."

"You stop anywhere? Even to take a shit?"

Bradley sighed. This fucking routine again. "No, Mr. Kramer. I didn't make a stop to take a shit or for any other reason."

"Aight." Stan shrugged. "Just please don't let me hear that you stopped somewhere. Not to take a shit, not for no other reason. 'Cause the money I'm paying you to specifically not stop somewhere will buy a whole lot of clean underwear. Basically, Brad, I'm saying to shit yourself before you stop somewhere. It'll be cheaper on you in the long run. You know, one call to Dewayne."

"Aight, aight," Bradley said. "I got it, Mr. Kramer."

Stan looked the boy over and then smirked like he was just fucking with him. Before the first delivery, Peach hadn't told Bradley what he would be hauling. Just gave him an address and told him not to stop anywhere. At the butcher, Stan signed for the shipment, the paperwork only itemizing the different cuts of venison so the delivery looked more legit in case Bradley was pulled over or had to go through a roadblock or something. Then Stan had asked Bradley if he had stopped anywhere, Bradley not knowing why so many fucks were being given about stopping. He admitted, because the evidence was sitting right there in the console, that he'd driven through a McDonald's because he'd missed lunch. So Stan cut the tape holding closed the lid flaps of the nearest box, sliced open the pack of venison inside the box, and cracked apart two frozen tenderloins. There Bradley saw the several small plastic baggies that had been lined up between the loins. The bags contained what at first looked like aquarium rocks for some exotic species of fish, but then Bradley realized the flat, jagged pebbles he was staring at were meth. A whole week's cook: one-point-six pounds already divided into teeners—one-sixteenths of an ounce—and spread across marked boxes of tenderloin, ground chuck, chuck roast, deer sausage, and ribeyes. That's why you don't stop, Stan had said, unless you want your own tenderloins disguising this shit. Stan might have just been fucking with Bradley but he also knew Stan was serious. The threat to call Dewayne was not an idle one. He had sent Dewayne to clean up Peach's outfit. Even had Dewayne chemically burn the poor son of a bitch who'd held Bradley's position previously so that his body looked more like lump charcoal than a corpse. Stan could just as easily get Dewayne to process Bradley, dissect him and cut him up same as any deer.

Which inspired Bradley to shut up and start loading Stan's dolly with the boxes. It only took two trips, but on the second load Bradley slipped some cash between the boxes. Bradley hung out in cover of the cold freezer while Stan opened the marked boxes inside the shop, unpacked and counted the teeners, and weighed the product. He wondered if Stan now knew about the old dead man. Probably if Stan needed to know, Dewayne was the one to do the telling. But really Bradley just wanted to talk to someone about it. He listened to the cheerful blare of mariachi music next door. Gearing up for happy hour. No ice storms in Little Mexico. Stan returned about fifteen minutes and another Newport later with two large cardboard boxes on the dolly, each with the word SCRAPS scribbled in permanent marker on its side. Each box contained dozens of forty-eight-count packages of ephedrine. A smaller box labeled GROUND CHUCK sat on top of the larger ones.

"You'll find your Vicodin and muscle relaxers in the middle of the chuck," Stan said. "Regarding the Valium, I'm not even curious so don't share your weekend plans with me. I won't ask you if Dewayne knows either cause I ain't responsible for you. Oh and tell Dewayne I'm a couple ounces shy again."

"Thought you was looking thinner, Stan."

"Tell him I ain't fucking around."

Bradley thought those couple ounces must be Dewayne's price to get a ride on Lori. Bradley wasn't curious or stupid enough to actually accuse that psychopath of skimming meth for Peach's sister. Almost told Stan as much. But then he remembered this would be the last time he saw Stan. Last time he saw any of them.

He mustered up his best shit-eating grin and said, "Will do, Stan."

Took Bradley over an hour moving through traffic that had slowed to a crawl over roads already patched with ice before he even got outside of Memphis, where Lamar Avenue stretched into US-78. Bodock still two hours away, probably closer to three this afternoon as he steered through sleet that loosened into a wintery mix the farther he drove into Mississippi. The last thing he wanted to do while hauling as much ephedrine as a small pharmacy was to wreck or stick the truck in a ditch or median. The digital clock on the console read 6:41 when he finally passed the Claygardner County sign. He exited off 78, drove down Highway 9, and turned left onto Twenty Mile Road, where home lay just eight more country miles away. Felt like he was close enough to hear the singlewide calling for him to come warm up, crack open a beer, watch some basketball or something. A magazine in his grip to hurl at the occasional moving pattern of a wood roach searching across gypsum walls painted the color of secondhand smoke.

But he didn't have any beer in the fridge. He had drank the last tallboy the night before.

He'd been drinking a lot more tallboys since Monday night.

His watch said he had a few minutes before seven. Bradley figured he ought to play it safe, just go on and park the freezer truck in front of his house and wait for Peach to get here. Peach would switch Bradley's pickup for the freezer truck and then, a few minutes later, Bradley could take the S-10 to the beer store and everything would be right with the world again.

But Peach wouldn't be at Bradley's until eight, and Peach had never been on time. What shape would the roads even be in after eight? There was no guarantee that Bradley could even make it to the store, so he ended up driving on past his driveway and kept on the dark two-lane that held the occasional slick patch but that had not started to ice over just yet. Telling himself he was doing this out of necessity. That he couldn't tolerate sitting in that decrepit shithole all night without a drink or four to push him over the edge and away from that old man's face, disfigured and frozen in his last agony, and on into sleep.

Four miles past the trailer, he saw the utility pole in front of Flick's

Bar dousing the dark with its yellow light. The bar was a cinderblock building in a bed of dust and gravel five hundred feet across the Lee County line where the purchase of alcohol was legal. The place looked dead but the OPEN sign still burned. Flick had on more than one occasion let Bradley buy a six-pack from behind the bar to save himself having to drive to the beer store farther into Lee County, Flick not caring much about the legality of how the cash ended up in his register so long as it got there.

Inside the bar, the walls were slivers of bare plywood between NASCAR and Atlanta Braves posters and advertisements of heavy-breasted tan bodies in string bikinis selling Budweiser and Miller Light and a God-given right to tap the Rockies. Extension cords looped through wires twisted around the aluminum framework of the drop ceiling, the cork ceiling tiles yellowed with cigarette smoke. The cords ran to a couple of Budweiser billiards lamps that lit vacant pool tables below. The felt and wood of the tables scarred with use like dogs had been gnawing on them. A Corona sign hummed its electric glow over an empty bar and Cinderella screeched hair metal from the stereo about being nobody's fool. From the music, Bradley figured Teej must be tending bar tonight before she even emerged from the walk-in refrigerator pulling an empty Igloo cooler behind her. She didn't acknowledge Bradley before she resumed filling the cooler with an assortment of beers from the metal trough behind the bar. Her black curls looked wet and a sliver of pale stomach squeezed from beneath her T-shirt.

Bradley shook a Newport out of his pack. "Sup?"

Teej kept on filling the cooler with cans and bottles to return to the walk-in where the beers would be stored for the next night of business. She might've shrugged, but Bradley couldn't tell.

"Y'all closing down already?"

She said, "Yep, ice storm," but still hadn't looked up at him. Her tan, tattooed arm didn't jiggle a bit while she raked her hand through the ice, searching for the necks of bottles.

"Need to grab some beer to take back to the house."

She was filling a pitcher of hot water and looked up then. "You see us selling six packs in here?"

"Call down to Flick. He'll authorize it."

Teej shook her head and poured the hot water into the trough to melt the ice. The clock above the bar read 7:09. Wouldn't take him more than ten minutes to abide the speed limit driving home, but he'd already been in here longer than he'd meant to be.

Bradley said, "Guess I could just sit here and drink six beers with you then."

"Flick already told me to shut it down."

"He know you have a customer when he told you that?"

Teej sighed and filled a third pitcher with hot water. "Be ten bucks."

Bradley stacked a five and five ones on the counter while Teej poured hot water into the trough again, the ice crackling and slurping as the runoff found the drain. Then Teej set the pitcher on the bar, pocketed the money, and rooted around in the beer that she'd transferred to the cooler. She pulled up a High Life that she set on the bar.

"Ten bucks for High Life is about like robbery," Bradley said.

Teej smirked and dug around the Budweisers and Banquets for five more High Lifes. Scanning the bar so he wasn't watching her, he glanced past a disassembled stack of today's issue of the *Bodock Post* and towards the pool tables before he realized he'd lost track of the day and hadn't checked the news. Teej had two more High Lifes on the counter and was still rooting around in the cooler, so

ROBERT BUSBY • 61

he pulled the paper near him. The main story was about the coming ice storm, which Bradley took as a good sign. An ice storm wasn't more important than a murder. At the bottom of the front page, though, he saw a story about a body that'd been found. His stomach dropped.

"Your lucky day," Teej said.

"Huh?"

Teej had only found four and stood the Champagne of Beers in a Dos Equis carton along with the last beer she'd grabbed: a Corona.

"Said it was your lucky day," Teej said.

"Oh. Thanks, I guess."

Bradley stretched his legs and lit a cigarette for the road as he hurried the six-pack and the newspaper out to the truck. The temperature had already dropped again and he felt the transference in his arms. Light sleet pocked at his face, the sound of it muffled against the hood of the Starter jacket pulled over his head. He breathed in the icy stinging stillness of the county line tonight that smelled cold and atmospheric, folks all huddled in their homes with families and loved ones, buried under blankets. His hands were cold, so after he'd cranked the truck, he looked beneath the seat and found a pair of work gloves anchored beneath a filet knife and put them on.

He punched on the cab light above him and quickly scanned the story. The picture that accompanied the story was of a young man in some sort of soldier's uniform. Bradley thought maybe another body had been found somewhere in Claygardner County sometime this week. But further reading informed that the old man had been a decorated war vet, a colonel in World War II, which didn't seem like a good sign to Bradley. After some more details about the old man's biography and the case of his death, the story got around to concluding that the sheriff didn't suspect foul play, which seemed like a plus. But the department was still sending the body off to Jackson for an autopsy to determine cause of death.

Bradley wasn't sure where that left them, but he felt a little relief in that, at the least, if his demise was inevitable, it was at least delayed for a while. His arrest one less thing he had to worry about at his empty place all by himself to endure a cold storm and the role he'd played in the life of the dead old man. He felt the need for a drink and twisted the cap off a High Life, deciding to save the Corona for when he got home. For when he heard Peach drive off. For when he would tell himself again that things would be better in the morning. That not even the cops would be out on a night like this one.

Twenty Mile Road coiled over ridges and dropped into hollows and ran narrow and pocked with potholes and washout that jarred the rickety spine of the truck's long wheelbase. The beers were cold but the cab lacked heat. Bradley downed his first one too quick and sailed the bottle over the truck into an oncoming speed limit sign. The metal sign shouted at the truck as another mile shuttered on the odometer. Then Twenty Mile swung around a curve and straightened out into a hollow for a little over a half mile so Bradley took the opportunity to nab another High Life from the carton, guiding the steering wheel with his knee while he twisted the cap. The bottle sneezed and Bradley slurped the foam head before turning the bottle up. The needle held at thirty-five, but when he lowered the beer, Bradley noticed too late the curve in the road that loomed ahead. He tried to wedge the beer between his legs and resume control of the wheel but the front tire clipped the rim of a deep pothole and leapt the steering wheel from his knee's grip. The beer tipped over, pooling cold in his lap. The pothole had also knocked the Ford out of the curve, Bradley having to pump the brake until the truck skated to a stop on the gravel shoulder. The shoulder was narrow and the grille of the truck overhung the edge where the shoulder sloped off steeply into a shallow ditch. The headlights burned against where the ditch sloped upwards again into a wall of kudzu that broke the light into a million shadows.

Bradley sat there in his soaked pants for a moment to curse his luck. He didn't think Peach would give much of a shit if the truck reeked of beer. What worried him was that Dewayne might find out that Bradley not only stopped for a drink but had been drinking behind the wheel. He shucked off his jacket, pulled off the white undershirt from beneath his red polo, and used the shirt to soak up whatever beer he could from the cloth seats. Bradley checked his watch. About thirty minutes and change before Peach arrived. No time to collect some quarters and carpet cleaner and clean up the truck at the nearest self-service car wash. Some Lysol or whatever was under the sink would have to do.

The truck had stalled out but on the second try Bradley caught what he could've sworn was his first lucky break ever when the engine turned over. He shifted to reverse and was about to toss the quarter-empty beer bottle into the kudzu and give the truck some gas when a light flashed over him and filled the cab. His first thought: UFO. In his side mirror he saw the beam of a searchlight sweeping the trees before gathering its bearings back on the truck. The origin of the searchlight sat about a half a football field away from the road. Bradley couldn't tell what kind of vehicle, could only see the searchlight and then a pair of headlights join it in the darkness like the wakened eyes of a predator. The searchlight flicked off and the headlights hovered forward toward the road. Bradley rolled up the window and put the cap back on the half-empty beer, which he placed back in the six-pack carton, praying the light was just some poacher he'd spooked who would turn the other direction.

But when the headlights reached the road, they aimed for Bradley instead. He heard the engine rev over that distance and the car came on faster, blue and red flashing now from the light bar on the roof, quilting the Ford and the trees that flanked the road. The cruiser squealed to a stop behind the Ford, which froze Bradley and slid his heart up into his throat. A black brush guard menaced from the grille of the cruiser but the glare of the headlights and flashing red-and-blues kept him from seeing much else of the car. Including the driver.

Bradley went over his options. He could chance the traffic stop and just hope the officer ignored the smell of beer and the vacant slot of the six-pack he was transporting into a dry county as an invitation to search the truck, eventually finding the ephedrine in the freezer.

He was only about a mile from his trailer. But he'd never outrun the cruiser.

At least not until the deputy approached the truck, putting some distance between him and his own cruiser. All Bradley would have to do then was disappear over the next ridge and run with his headlights off. Then he might be able to haul hell down the decline of his driveway and swing the truck around back behind the trailer.

Really that was the only option he could come up with.

Bradley watched the cruiser in the side mirror. The car door opened and a hulking figure stepped out and walked around the hood of the car, breaking the glare of headlights.

Fuck this, he thought, and wrenched the wheels to the left before he punched the damn gas.

Dirt and gravel pelted the chassis of the truck as it lurched backward.

Bradley saw the needle still pointing at R and slammed the brakes but not before he felt the soft thud of a body against the Ford's bumper.

Bradley yanked the truck into neutral and set the parking brake. When he stepped out, the cold wind chilled his beer-soaked crotch. The sleet picking up now. The officer lay between the cruiser and his truck, hips twisted in khaki cargo pants, his brown jacket unzipped, a thick slat of pale arm hanging limp from a short-sleeve black polo. A six-star badge clipped to his belt. And stitched just above his right pec was his rank and name: Deputy Phil Innes.

They'd graduated high school at the same time. Folks would joke that Innes was gay, would call him Phillip Innes but would say it like "Feel-a-penis" even though Phil wasn't short for a longer moniker and no one had ever come forward with first-hand evidence of Phil giving hand jobs or anything like that. Still, when Innes joined the sheriff's department, the same folks who'd called him a faggot in school and who spent their weekends shooting the shit and getting elbow splinters on Flick's plywood bar said Innes was just using the badge to compensate for the fact that he woke up every morning from a wet dream where he got plowed by a prison cell full of bulls.

Innes's barrel chest filled his black polo and throbbed up and down with his breathing. The asphalt had eaten his ass up pretty good, the skin on his forearms a road map of scrapes. He had dropped a small notepad. A license plate number had been written on the paper and Bradley had to compare it to the Ford's before he realized it was a match. He crammed the pad into his back pocket and looked around. No one had seen them. No one was even coming down the road.

He tried to think of a plan fast. His first option involved some variation on him dragging the deputy's body to the side of the road or propping him up in the car and him hauling ass home like nothing ever happened. The deputy didn't have his name or his driver's license, and Bradley wasn't even registered to the license plate. Hell, the deputy hadn't even seen him. But if the deputy woke up and remembered the plate number or the Ford refrigerator pickup truck then this would spray back on him like shit through a fan. Dewayne or Surgan wasn't going to take the fall for him. Peach wouldn't, either, and Bradley was stupid if he entertained a thought to the contrary.

He languished about leaving town in a day or two. About how he wished he'd already left now, how this little fuck-up would fuck up his larger plans to get far away from here and the old man and those stilled blue eyes that would not stop burning a hole in his mind's eye. Bradley observed the musculature of the deputy's thick throat and thought of the old rusting filet knife beneath the seat where he'd found the gloves he still wore. He guessed he could make it look like the deputy's jugular had been severed during impact. He didn't want to murder someone, but he didn't want to be murdered by Dewayne either. For sure didn't want to go to jail. He didn't see much other choice.

If the deputy was dead, he wouldn't remember nothing. Couldn't trace this back to him.

But Bradley would remember. Wasn't like the Colonel had left him alone. And Bradley had only been a witness to that murder.

His watch read 7:36. Was twenty minutes long enough for him to convince a knife to another person's throat, bleed a whole life out right there on the pavement?

Bradley steered himself away from that darkness.

If Bradley wasn't going to slice the deputy's throat, then he decided for the same reasons that he couldn't really leave the deputy out here or drag him into the ditch or something so he didn't get run over just to freeze to death either. What the deputy needed was a hospital. Bradley didn't have a phone at his house to call from but thought that was probably for the best because he'd heard calls could be traced now anyway. He could call in from a payphone, say he had just been driving by, got out to check on the unconscious cop lying in the middle of the road but didn't have one of those car phones or nothing. But there wasn't a payphone close enough for him to use and still be at his house by eight.

Which was also why he couldn't drive the deputy to the hospital himself. Not that there was an inconspicuous way to drop off an officer of the law in a Ford refrigerator truck, the name of the processing plant stenciled on one side.

But he could drive him in his S-10 after Peach dropped it off.

In the cab of the cruiser, he tried some switches on a small control panel and accidentally triggered the siren before he found the off switch for the light bar. After he turned the headlights off as well, the engine still running, he threw the cruiser in neutral then killed the ignition and pushed the car toward the roadside. He figured he'd just slide the cruiser onto the shoulder, but it caught some momentum and got away from him and, once it hit the slope, rammed down into the shallow ditch. On impact the driver-side door bounced like it was about to shut but lacked the impetus and swung back open. He stepped into the ditch to close the door and hopped back up on the road where he hefted the deputy up beneath his arms, the tall fucker's legs dragging as he pulled him over to the passenger side of the truck. His breaths hard to come by already when he lifted with his legs to push the body in.

At the trailer, Bradley parked the truck so that the passenger-side door opened only a few feet from the front door. At night the only sign of any neighbors was their porch lights burning from an acre away and the carry of their voices. The ravine was mostly quiet tonight except for the freezing rain, everyone huddled indoors where they wouldn't see him carrying an unconscious hulk of a deputy uniform up the cinderblock steps and through the door.

Inside the sleet drummed a low roar against the roof that filled the singlewide in a vacuous echo. Bradley dumped the deputy on the bed, which was just a mattress and box spring that lay flat on the carpet and pinned a gold, flaking headboard against the wall. The deputy was still unconscious and hadn't stirred at all and Bradley hoped he stayed that way until he could get him to the hospital.

He checked his watch. 7:49. He needed to remove everything from the truck before Peach arrived. First Bradley grabbed the beer-soaked T-shirt, which he had pressed against the back of the deputy's head after he'd picked him up from the pavement and saw a little island of blood there on the road. Also grabbed the six pack and in the kitchen cleared a space on the counter and clanked the six-pack down next to the .30-30 rifle. He buried the T-shirt at the bottom of his dirty clothes and grabbed an old towel and some Lysol. He didn't have time to deep clean the seat, definitely didn't have the time for it to dry, so he sprayed lemon-scented disinfectant over the damp beer spot before adjusting the towel over the driver's seat.

Then he grabbed the box of Vicodin and muscle relaxers from the freezer, locked the door again, and carried the narcotics and Lysol and keys into the bedroom where he set them on the dresser. The deputy was still unconscious. Still hadn't moved. Blood matted a patch of thick black hair near the scalp where his head had bounced against the pavement. He wondered how bad the gash was, but it wasn't bleeding now and he was afraid he'd wake up the deputy if he touched it. A small V had been cut in the elastic arm of both the deputy's short sleeves to accommodate the large muscles of his biceps and triceps, which only made Bradley hope the deputy at least waited until the hospital to wake up if he ever would.

After he took the bag of pills from the box, Bradley pulled the carpet back from the wall and removed the animal crackers tin from a hole in the floorboard. Inside the tin were $8500. He stashed the painkillers and muscle relaxers in the tin. Then he realized there was a good chance he wouldn't make it back here once he dropped off the deputy. If he had to get away quick, he figured he could take it all with him, but what if he got away with this whole thing only to get pulled over again with opioids and downers. So he only took the money from the tin, leaving the pills in there before he pushed the carpet back over the stash.

He set the roll of cash on the dresser next to the Lysol and keys and a roll of duct tape he'd used to fasten rabbit ears to the television-VCR combo. He shed his beer-soaked black slacks onto a dirty pile that spilled toward a garbage can, dug a pair of light baggy jeans from the closet floor, and slipped the cash and a pack of Newports from his sock drawer into his jeans pocket.

The time was closing in on eight. As soon as Peach exchanged vehicles, Bradley would drive the deputy to the ER in his S-10, drop him off in some shadow at the far end of the parking lot, and call in the deputy's whereabouts from a payphone at the first convenience store he saw while gas pumped into his pickup. He'd carry his own damn self a hell of a long way from here after that. But then he thought what he really should've just done was to put the deputy back in his own car once he'd pushed the cruiser into the ditch.

The simplicity of that plan compared to the one he'd chosen just made him want another beer and to vomit simultaneously. Instead of doing either, he waited in the bedroom in case the deputy woke up and removed the pistol from the deputy's holster in case he startled and needed a longer time being convinced that Bradley meant him no harm.

Standing in the bedroom with the semiautomatic at his side, he listened to tires crunch gravel outside. Aluminum foil covered his bedroom window so he hadn't seen the headlights. A car door opened and slammed. Bradley watched the deputy but the noise didn't stir the body. Over the previous seventeen exchanges, Peach had had always insisted on being quick, never once coming up to the trailer. Bradley prayed this eighteenth time was no different. He heard the dry hinges of the Ford's driver-side door creak open and thought he was in the clear. But in a quiet that went on too long he didn't hear the Ford crank up.

Instead, a knock pounded on the trailer.

About ten thousand volts shot down Bradley's spine, palpitating his heart along the way and pinching his asshole closed tight. He scooted out and got the door to the bedroom closed just as Dewayne pushed through the front door where Bradley stared mouth-gaped at Dewayne's face in the doorway, all beard and angles, his eyes like bug zappers humming static energy, just waiting to strike. A red Razorback leapt across his cap.

Dewayne nodded at the pistol at Bradley's side. "You expectin some troublesome company?"

"Nah, Dewayne." Bradley had to work to keep his voice from cracking. Had to make himself pause before each sentence so the words wouldn't just spill out. "Didn't know who it was. Peach don't usually come to the door."

"He's waitin in the truck. Where the keys at?"

"I left em under the mat."

"Nah you didn't."

Bradley said okay and then remembered. He'd left them in the fucking bedroom.

"Must of brought em in and set em on the counter. Let me go grab em."

"Leave the Beretta," Dewayne said.

"The what?" Bradley said then looked at the pistol in his hand. "Why?"

"You need it or something?"

Bradley shook his head, said he didn't guess, and watched Dewayne wrench the Beretta from his loose grip. His heart still pounding too loud for his brain to work out a good way out of this. He went on into the kitchen where he made it sound like he was rooting around for the keys.

"Know what?" Bradley said, turning from the counter. "Think I left em in the bedroom. You want a beer or something for the road while I grab em?"

"No beer for me. Might have to go through a roadblock or something. Smelt like you done left me one in the truck somewhere anyway though. Cops smell that and they gonna search the truck, find them a felon haulin Sudafed and several grand in cash. Ain't exactly geniuses patrolin this county, but even they could put two and two together. Can't have it."

Before Bradley could respond, Dewayne pounced to the left and opened the bedroom door. Bradley felt like his heart had knocked itself out against his sternum. Dewayne took his time surveying the room then turned to face Bradley. His expression hadn't changed. Had always unnerved Bradley how he could never tell what Dewayne felt or thought. Bradley could bring in a spike or an eighteen-point and Dewayne would wear the same mile-long expression either way.

Dewayne said, "So you bangin a deputy?"

"No!"

"Why else you got Innes knocked out in your bed," Dewayne said, "if it ain't 'cause you want to feel a penis?"

Bradley spilled what happened then. "No, it ain't like that, Dewayne. I ain't no faggot. He knocked his head pretty good. Don't think he gonna remember anything to tell em at the hospital."

"How he gone get to the hospital?"

"He needs to go, don't he?"

Dewayne shook his head. "That ain't gonna happen. Should of left his ass out there. Made sure he was dead first."

"Well what should we do now?"

"We gonna get you taken care of, Brad. Clear this mess up. Don't worry."

Bradley asked how but Dewayne held a hand up at him to shut up while he studied the bedroom from the entryway.

"You got a pair of gloves?" Dewayne asked.

Bradley had worn the work gloves inside. He fetched them from the counter. Dewayne slipped them on.

"Bring me your shoes," Dewayne said, and Bradley went into the bedroom and picked up the high tops Dewayne was pointing at. Dewayne took off his boots, set them on the stoop outside, held up a finger to Peach in the truck, then closed the door again. He slipped his small feet into the black Nikes, and Bradley noticed how his heel bounced out of the size-twelve shoes as he followed Dewayne into his bedroom. He felt a little like he was watching from underwater as Dewayne tore a length of duct tape and smoothed it over the deputy's mouth, then took a knee on the carpet next to the bed, where he wrapped the duct tape around the ankles of the deputy's black boots. The work gloves smearing printless shapes into the gravel-dusted leather. He looked in the holster then the Beretta he'd set on the floor. He held the semiautomatic up to Bradley.

"This his?" Dewayne asked.

Bradley nodded.

Dewayne wiped the pistol clean with a T-shirt he found on the carpet. "Dump out that garbage and bring me the plastic bag."

"What for?" Bradley asked.

With a gloved hand, Dewayne aimed the Beretta at Bradley. Bradley nodded. The can was lined with a plastic takeout bag that overflowed with Hardee's wrappers and the crusts of partially-eaten burgers and Kleenex he'd shot off into while watching porn on the TV–VCR combo. He spilled the trash on the floor, removed the bag, and handed it to Dewayne. When Dewayne had removed the handcuffs from the deputy's belt, he used them to shackle only the deputy's left wrist to the headboard. Then he removed one of the gold rungs from the headboard frame and duct-taped the wrist of the deputy's free hand to the bar. Bradley watched him slip the bag over the deputy's head and duct-tape the bag around the deputy's throat and leave what remained of the roll hanging from his neck. Bradley watched the plastic bag pulse along with Innes's shallow breathing, contouring around his nostrils as he inhaled, the bag recessing from the deputy's face when he exhaled. Bradley wanted to object but he reckoned with what authority. The .30-30 was in the kitchen. Might as well have been a hundred miles from here.

After Dewayne pulled back and released the slide on the Beretta, he picked up the deputy's free hand that had the gold-colored rung duct-taped to his wrist and fit the Beretta into the deputy's hand and formed Innes's thumb and each of his fingers around the grip, except for his index, which Dewayne slipped between the trigger and its guard. Bradley felt sick.

"Whatcha doin, Dewayne?"

Dewayne aimed again at Bradley.

"Fixin a situation."

Then he fired a round into Bradley's gut. The impact felt like Bradley had taken the nose of a hard-thrown football just above his belly button. He looked down and took a breath and the wound started to burn like his belly had been opened and hot grease got poured in. He took another breath before stumbling backward at the gut-shot pain. The discharge aroused the deputy then. He thrashed against the force of Dewayne's sinewy forearm across his massive chest, but in his disorientation and deprivation of oxygen, he was no match for the Razorback pushing him down against Bradley's rotten mattress. Meanwhile, Bradley's back landed on the wall and something inside him broke loose a bunch of blood and hurt. He blacked out for a moment until the excruciating hurt of his next breath jerked him back to consciousness.

Bradley watched Dewayne rip the deputy's left arm up to the headboard with one hand and with the other hand slam the lamp from the milk crate next to the bed down on his head. His unconscious body sucked about the rest of the oxygen from the plastic bag. Then the bag stayed contoured to his face and the scene seemed all too distant to Bradley, so he watched a puddle of blood form on the carpet in front of him. Watched it spill too quickly for the fabric to soak up. He didn't wake up this morning thinking he would die.

"Think I'm gonna need a hospital, Dewayne."

Dewayne stepped over the blood and squatted down in the doorway just behind Bradley. Bradley waited for a shot through the back of his head and started crying. He could feel the stream of tears as they cooled on his face. The taste of salt gathering at the corner of his lips. Dewayne was digging through Bradley's pockets now and Bradley felt the heft of the roll of bills remove from his pants and then the pack of Newports. Dewayne wedged one into Bradley's lips and lit it for him. "Where them pills you been skimming off the Jew?"

Bradley struggled to focus on Dewayne. "Huh?"

Dewayne sighed and calmly said, "Don't fuck around. Soon as you tell me where they are, I'll call you in a ambulance."

"Just take me with you. Drop me off at the hospital. You ain't even gotta go in."

"Can't do it, Brad."

"I don't wanna go to jail."

"Ain't gone let that happen," Dewayne says.

The pain building in this stomach and the urgency that he may die made Bradley forget that it was Dewayne shot him in the first place. Bradley relented and watched as Dewayne threw the pile of clothes in the corner to the middle of the room and pulled back the carpet, reached in, and removed the animal crackers tin. Dewayne squatted there a moment longer staring into the bag he removed from the tin before he stood and kicked the pile of clothes back into the corner over the hole. He left the room and returned with the .30-30 and approached the bed. The rifle he dropped a ways from Bradley's reach, about where Bradley was first shot.

While Dewayne slipped the hightops on Bradley's feet, he said, "You got anything else in here that could incriminate me?"

Bradley thought about the black Burger King uniform pants that sat away from the clothes pile. Beer soaked, Dewayne's license plate number scrawled on the yellow paper from Innes's notepad. He shook his head. "You call that ambulance, Dewayne?"

"They was busy. Sorry about all this, Brad."

Dewayne walked out. Bradley knew he was about to turn to nothing and slip on off into the blackness flickering in front of him. He felt so shitty about damn everything. He yelled for help. Yelled and yelled and yelledyelledyelled.

He stopped yelling when he began to black out.

He had the thought to crawl to his beer-wet pants and remove the lined yellow paper from the back pocket where the blue numbers, hopefully not too thick with smudge, spelled out a plate number for a truck other than his own. Just to make sure it got found. To clear his own name.

But then he remembered he wouldn't be alive to clear anything. All that would do was ensure that Dewayne and Peach went down with him.

He searched out the deputy on the bed. Couldn't tell if it was his own blurring vision or if the plastic bag around Innes's face was really lifting. So Bradley pulled himself through his own blood and puke and chipped a molar gritting at the pain. At the bed he had to hold his insides in with one hand as he reached with his other to grab at the bag which his palm slipped against at first, trying to find a grip against the plastic stilled against the deputy's face.

A fingernail caught a pocket of air where the plastic rose from his jaw to his ear. When Bradley was sure of his grasp, he rolled his body away from the bed, the bag stretching and tearing away from the deputy's face.

He blacked out then but came back to, unaware how much time had elapsed. Innes hadn't moved and Bradley tried to steal a glance to see if the deputy was breathing now. If his chest rose with inhalation. But the prior exertion had spent him for good. Bradley didn't see himself making another move ever. With the spittle of his own sick slick against his lips, he apologized aloud to Innes that it had come to this. That he backed into Innes. That he didn't just radio in for help. That he placed a monetary value over the life deflating in front of him. But his remorse felt insignificant. So he settled in for whatever came next, the pain of weakening breaths too much to let him steer off into that darkness just yet.

SEASONUS EXODUS

FEBRUARY

Power and telephone lines hang limp from utility poles. From the window, the old wife can see for hundreds of yards through a clear-cut emptiness where before much couldn't be seen past twenty feet. In the wake of the storm, oaks and cedars lie uprooted or snapped in half or, in the case of the young pines and firs, doubled over completely, held to the earth like a winded runner by the twelve-hour strain of ice settled in their branches.

Their first year of retirement, she and her husband had taken a charter bus tour through the northeast and found themselves stranded and forced to hole up in a Days Inn to wait out a late-autumn snowstorm and a ten-below wind chill just outside Freeport, Maine. That brutal cold had produced something tranquil and beautiful in their motel window. But this one that snuck across the Mid-South last night, she thinks. Looks more like some tornado had blown through than any ice storm. Like cancer in marrow had escaped bone.

April

Condensation veils the windows like partial glaucoma. The white blanket of a strange, early spring frost draws back now into the shadow of the forest, persuaded there by the sunlight crawling across the backyard and glistening the length of wet blades of grass. The ground looks like a candy wrapper.

"What about the car again?" her husband says, his hand on the handle of the sliding patio door.

"I said," the wife calls from their bedroom, "don't forget your cardigan. There was a frost late last night."

Her husband nods at the vines, their fruit rock solid and crying dew in the mid-morning light. Dreaming of fresh tomato sandwiches. Lunch on the beach.

August

A storm brews off the Gulf Coast. A gull beak-shovels guts from a dead seal half submerged in the warm sand. Purple flesh clings to the bird's lower jaw. The couple makes dinner plans the clouds threaten to postpone.

"I hear Harborside Landing's good," the old wife says. The gull knocks back more carrion. She brushes sand from the swatch of half-calf below her capris.

"Is it safe to eat there?" her husband asks.

She shrugs. "It's on the bay. Where better to get seafood than by the water?"

A wave thrusts towards the shore like a clenched fist and the froth unfolds before the couple. Suddenly young, the wife dips a toe in the tide and laughs, rubs her wet, bare foot on her husband's calf.

Water maps a trail down his sandy varicose vein. He holds her wrist in silence, frozen beneath a gray sky like Pompeii lovers.

He says, "I just don't know about eating at a place called Herbicide."

October

The wind shifts oak leaves towards the heavens, braids them into some combusted cyclone that sends a squirrel bobbing like a cork back to its winter stash, acornless. The widower watches the unfamiliar parking lot from a chair at the table of their breakfast nook that's closer to their bedroom than he remembers but regardless would be across from where she would've sat. Legs crossed, his argyle socks interrupt khaki hem and Rockports. The brief solitude that he had sometimes sought, that his trouble hearing would allow, now crowds the shrunken space. Between two cars the squirrel reappears at the acorn it dropped, massages it back into the cavity of its jaw, and returns to its stash beneath what the widower imagines is the tree still doubled over from last winter's storm. Providing, the man thinks. But who does he provide for now? Who provides for him?

He drops his hand on the table, palm flat, a prelude to motion. The leaves do not rake themselves. Get your cardigan, he tells himself in her way. And then the rake.

BODOCK, 1816–1834

EXA CLAYGARDNER HUNCHED OVER the dutch oven behind their cabin and pled for the men harvesting corn in the hollow to dissolve from view into the stalks that wound the bend. She needed to steal off unnoticed, get the herb that would incapacitate her husband, Cyrus, and keep him from making the trip to Gum Pond in the morning. She figured to disguise the herb in the pot of mustard grits she had stewed now into the tomato-braised reduction of several squirrels. The squirrels she had trapped where the still hid in a shed disguised by foliage, dug into the far hill that defined their eight acres. A monument to the memory of her first two born.

She had borne Dob and Rufus before Leon. Then six years ago, starved and frustrated at the scant return cotton yielded at the gin in Gum Pond, only half of their acreage having been carved from the red clay ridge into soil favorable enough for farming, Cyrus had declared he was making the switch to corn, figuring to set up distilling. The next morning Cyrus rode Dob and Rufus to Gum Pond and returned them to Exa two days later as the copper-lined kettle and coiled worm and the wagon carrying the equipment.

Now Exa turned her attention to the harvesters. There were

Cyrus and their youngest, Leon, who would be fifteen soon. Also their enslaved: Mose Eutuban, and Mose's only son, Beauregard. She watched them pluck ears from the pods and shuck what they could of the husks and deposit the ears into ragged sacks wrapped around necks and shoulders knitted with sweaty ropes of muscle. Tomorrow the week's harvest would soak in water beneath the sun for five days in barrels covered with cheesecloth where they would sprout tails like tadpoles and ferment into mash. Meanwhile, Cyrus would travel to Gum Pond to haul back the yeast and sugar to add to the mash once it had been ground into malt.

For six years now, Cyrus had taken Mose with him on that trip. But last night at the kitchen table, Cyrus announced that Mose would stay behind this trip. That Leon would go with him to the gristmill. Boy's on his way to being a man, Cyrus said. Said it was about time he was treated as such. Cyrus had gone on about how it was time to show Leon the trade proper, but all Exa heard was that her last son would share the same fate as her other progeny, that Cyrus would sell him in Gum Pond tomorrow to some impotent or infertile couple like he was some damn enslaved worker himself. For eighteen years Cyrus, now in his sixties, had worked elbow-to-elbow with their enslaved. He could use the money Leon would bring to spend his last years no longer having to work the same land he owned.

The four men disappeared around the bend where the remaining acre of the property folded west. She had about an hour before dusk halted their work. Exa cranked the bubbles from the boiling broth and wiped her hands on her skirt and made for the dirt path leading to the Eutubans' cabin across the hollow.

Eighteen years ago, Cyrus arrived in North Mississippi by way of the Natchez Trace after a bout of middle-aged anxiety he couldn't verbalize drove him from his banker job in Nashville. At Gum Pond he took an obscure Chickasaw road that had once been a buffalo trace and camped in the last of the gullies along the route. The next morning he greeted daylight and looked for grub, which he thought he'd found in Exa's father, draped in whitetail fur and bearing a five-point crown of antlers. At fifteen years old, Exa had begun to fill out the cotton dresses she'd inherited from her mother—the third daughter of a lesser Chickasaw chief, who had died in labor—in a manner so similar to the original that it pleased Exa's father in ways he had not trusted himself to deny. He took to wearing the pelts his half-breed daughter had trapped and wandering the woods each morning in the hopes that someone like Cyrus would shoulder a smoothbore musket and provide him death without that sin on his soul.

Later, Exa answered an unfamiliar knock and had known enough about the world to understand she was more likely to survive in this land with the help of a man such as the one who stood before her, red with clay and her father's blood, hocking the chilled air from his lungs. She had gazed upon the long stretch of winter ahead with little food and no money and now a husband who would suffer from gun shyness for the rest of his life and never take aim at any fur-covered thing for fear of it being another person. Who would fall into drunkenness every night to forget the thing ever happened. Who even though it was late November when nothing would grow would steal away one night far southward into more fertile flatwoods region and acquire Mose Eutuban and Mose's wife and a pair of young sibling mules that couldn't breed on a loan with terms Cyrus didn't worry waking the plantation owner to discuss.

All Exa saw was that he had brought back four more damn mouths to feed.

Exa froze through those first winter months hunting deer and trapping rabbit and squirrel without her coat, which Cyrus had buried with her father out of misguided respect. One evening over a bowl of braised squirrel, Cyrus told her about some strange squat tree the Eutubans had built their cabin into. How the notching on the cabin planks was seamless, like the cabin had just been stretched from the tree. How the tree bore some kind of cobbled fruit.

"Asked Mose what was the kind of tree they built they's cabin into," Cyrus said. A thread of squirrel meat hung from the corner of his mouth.

"What he say?" Exa asked.

"Called it a bo-dock tree," Cyrus said. "Ain't never heard of it. Asked him where it come from."

"What he say?"

"Just shrugged."

Exa was familiar with the bois d'arc tree, which her people had named ayac, and knew the enslaved would've pronounced the tree bwo-dark, not bodock. But Exa carried their first child—whom they would name Dob—in her belly by then and because Cyrus was the father of Dob she didn't correct him. But she'd also lived her whole life on that land and knew that no bois d'arc had inhabited any nook or crannie of the acreage. She grew suspicious of the Eutubans, how they conjured a tree to spring up full in less than a week.

Now the setting sun had unfurled an autumn chill into the hollow as the arcane bois d'arc came into view. Hanging from the bois d'arc was a cage with bars carved from thick twigs of the same wood. A mockingbird palpitated around the inside of the cage. Esther Eutuban was not to be found and Exa ducked the low-hanging branches, paying mind not to roll an ankle on the horseapples the bois d'arc had deposited on the ground. Some of the horseapples had already been trampled and exhaled the sweet rotted breath of their bitter, blackened fruit.

A garden should have been at the back of the cabin. Exa first discovered it while pregnant with Leon. That was seven or eight years ago—before Cyrus separated her from Dob and Rufus as if her boys were just so little alcohol distilled from fermented mash, back when she still felt blessed and wanted to surprise Cyrus with a diversion from one of her usual gamy dishes. The Eutuban garden had been pregnant with aesthetics and smells completely foreign to her. She settled on a leafy plant similar to turnips in appearance but was more akin to the sorrel herb. The large quantity she served to Cyrus, that potlikker he drank like whiskey, incapacitated his urinary tract. He went on a three-day binge of sour mash to pass the stones. His quick-triggered temperament turned violent just that once.

Exa had not been back to the garden until now and found it had been reduced in size and sat caged in twigs knitted into chicken wire and carried only familiar things: snap peas and butter beans and late-season tomatoes coiling their vines around tall stakes.

Footsteps snapped kindling behind her.

"What it be, ma'am?"

Exa jumped, saw Esther Eutuban kicking horseapples from her path. She was short and slender and spoke in a Creole accent, her second-generation Haitian skin diluted with her former master's blood.

"What happened to the garden?"

"It be gone, ma'am."

"Need something from it."

"Burned," Esther Eutuban said and gesticulated with one hand the smoke that had curled away from the small flat brush fire that day Cyrus had stormed down to the cabin, slashed and burned the garden from which his kidney stones had burgeoned, the gray exhaust that took with it remedies like the one that may have cured Esther Eutuban's infertility, having only had the one son, Beauregard.

Exa said, "Cyrus got the stones."

Esther Eutuban nodded and Exa watched her enter the cabin. When she returned, she carried in her apron only a handful of sorrel-like leaves. The Eutubans had found the seeds beneath the charred earth but had been too wary to plant them outside again for Cyrus to see.

"Need more than that."

"Big stones," Esther Eutuban whistled. "Small stones. This do for either."

The mockingbird continued singing. The thick red freckles on Esther Eutuban's face and neck glowed in the false-purple dusk beneath the bois d'arc. The men would soon conclude the harvest.

"He ain't got stones," Exa said. "Need him to not make a trip tomorrow."

"Trip?"

"To Gum Pond. Taking Leon to do the same he did with Dob and Rufus." Exa stared at Esther Eutuban but saw no sympathy there and fought back the compulsion to slap those purple freckles off her face. Exa conjured a lie and reasoned to her father's God—who couldn't be hers as well, not after all that had happened—that it was a necessary fib.

"Cyrus say he gone take Mose as well."

"Don't he usually?" Esther Eutuban asked.

"Reckon he figure he can get a couple slaves in exchange for him as well. Maybe a female for that young 'un of y'all's. Get us some more hands round here."

Esther Eutuban seemed to buy the lie and stood quiet for a long stretch.

"Dammit, hurry," Exa said. "We ain't got much time."

"How was you gonna administer the sorrel?"

"Having stew for supper."

"What you flavor the squirrel with?"

"Little hickory."

"Mustard in the broth?"

Exa nodded and Esther Eutuban told her there was another way. She walked through the house again and ground some hickory and mustard from a tin jar into a small seed bag. Outside the house, she worked an axe out of a nearby stump, swung the blade down into one of the horseapples lying on the property. The horseapple lodged itself on the axe head, flecks and threads of milky white sap sticking to the metal. She swung once more and the horseapple split. She retrieved one half and told Exa to get the mockingbird and Exa cooed the bird from the cage into her hand. The bird pecked her flesh. Esther Eutuban handed her a paring knife wrapped in a swatch of burlap in her front apron and instructed Exa to slit the creature's throat.

"Why?"

"You'll see."

Esther Eutuban held the halved horseapple under the bird and once the avian blood had drained into it, Esther poured in the hickory and mustard and muddled the ingredients into the white sap and fruit with a thick squat stick smoothed and fashioned into a pestle. She dumped the concoction into a magnolia leaf and like a midwife gathering a newborn in swaddling clothes she wrapped and handed the package to Exa.

"Make sure only Cyrus eat it," she said.

Exa contemplated the bundle in her palm. "This won't kill him?"

"You want to keep your boy aight?"

"But I don't aim to kill Cyrus." This was gospel: not even during these last couple days had she entertained any of her inclinations to kill Cyrus. She did not fear solitude or the prospect of fending against nature itself or the nature of the men who would soon immigrate to the surrounding acreages in the wake of Indian Removal, men who would perhaps stumble upon her place to find a husbandless woman, equate hers with a loneliness only they could cure. That contentment that had first brought her to the Eutuban garden had in time transcended into a matrimonial devotion in which she placed her own absence of her father's faith. "I just aim to make sure he don't make the trip."

The whites of Esther Eutuban's eyes swelled there in the growing darkness. "You think cause he don't make that trip one time it's fixin stop him from never tryin to make that trip ever again?"

"I don't want him dead."

"Use half then."

"That won't kill him?"

"Just make him bad sick again," Esther Eutuban said. "Root him here for a long while."

Exa pondered what the enslaved meant in the departing light in which she had no time to ponder.

The trail coughed dirt around Exa's brogans. At the top of the knoll of their cabin, she found Cyrus already up from the field, bent over into the barrel to reach the water at the bottom. The barrel was planked together with pine and the men had been too busy harvesting corn the last few days to refill it.

"Where you been?" he said and whipped water over his back. His shirt hung unbuttoned. The slight bulge of his liver above the waist of his pants.

"Checkin traps."

Cyrus dipped the tin cup back in the water and rinsed his mouth and poured the rest of the cup over his head. It gathered in his long beard. He nodded in the direction opposite where she'd come. "Traps ain't that way?"

"Set up some new ones."

"Huh." He looked down into the barrel. "Water needed replacing yesterday. Get Eutuban to do it for you tomorrow before they get working on the mash while we're gone."

She nodded. The weight of the bundle hung in her apron. Leon walked up from the barn where he had been directing the Eutuban men over the last of the day's chores. He approached and addressed his mother, assumed a spot next to his father at the barrel, and massaged water into his face and through the crimson hair he inherited from Cyrus. Cyrus's hair and beard were an off white now. Leon patted water into the back of his neck and arm pits, the hair gleaming like knives. Leon's tan denim pants were slung low beneath his waist, his hip bones cavernous, a stream of peach fuzz between them. He was young but could run the place just fine. Why should Leon leave when Cyrus could, she thought.

While Leon and Cyrus went to study over the wagon, to inspect the ties and axle and wheels, Exa eased inside, took a tray and three wood bowls from the kitchen. She filled first Leon's bowl and then her own before spreading half of the paste across the bottom of Cyrus's bowl and as she filled her husband's bowl with broth her hand sloshed the ladle with nerve and conviction that what she was doing was neither right nor wrong but necessary.

At dinner, the Eutubans' singing spilled up to the Claygardner cabin earlier than usual. Cyrus allowed a few moments to pass before he pulled from the whiskey jug and excused himself from the table. Took the sling of tear-cartridges hanging by the door and the smoothbore flintlock leaning against the frame and stepped out behind the cabin like any other night he got piss drunk and fired blank warning shots a safe distance over the Eutubans' dwelling. He actually enjoyed their singing but felt it his duty as master to establish some sort of pretense against what he assumed other masters might view as defiance. It was his first and only experience owning people and he felt he'd never gotten the hang of it.

Out of the corner of his eye as he stepped out the back door, he saw Exa nod at Leon to follow. Cyrus had the cartridge torn open and was pouring the powder into the barrel when he heard the chair squeak backward against the wood floor. He pinched the lead ball from the paper cartridge. Instead of inserting the ball down the barrel, he flicked it onto the ground and eased the rammer into the barrel. Pushed the powder home, drew the rammer out. The cool had come on suddenly and fireflies oblivious to the change in temperature navigated the ravine in patterns of erratic flight between their cabin and the soft faint glow from the Eutubans about eight acres away. Rings encircled the full moon. Would rain soon, he thought.

"Gone need to remind em to camp out with the barrels," Cyrus said. "Eutuban and his boy. Keep that water warm at night while we gone. Would you know to do that?"

Leon said, "Bet Beau's daddy already know to do it."

"Ain't asking what Beau's daddy know. What would you do after that?"

In his own words Leon explained the distilling process.

"Good. When you plant the corn?"

"March."

"Unless."

"Unless the rains is late. Then wait til April."

"Huh." Cyrus cocked the flintlock hammer back. Pointed the smoothbore well above and to the right of the candlelight of the Eutubans' house even though he was shooting a blank. "Know why I do this?"

"Cause you think you need to remind em what would happen if they was to run?"

"More ritual than anything else."

"They ain't gonna run."

"Cover your ears anyway."

Leon did. Cyrus pulled the trigger. The echo of the smoothbore's report curled through the wooded hollow and bounced around the trees before losing itself in the maze. The spirituals or what have you halted a moment before the Eutubans resumed.

"Persistent tonight."

"Or deaf."

Cyrus chuckled, stretched his jaws, popped the ringing out of his ears.

"Beau says they sing like that cause they singing their way into heaven."

"That right?"

"What Beau said. Beau says you want to get to heaven cause you live there forever."

"That's the rumor," Cyrus said.

"So why ain't we just go straight there then stead of coming here first?"

"Coming where?"

"I dunno. Here."

"You already believe life's pointless?"

"What you mean?"

"Nothing," Cyrus said. "Too young to understand."

"Ain't that young."

"Ain't too young to run this place?"

"Think I could."

Cyrus reached out the smoothbore. "Here then."

"Don't know that it's necessary."

"You asserted that already."

Cyrus raked his fingers through his beard and winked at Leon as he handed off the smoothbore. Leon accepted it reluctantly. Cyrus tried to show him how to pinch the ball from the paper without losing control of the bearing even though they weren't using it. Leon told him he already knew, that Beauregard showed him once.

"When?"

"Couple years ago," Leon said. "When you and Beau's daddy was headed to Gum Pond."

"Didn't know nothing about that."

"Guess it was about three years maybe. Beau said best not to tell you."

"You kill anything?"

"Got a rabbit."

"You sure it was a rabbit?"

"What else would it'd been?"

Cyrus shrugged. He tried to recall how he'd ended up here, with visions of strange deer-men stuttering up his little knoll of earth every night toward the house, steam throbbing from their snouts. Two sons he'd likely never see again and a wife as likely to slit his throat tonight in bed as Cyrus was to piss out every ounce of blood in him like he'd been doing since summer heat had cut short spring. He wished he could explain to Exa that this trip wasn't like the other one. But to claim there would never be a reason to indenture Leon would be to acknowledge that he had indentured the others. And he had only spoken of that once, to assure Exa that her boys were safe on some spread of tobacco farm way off in South Carolina. Although how could he ever know.

Leon lifted the musket and Cyrus covered his ears and waited for the second round to blast through the hollow. Once the resonance had fizzled, Cyrus listened for the spirituals to resume once more. Hoped they would. They reminded Cyrus of how Exa had told him that the Chickasaw, upon burying their dead, not only sang for two hours a day for three months but that they would fire three shots into the air to warn off evil spirits. The spirituals did not start back up tonight.

"Once more," Cyrus said.

"But they ain't singing no more."

"Just shoot the damn thing. And something ever happens to me. I wake up dead tomorrow or die on the way back from Gum Pond, you be sure to come back here and do the same."

"Do what?"

"Fire into the sky three times, boy."

"Is that what we did for Dob and Rufus when they drown in the creek down there?"

ROBERT BUSBY · 95

The Eutubans sat with their hands held in a circle around the table a few feet from the silent potbelly and in the middle of the dinner prayer Esther Eutuban began her short, venerable hum. Grew that into an infectious timbre that sprawled like the bois d'arc that shaped the tapered wall of their cabin. Eutuban was not immune and joined in. When his wife sustained their song even after the first gun shot, Eutuban had to inquire why. She sang through his inquiry. He asked again and she sang and he banged his fist on the table and she hummed down the octaves to silence. Told him what she'd done for Exa.

"Why you done that?"

Esther sat silent.

A third gun shot rang down into the hollow.

"Don't he know we quit?" Eutuban said.

Esther Eutuban told him then about how Cyrus had planned to sell him off tomorrow in Gum Pond.

"When was this gonna happen?"

"Tomorrow."

Eutuban shook his head. "I ain't even goin to Gum Pond tomorrow. They boy is." He folded is napkin on the table. "I gotta go fix this before I can eat. Keep my greens warm, Momma. Son," he says.

"Yessuh."

"You comin with me."

"Nah." Esther Eutuban grabbed at the back of her mister's thin cotton-denim shirt. "What you fixin to tell him, huh? 'Don't eat whatever your wife fix you cause my damn wife be tryin to help her hex you?'"

Eutuban had already stood but what his wife said paused him. "Go on wait outside, Beau."

"Please," Esther Eutuban said before their son could get out the door good. She grabbed the front of Eutuban's shirt. A button popped off.

When the boy had closed the door, Eutuban said, "What did you do, woman?"

Esther Eutuban had been looking at the dirt floor where the button had landed but raised her eyes to her husband now. "Come morning he gonna be a tree. Just like I done our former master."

The plantation owner Cyrus had stolen them from had eventually come looking. The same owner who had permanently allotted Esther Eutuban's father to another master, never to be seen or heard from again. The same master that, when Esther Eutuban's mother hesitated to remarry, took into his own hands the matter of rearing himself additional labor. Esther Eutuban had not wanted the same fate for her beloved or herself. Had taken Esther Eutuban two blows with a frying pan to lay that enslaver out before she transformed him into the bois d'arc their house stretched from now. All evidence hid. She did not regret the actions she took this afternoon either.

Eutuban said, "You think about what that half-grown white boy or his momma gone do to us?"

"She came to me."

"She say specifically she want him to be a tree?"

"Of course not."

"Dead then?" He waited for that to sink in and Esther shook her head. "There a way to reverse it?"

"No," Esther Eutuban said. "Not unless he purge it quick."

Eutuban looked across the table at the plates of food, at the potbelly digesting fire at the end of the table. Took his night–walking-stick from the pot next to the door.

"What you gone tell im?"

"I'm gone tell im we need Leon for something. Then I'm gone stay up there and see if I can't get him drunker than usual. Maybe he'll toss that shit up then. We gonna be aight, momma," Eutuban sighed and opened the door.

Exa watched as the fire pit still burning outside slung the light of its flames through the doorway and cast shadows of Eutuban and his son about the pine wood floor. They had still been eating and now that she knew she had done everything she could to keep Leon, her heart ached for her drunk quick-tempered, near-incompetent husband who mistook her even more incompetent father for a deer and brokered their children for equipment. But that had been six years ago and out of a necessity for survival that they obviously were not encumbered to now. All through the meal she had wondered if there was still time for him to purge the bane. Had wondered if he would forgive her. Had wondered if she could ignore history and give her husband the chance to take Leon to Gum Pond tomorrow and then wait three days alone and a lifetime after that to see if Cyrus would always bring her last son back to her.

She didn't think she possessed that kind of faith and her heart regretted having to choose between the two.

The door opened and the wind brought a draft of cold air behind the Eutubans and flakes of white ash into the cabin.

"Hey Beau," Leon said. Beauregard nodded at him.

"Eutuban," Cyrus said. "What you doing up here for?"

"Autumn done come, sir," Eutuban said. "Smoked ourselves out. Need a extra pair of hands smaller'n my own to get our chimney cleaned."

"Shit," Cyrus said. "Needin ours cleaned too then, I guess. Y'all need it done tonight though? Needin us rested for in the morning."

Eutuban said something about his missus coming down with a cold. Feeling feverish. While the men spoke, Exa watched Leon. Saw a boy about the same age she had been when she was orphaned. But he would soon become a man if he had not already reached that age to fend for himself without his father's or her help. A plan came to her. Under the table, Exa unfolded the leaf from her apron, smeared the rest of the concoction into her hand and brought the bitter paste to her mouth behind the disguise of a napkin. In case that didn't work, she would get herself and Cyrus riproaring blackout drunk tonight. Would build their hearthfire high first. They would pass out from drink and lovemaking and the smoke would suffocate her and Cyrus before the fire burned their bodies and any evidence that might indict the Eutubans. Leon would stay in the Eutuban cabin and would have them to help him rebuild a house and a life of his own to prosper from or fuck up. Cyrus had given him the tools for either.

"Leon can go," Exa said. "Got our chimney cleaned this afternoon."

Cyrus looked at Exa. "When was that?"

"While y'all was harvesting," Exa lied.

"How come your clothes ain't dirty then?"

"Wasn't wearing none when I cleaned it." Exa reached for his hand. "Need someone to clean me up when Leon's gone. Won't see you til y'all get back."

Exa hugged Leon for too long before her son followed Beauregard out the door. She watched as they made their way down the hill until their forms had moved beyond the summer kitchen fire into the swallowing darkness. She felt a tear and caught Eutuban still in the doorway, watching her.

"Needin something else?" Cyrus said.

"Well."

"Can wait til morning," Exa said.

Cyrus echoed his wife. Her hand still gripped his. "Morning, Eutuban."

Mose Eutuban stood outside after the door closed, realizing he had not thought of a strategy on the way here for why now, after seventeen some-odd years of servitude, he would've been offering himself as a drinking buddy for the evening. Esther Eutuban had been right as she often was: to save Cyrus, Eutuban would've had to betray the very person he was indebted to him for.

Still Eutuban did not return to his own house. He sat cross-legged behind the shadow of a stand of trees just beyond the cabin and waited in the event another solution would reach him.

Sometime later, the glow of the candles through the oilpaper window extinguished. Sometime after that, Eutuban blushed when he heard them rooting around in the attic space of the cabin. Eutuban prayed that Exa had second thoughts at dinner and had never gone through with it. But then the moans became more audible, guttural, until Exa screamed in agony. Eutuban untangled his legs and made for the cabin.

In the loft, the two of them were still attached biblically. Both their skins shifted into long gray ridges of bark that melded and locked into the other. He got a good look at the side of Exa's pale tits before they became encased in stripy, orange-brown bark with thin ridges and fissures that would deepen with age. The couple's skulls molded over into bark as well and their arms stretched past their normal reach and branched out into smaller limbs and branches and kindling. Their torsos infused into two boughs that drove through their marital bed to release the dried wrinkled corncobs shaping the mattress. The cobs rebounded off the wood floor and down the attic ladder. The couple's now-singular torso reached the topsoil where Cyrus's legs took root and anchored into the red clay earth.

One of Exa's legs had splayed over the footboard of the bed, kicked out and then up into its own sort of skinny trunk that branched out into smaller limbs and branches and twigs.

From this limb, horseapples would sprout and then drop every fall for the next 159 years.

THE PARABLE OF THE LUNG

Hunched over my ex-father-in-law's front yard, molding a layer of pine straw around the purple lilac hedges and crawl space grates wrapped around Lafayette's sprawl of brick one-story rancher, I heard the tires of Erin's rental car massaging the gravel drive leading up to the carport. Erin had found a new breath of life after our divorce, quit her job as first-grade teacher at Bodock Elementary to pursue her PhD in American folklore at Oklahoma State University. Except for the semester she took off after Betty, her mom, was murdered a year and a half ago, she'd been in Stillwater for four years of the five we'd been divorced. I was between gigs. Holding out for that management position, as they say.

Erin eased the car to a stop just short of the carport even though her father's El Camino had not been parked there when I pulled in this morning. I'd assumed Lafayette was at the Feed Mill just off Main Street, slugging coffee and shooting the shit with the other old timers. Lafayette's lungs were bad sick, figured he'd want to get in all the breakfasts he could. But it wasn't like him not to welcome Erin home. The car door slammed. I stabbed the shears through the pallet of pine straw into the red clay underneath, made my way around the house along the stone path embroidered with monkey grass I'd planted for Lafayette last spring.

"Thought you might be over here," she said.

She pushed herself off the hood of the blue Saturn. She wore a black wool turtleneck and when she uncrossed her arms her tits became ambitious. Her teeth gripped a peppermint candy. I folded my work gloves into the back pocket of my jeans and gave her a hug.

"I just came from the hospital," she said. "Dad shot himself last night."

"He all right?"

"He was cleaning that damn .22 revolver of his," she said. "He forgot to unload it first. I flew in as soon as I got the call from the hospital." She removed her plaid-lined parka from the car hood. "The bullet only got his ear."

"Shit," I said. "Should of called.

She tumbled the set of keys around her finger. "Wasn't so bad he couldn't drive himself to the hospital. They're keeping him there another night. I came by to get him a change of clothes."

Erin invited me inside. A short, lopsided pyramid of empty beer cans squatted next to the garbage can. A tower of newspapers and dirty plates each had been erected on the dining room table when the kitchen sink had refused further occupancy. Erin reheated the leftover coffee in the carafe on the burner while we rinsed the dishes and sorted them into the dishwasher. Erin had always been attractively one diet away from what might be considered hungry, filled out her jeans as if she'd been dipped up to her waist in a vat of liquid denim and left to air dry. Considering she'd flown into Memphis the night before and had immediately driven two hours south to the North Mississippi Medical Center in Tupelo, twenty-five miles east of Bodock, and slept all night in a hospital room because her father had grazed a bullet off his head, she looked pretty damn good.

The first thread of steam rose from the coffee. Erin poured two cups and leaned against the counter. She grimaced at the stale, scorched Folgers. She said she needed a favor.

I smirked. "You want me to be Lafayette's emergency contact?"

Erin fingered some coffee off the edge of her lips. "I found Lafayette a donor."

The night Betty was shot, Lafayette had ambled into their house after work to find a pair of men cranked up on methamphetamine holding her at gun point in their living room while robbing the place. Lafayette startled the man training the .357 on Betty into pulling the trigger. The Black guy managed to make the back door but the old boy who put a bullet into Betty's sternum tripped and fell. Lafayette had just enough time to retrieve the revolver and put a round through the back of the man's skull as he scrambled away. Lafayette chased the other meth head down two backyards over, lodged a bullet in his spine while he climbed over a limestone retaining wall to the backyard of Gray Sherman, the neighborhood queer. The man fell unarmed and off Lafayette's property. Before the trial started, the black guy died in ICU at the hospital, which elevated the case from attempted murder or manslaughter to committed. Lafayette probably would've won against either charge given the circumstantial grounds of his case and his standing in the community. He stunned everyone when he insisted on a plea bargain, took two years for involuntary manslaughter. Nobody understood why he'd want to go to prison for defending himself and his late wife, but he wouldn't explain it or let anyone stop him. The best most of us could figure was Lafayette just wanted to move past the ordeal.

Erin and I were already three years into our divorce when Lafayette was admitted to the minimum-security wing at Parchman. A little over six months into Lafayette's two-year sentence, he nearly keeled over during a physical. His blackout led to a biopsy and the diagnosis that sarcoidosis had completely scarred his upper respiratory. Lafayette's sentence was commuted to probation by the governor at the urging of Judge Polk, who'd played football with Lafayette at Ole Miss. The convenience mattered little: as a seventy-year-old felon still technically serving out a manslaughter sentence, Lafayette had a lung allocation score—determined by a number of variables set forth by the United Network of Organ Sharing—that was too low for any viable shot of finding a donor in the seven months the doctors gave Lafayette to live.

Erin sipped her coffee and explained how she had discovered this loophole called the Good Samaritan Clause, which allowed a donor to bypass any UNOS regulations and choose whatever non-family recipient they wanted at their own discretion. In Lafayette's case, that donor was a Pentecostal preacher dying of liver disease. The preacher's church had burned down last year. Erin had set all this up over the phone from Stillwater. Said the man was crazy, obsessed with all the old martyrs or something, had agreed to donate his lung to Lafayette on the grounds he turn over the deed to his house to the First Pentecostal Church of Bodock so that the preacher's ministry could continue in his absence.

"Huh." I nodded at the rest of the house. "So this place is going to be filled with snake-handlers this time next year?"

"They're not those kind of Pentecostals."

"So you want Lafayette to trade his house for a lung," I said, "and you explained all this to Lafayette over the phone yesterday morning, after which he shot himself in the head?"

"It was his ear." Erin considered the window above the sink, the white oak limb framed there like a pillar of cigar ash. "What am I fixing to do, sit on my fat ass and do nothing? He's all I've got."

Our marriage had not so much dissolved as imploded after a streak of impulsivity landed me between the thighs of a stripper named Sugartits one night just about a month shy of our five-year anniversary. We'd married young, while she was still studying elementary education at Ole Miss, a compromise of ambition I wasn't aware of until she enrolled in the doctoral program at OSU. I was still building pinewood couch frames then at National Furniture out on Highway 15. We weren't living hand-to-mouth but I'd lost out on a supervisor promotion one Friday afternoon to a man I still regard to this day as a fundamental douche bag. Because I was young and dumbass enough back then to think Lafayette was the barometer by which Erin measured me, I said hell with it and drove a few counties over to DeWerks La'Rey—spelled backwards: Yer Al Skrewed—and spent a good chunk of my paycheck crafting a dollar-bill hula skirt out of Sugartits' thong. Got drunk and self-deprecated enough for it to seem perfectly justified to hand over what was left of my paycheck if Sugartits would just keep me from getting lonely at a nearby motel.

Erin explained her favor. There was no guarantee she'd be granted enough of a heads up to fly back in time. I assured her I'd see that Lafayette made it to the transplant center two hours north of here.

A little bit later we ended up on the kitchen floor, our clothes half-on to protect against the cold brown linoleum. It wasn't the first time since the divorce: Every few months or so when she came back home, we'd get together to fulfill the more carnal of marital conditions that somehow manage to slip through the cracks of a divorce.

"Have you thought about starting a landscaping business?" she asked afterward. "You've done a hell of a job on my father's yard. Seriously."

I told her I hadn't. But I'd be lying if I said my heart didn't swell a little that she saw some kind of potential in me. That she was thinking about the future.

Erin stayed at Lafayette's through the weekend to get everything squared away with the preacher and to make sure things with Lafayette were settled down. Monday morning, she headed back to Stillwater to teach her evening composition class. The class canceled on account of some arctic front from Canada pairing up with a wet weather system before sweeping through and shutting down the whole state of Oklahoma, delaying all incoming and outgoing flights. The storm then wound its way southeastward, gathering strength the entire time.

The preacher went into a coma Wednesday evening about the time the crackle of sleet reached Mississippi and dumped six inches of ice and knocked power out across the Mid-South. Hospitals would retain electricity, but the Pentecostal preacher had a living will instructing not to put him on life support. The preacher lasted thirty-six hours before he suffocated early Friday morning. The Memphis International Airport was still closed when the lung was harvested a little after eight a.m.

When I wheeled into Lafayette's yard Friday morning, his lung was already hurling through the air in a helicopter a few thousand feet above us. Lafayette was standing on his roof in a pair of Clorox-stained boxers, a loosely knotted noose around his neck, the end of the rope tied to a branch of the sweet gum stretching its bare, knotty limbs out over the front of the house. His wrists cuffed behind his back. Gumballs from the tree overcrowded the gutters and piled up the slanted roof and accumulated around his bare feet. The tree had largely survived the storm but the branch he'd tied up to had sustained substantial damage. Probably Lafayette would take the branch with him to the ground and bust his back or fracture a hip or bulge a disc from his spine like a pea popped from its pod instead of stopping midair and snapping his neck in that pivotal moment when the rope and gravity became acquainted. Well goddamn, I thought. Lafayette's efforts to mount the roof had pulled loose the stitches in his ear. Skinny swirls of blood colored the white bandage like a peppermint. I stepped out of the truck and asked him what the shit it was he thought he was doing.

"Had been contemplating killing myself," he said.

"Yeah, I gathered that much. You forget about us fishing?"

"Nah," he said. His breath pulsed like a chimney pipe in the chilly morning air. This was the dead of February, when fish hunkered down at lake bottoms, barely moving in their dormancy. But Erin had insisted on the fishing euphemism, something about perceived reality and helping her father to feel as comfortable as possible riding with someone other than her to his transplant surgery.

Last night, I went over to check on Lafayette and crash on his couch after the hospital pager Erin had given me alerted us that the next incoming page would mean the lung had been harvested. Lafayette and I ate a supper of hot dogs roasted on clothes hangers over the gas wall heater in his living room, and I hung around for a long while after in the dark house, not really much to say and even less to do. I knew I shouldn't leave him unsupervised, fending for himself in a powerless house, only the specter of his murdered wife for company. But it was fucking awkward just sitting there, no sounds but Lafayette's wheezing and the jabs he took at me about babysitting him. When you fixin to run my bath? Will you warm me up some milk first? That sort of thing. We couldn't watch television. Hell, we couldn't even drink beer. I mean, I could—I wasn't getting a new lung tomorrow. Lafayette might've disagreed given what I'd done to his daughter, but I wasn't that big of an asshole. I guess we could've read but the only books Lafayette had lying around were a Bible and some old devotionals stacked on the tank of the toilet. I saw the *Upper Rooms* when I got up to go piss. Could've held us a little prayer group, ask the good Lord to bless our journey and for His healing grace during the operation tomorrow and all that. But there in the wake of candles, it already felt too much like we were holding vigil.

I finally said something about hitting the sack if we was going fishing tomorrow. I felt silly saying it. I hadn't even led into it, just kind of blurted it out. I couldn't really see Lafayette's face, just this disembodied voice that said, "Just what kind of a dumb sumbitch you and Erin think I am? Y'all think I'm the kid y'all didn't have or something? You waiting to come over here and tuck me in too? Say my prayers? Please God, go the fuck home, Topher, so I can get some goddamn rest."

I felt shitty about abandoning him. Felt even shittier now, seeing the result.

"Nah, guess not," Lafayette said again from the roof. "Suppose we can go fishing now."

Lafayette's operation was scheduled for some time after noon. He was due in Olive Branch at 11:15 to get prepped for surgery: blood tests conducted to determine the type and strength of anesthesia, a tissue test to make sure Lafayette's body wouldn't reject the lung. It was 8:45 now. I'd filled the gas tank that morning on a generator-run pump at a buddy's farm, which left Lafayette and me plenty of time to make the hour-and-a-half haul up US-78 to the transplant clinic just outside Memphis. I called up to Lafayette to get a move on then. He stepped forward and twirled his fingers to remind me of the predicament he'd gotten himself into. "Be right up," I said.

I retrieved the ladder lying out in the front yard and propped it against the house. When I reached Lafayette, he had his head down. The plow lines of his gray comb-over revealed freckled sections of scalp. Erin could write a thesis on the number of tales her father contributed to the community mythos, like when he very nearly pummeled the testicles of an unfortunate rival while in a dog pile on the thirty-yard line during the county football jamboree. Rode through pharmacy school at Ole Miss on an athletic scholarship, where he played for the legendary Johnny Vaught. Returned to our good town after graduation to open Bodock's second drug store. That was all before I was born, thirty years ago about. But Lafayette wasn't indomitable. The inflammatory lung disease and his wife's murder and six months in a low-security prison wing had left him a pathetic reflection of the man he used to be.

When I removed the noose from his neck and asked what pocket the handcuffs key was in, it was still hard not to show my frustration when he raised his head and said, "The yard, somewhere."

"You not think to tell me that before I got up here?"

"Shit, Topher. This ain't exactly one of my better days."

The key had landed on some plastic sheeting I'd covered the hedges with when news of the possible storm first reached Bodock. After I got him off the roof, I brushed the asphalt grit from my hands on the legs of my jeans and looked at him bent over in the lawn. The scar on his calf from an incident the last time he went hunting and his bare feet positioned on the spiny gumballs. Chest heaving whatever was left of his lungs.

When he was finished coughing, I said, "You ready to go?"

Lafayette Cummings stood as straight as he could in the front yard and wiped a spot of blood from the corner of his mouth on his boxers and said, "Been waiting on you."

While Lafayette was in the house getting dressed, I waited out in the truck and honked the horn once and rested my arm on the Igloo cooler I kept in the truck.

It wasn't quite nine o'clock, but I appreciated the obvious sense of urgency lent to the task of escorting a transplant patient. I honked again.

Gave it exactly two minutes. Then honked a third time.

Lafayette appeared on the front porch then. He wore a denim jacket over an Old Milwaukee T-shirt tucked into his beltless jeans and a pair of sunglasses draped around his neck by a red Croakie. Boat shoes on his feet. I retired the cooler to the backseat. In one hand, Lafayette had a Shakespeare rod-and-reel that he set in the truck bed. In his other hand was a half-case of Old Milwaukee which, when he tucked the box between his feet in the floorboard, I saw held only four bottles.

"Lafayette." I nodded my head as I turned over the ignition.

He inspected the cab as I backed downhill out the long drive. Just the walk from the house had spent him. The hell sort of adrenaline that had to have pumped through his old arteries this morning, allowed him to climb up on his roof without keeling over.

"Notice you ain't brought any fishing gear with you," he said. "Don't think it would've helped the illusion some if you'd at least packed a fishing pole in the back there? A tackle box at least?"

I forced a laugh. "I think you got the imagination for it, Lafayette."

"Shit. I see you got the cooler though. I guess that could work. Coolers're essential for a day on the lake."

At the end of his street, I threw the truck in park. "You want, I can go back and get my damn fishing gear, Lafayette."

"Nah." He winked. "I'm just yanking that rod and reel you did bring with you."

I shifted back to drive. "You was easier to get along with on the roof."

I made a left out of the neighborhood and then hung a right, which put us northbound on Highway 15. Lafayette cracked open a beer. The bottle sneezed. He cleared the neck and said, "Want one?"

"They ain't going to use anesthesia on you if you're drunk."

He bent down and handed me a beer. "So help me drink em then."

I imagined the shit storm that would be arriving in Olive Branch only to have Lafayette denied for surgery because I didn't deny him a pre-op beer or a mock–fishing trip beer. Figured I should be less worried with whatever condition he arrived in so long as I got him to the surgery. Further, there were all the stories of Lafayette's drinking exploits before a pregnant Betty ultimatumed him into sobering up. Hauling ass down back roads with a fifth of Evan Williams between his legs, the green cap discarded out the window miles behind him in a sort of insurance the bottle would be emptied in that single sitting. Usually it was. That kind of tolerance doesn't desert a man. He only had four beers on him—two if we split them—which I reckoned would leave plenty of time in the next couple of hours or so for him to piss it all out.

I nursed the Old Milwaukee and we rode in silence up Highway

15 except for the news station out of Memphis and something between a wheeze and a growl from Lafayette's chest. According to the news lady's voice, power had been restored to Nashville and parts of Memphis that morning and some of the larger towns in North Mississippi: Corinth and Tupelo, Oxford. We hit the US-78 on-ramp in New Albany at 9:15, which would take us north all the way to Olive Branch. Out on the four-lane we saw not one wooded acre had been spared. Many hardwoods—oaks and hickories, some of the older, more resilient gums—were still standing, but even their spread had diminished some. The bright wood of their exposed flesh marked their shed poundage to the pallet of broken trunks and branches carrying for miles across the roll of ridges. Besides the occasional eighteen-wheeler, there wasn't much traffic out. Ahead of us, one of the clean-up crews set up every ten miles or so was removing branches or the occasional utility pole that had fallen into the right side of the highway. I merged into the left lane and looked over at Lafayette.

"Be better if we could keep them beers cold." He nodded in the backseat. "There ice in that cooler?"

I told him no.

"Too bad we couldn't transport the lung ourselves. Would've appreciated seeing what a Pentecostal lung looked like."

"If you ask nice they might let you get a good look at it just before surgery."

Lafayette gulped the last of his first beer as we passed a group of orange vests catapulting branches into a dump truck. Then northbound US-78 relaxed back into two lanes and Lafayette rolled down his window and sailed the empty beer bottle at the Myrtle corporate limit sign. The bottle missed high and got swallowed up by the kudzu spilling from the tree line, where some of the more flexible pines made top-heavy by the ice collected in their branches were bowed over towards the highway like the Pentecostals who'd soon be congregating in Lafayette's living room. Lafayette took a handkerchief from his back pocket and coughed violently into it, wiped his mouth and folded the handkerchief back behind his wallet.

"Be too drugged up by then to remember what it looked like."

The .357 that drilled Betty's chest belonged to Lafayette. He wore the piece everywhere as if it were a nickel-plated watch: sitting in the concrete stands during high school football games, depositing his pharmacy's weekly cash flow at the Peoples Bank. Fighting off sleep in the back pew at First United Methodist where Betty dragged him every Sunday. He even pulled the hand cannon on a customer once for being generally disruptive because the man didn't want to wait five minutes over the estimated hour for his prescription to be filled on account he was a distant cousin of Mayor Duff's.

But Lafayette would leave the gun at the house that morning, probably for the first time in years. That evening two unarmed men, high on crank and thinking the house vacant, would break in. A kitchen light sparking to life, perhaps, Betty's voice addressing whom she assumed was Lafayette home from work. And instead of abandoning their mission, one of them men would see an opportunity in Lafayette's pistol on the side table next to the recliner.

It was nearing ten o'clock when we passed Hickory Flat, about halfway to Olive Branch.

"How bad did that hurt?" I said, pointing at his bandage in the side mirror.

"Ashamed to admit I cried some," Lafayette said. "Was a lot like getting your ear flicked in cold weather, except instead of thumping you with their finger, someone shot you. Still hurts like hell. I ain't never fallen asleep with my head in a fire ant bed before, but I'd venture a guess that the two was comparable."

"You mean to do it?"

"Why the shit would I mean to shoot myself in the ear?" he said.

"Meant why'd you have a loaded revolver pointed at your head in the first place?"

Lafayette reached down to get his second beer, popped the cap, and offered it to me. I declined. He shrugged and hooked his fingers on the oh-shit handle above him. "Don't get me wrong," he said. "I'd do anything for Erin. She's my daughter. If she'd requested back then to filet your pecker with a rusty boning knife or to simply shoot you in the face, I'd of obliged her. No questions asked. No offense." He pulled on the bottle. "So if she wants me to get my sternum cracked open or my side split like the underbelly of a bream or however the hell them doctors plan on fitting that crazy Pentecostal son of a bitch's lung inside me just so all his hair-legged-and-armpitted, ankle-length-denim-skirt-wearing female disciples can speak in tongues like certifiable nuts, so be it. But it ain't what I want for myself. Ain't about to feign enthusiasm for it neither."

"So how was jumping off your roof this morning with a noose around your neck doing what's best for Erin?" I asked.

"Ain't what I said."

"Huh?"

"Ain't said I'd do what's best for Erin," Lafayette said. "Said I'd do what she wanted." Lafayette stared out the window and took two quick pulls on his beer and said, "I admit I wasn't in the most logical frames of mind this morning." He held his bottle up to me. "Stayed up last night drinking the other eight of these."

"Shit," I said.

"What? Power was off. You left."

"You told my ass to leave."

"And I didn't have *Sanford and Son* reruns to distract me, I guess. Guess at some point I thought it was a good idea. Thought better of it once I got up there on the roof."

"You would've taken that branch down with you anyway," I said. "Guess it's good you ain't gotten any better at committing suicide."

"Keeps me entertained at least," he said.

"How long was you up there this morning?"

"About an hour," Lafayette said. "Maybe two. It hit me what extent of bad idea it was soon as I tossed that key out in the yard."

I felt pretty shitty for pressing the issue and waited for Lafayette to say something else. But he seemed done with that talk. My beer had gone lukewarm. I finished it and held it between my legs and waited until we'd passed another clean-up crew before rolling down the window. For all the debris we'd passed, it seemed the crews' efforts at present were futile and they'd caught on to that fact as well. The crews this far north simply removed the fallen timber from the highway into brush piles ten or so feet high instead of fighting to stack each piece in a dump truck. The rush of air through the window was a welcomed relief to the silence that'd swelled the cab.

It was twenty minutes after ten when we passed the Holly Springs exit. Thirty, thirty-five minutes from the transplant center. I asked Lafayette to hand me the last beer.

"What?" he said.

I pointed down at the box.

"Roll that window up," he said. I obliged. He popped the cap and handed the beer to me. On the radio, reports on the storm's aftermath continued. Some of the more rural areas of the state would be without power for upwards of a month. Lafayette turned the volume down.

"Tired of hearing about that damn storm."

"All right," I said. Beads of sweat big as ball bearings had formed on his brow. "You all right?"

He fiddled with the heater some, trying to turn it down. I intervened.

"That better?" I said. "You want I can roll the window back down."

Lafayette said, "I ever tell you the story about the time I lost that old bird dog of mine?"

He had on several occasions. About how he and his black lab, J.R., were headed in from the field when a pack of feral pit bulls intercepted them, appearing from the tree line like gray ghosts. How Lafayette couldn't have taken them all on at the same time by himself, how the lab's efforts distracted the other pits long enough for Lafayette to defend himself, first with the over-under, then with the .357 which was easier and quicker to load. Lafayette had to put the lab down right there in the hay patch, not fifty or so yards from the safety his truck would've offered. Would end the story each time by showing a large chunk of his calf missing from where one of the pits stayed latched onto him even after he mowed the top of its head off point.

"I'm a little blurry on the particulars, tell you the truth, Lafayette."

"Was going to make you listen anyway," he said. He hung his arm on the oh-shit handle above him and commenced his detailed account. "Not thirty yards from us I remember J.R. and see him fighting the good fight but just getting tore at by about half the pack. Four of em had abandoned the crowd around J.R. and was headed my way. I popped off one of them with the over-under and abandon it for the .357 because the over-under you know's too slow and bulky. Get three of the cocksuckers before the other one runs off. Then I hobble towards J.R. but only make it a few yards because of the pit that's jaws're still attached on my leg like some badass tick. I shoot the two pits around J.R. but can barely see him for the pit on top of him. Looks like it's already dug into J.R.'s throat. Only a matter of time. So I put a bead on the pit.

"But let's just say," Lafayette said, tapping his middle finger on the dash twice for dramatic effect. "Let's just imagine for a moment it only looked like that pit had a hold of J.R.'s throat, and just as I feel the trigger in the bend of my finger, that J.R., in some impressive maneuver and demonstration of resiliency, somehow manages his mouth around that pit's fat face and the pit rolls over to break free and it's my round that goes right into J.R. So that it's me who kills my dog out of no necessity whatsoever."

He paused and looked for me to answer.

I said, "I mean, that'd change the whole dynamic of the story, I guess, Lafayette."

"About would, yes," Lafayette said.

Out of the corner of my eye, I saw Lafayette drape back his denim jacket to make for the handkerchief again. I directed my attention back to the road. When my eyes drifted back towards Lafayette, I saw a black semi-automatic pistol resting on his leg. Had never known Lafayette to own a pistol—just the revolver and shotguns, some hunting rifles. Knew with his record now he couldn't have bought the pistol anywhere legally.

"Why the hell did you bring a gun with you, Lafayette?"

Before he could answer, he suffered another violent coughing episode, this time before he could reach the handkerchief. Traces of blood and phlegm sprayed on the glove compartment. Lafayette's beer tipped over into the floorboard. In his fit, I grabbed the gun away from him. He didn't fight me for it. He took out his handkerchief and wiped the dash.

"Shit. Sorry about that," he said.

The heft of the gun in my hand. "Why the hell did you bring a gun with you?" I asked again.

When he was finished smearing his muck on the dash, he dropped the handkerchief into the empty beer carton and deposited the beer bottle he'd knocked into the floorboard in the carton as well.

"Don't know anymore," Lafayette said and removed the carton to the backseat. He closed his eyes and leaned into the headrest. "Don't know. Had my .357 on me as always, Topher." Lafayette pointed at the gun in my left hand. I could tell he was fighting back tears his chest was trying to convulse out of him. "So that white trash piece of shit was holding that gun on her instead. Didn't know there was another man in the house, so when his Negro buddy saw me, sumbitch registered his friend's surprise, moved just as I pulled the trigger."

Ahead of us, an exit sign bounced like a green buoy in the waves of cool air thawing off the highway. I took the exit and turned right on Hacks Cross Road. Power still hadn't been restored. Truck stops sat squat and dead and empty. The only life some smoke pillaring from the side of one of the stores. I pulled around. It was 10:45 and we were only ten minutes away from the transplant center. Olive Branch was the next exit down 78. But the beer in my empty stomach reminded how I hadn't eaten anything yet that morning. I felt damn claustrophobic, like I was fixing to have a panic attack or something.

A red horse trailer was parked back behind the truck stop. A gas generator growled power into the trailer. MALONE'S CATFISH AND

OTHER FINGER LICKIN GOOD STUFF was painted on the side of the truck. Only a few customers were standing in line. I pulled back around the building and parked in a space facing the large panes of glass at the front of the store. The tires nudged the curb. A pay phone stood just beyond the truck grill.

"Shouldn't of told you that," Lafayette said and opened his eyes. "Don't tell Erin."

I guess I was still in shock. "Of course."

"We there?"

"Sit tight," I said. "Got to get some food in me. You want something?"

"Probably shouldn't eat before surgery."

"But you can drink beer?"

"Just a little something to snack on then. A biscuit, pack of Nabs. Whatever they got."

Two ladies were working the truck. The Black woman manned the register and the other one, a Mexican, held a pair of tongs over a pair of matching beige Crock-Pots. Both women were wearing hairnets. Not so much the smell of frying catfish wafted from the truck as chorizo and what I recognized as tamales. The first man in line paid and carried away a Styrofoam box. Two customers remained in front of me. The next customer ordered. The Mexican lady with the tongs waited for her co-worker to indicate which Crock-Pot. The black lady pointed with three fingers at the one on the right. Aluminum foil draped from the Crock-Pot. I handled the change in my pocket and watched the Mexican lift the lid and produce as many tamales.

Perhaps the pay phone actually did work, fed from lines below the ground, safe there from the storm's devastation. What would I tell Erin then? That the best possible result today would be the operation going just about textbook and Lafayette living out the five years his new lung might afford him at a retirement home, all while the guilt over having shot Betty continued to consume him much less quietly than the sarcoidosis had or ever would. Blame laid as much with me for how far this had gone. I ignored what Erin couldn't see with Lafayette's first suicide attempt because I still and always would love Erin enough to harbor some hope of a past revisited despite what that would mean another man, who had not so much broken his wife's heart but damn gored it with a bullet, would have to be wrung through.

My reflection caught in the rear glass window of the quick stop. I needed more time than I had to figure all this shit out. I focused past my reflection and examined the inside of the vacant store. All the usual suspects of quick-stop merchandise were present: junk food and beer, videocassettes and country music and gospel and gospel country music cassette tapes and CDs. CB radios and wiring, exaggerated antennas and bracket mountings. Several cheap brands of fishing poles hanging on the wall.

Back behind the wheel, I told Lafayette we had some time to kill, that the lady at the food truck said the store owner's catfish pond was nearby, a place we could cast a few quick lines in while we ate the tamales. They were selling hotdogs from the other Crock-Pot and I bought an opened pack of raw ones to hook on our lines. A couple of miles down the frontage road I made a left onto a narrower gravel road, maneuvered the truck like the lady said her old man did sometimes around the padlocked gate that didn't stretch across the entire width of the path and wasn't met on either side by fencing.

Branches slapped and scratched the side panels of the truck before the path yawned into a cove and a man-made lake of about fifteen squared acres sprawled out before us. At the far end, two tractors held between them a seine which would drag the length of the lake during harvest. A wire-netted hopper waited at the other end of the lake to lift from the water the catfish caught between the seine and the bank. I parked. Tall pines untouched by the storm darted from the ground around the rectangular perimeter of the lake like the makeshift walls of a medieval keep. There was some cloud cover and from the truck the water looked murky. Lafayette tried opening the door of the truck while managing the last of his beer and balancing the hot dogs on top of the box of tamales in his lap.

"Don't worry about all of that," I said, reaching for the food. "I can get it."

"I ain't completely helpless yet." He swung open the door and stepped down and the opened pack of hot dogs slipped off the Styrofoam and landed in the grass. Two of the hot dogs rolled from the plastic. Bits of dirt had already clung to them. "You can get them," he said.

We walked to the far end of the floating pier that would retract onto the bank during harvest. Lafayette's breathing was labored and he set the tamales and his pole on the dock, propped himself up on his knees and wheezed. When he could manage, he sat down on the pier. I handed him my pocket knife. He cut up one of the hot dogs against the pier and baited his hook before casting out into the lake. His arm jerked the rod in his hand, the other reeled the slack out of the line. I offered him another tamale.

"Can't say I've had any of these before," he said.

I told him the first time I'd ever tried them was when Manny, a co-worker at the Bodock Country Club back after I got fired from the line at National Furniture, offered me one from his lunch box leftover from his dinner the evening before.

"They ain't bad." Lafayette licked tomatillo salsa from his fingers. "You know? A little different but taste good. You still got that Ruger on you?"

I slipped the gun out of my pants and debated telling him I didn't feel comfortable with him having a loaded gun. But he'd been through enough. "Long as you ain't fixing to shoot me or you with it."

He cast the line. "Would you believe they broke in with only one bullet in that gun?" He swiped a finger across the bandage on his ear. "Used it to pull this here van Gogh what's-his-face."

I broke the breech of the gun and ejected the clip. The chamber and clip were empty. I handed the gun to him. He looked at the unloaded Ruger and tossed it off into the water. Then my ex-father-in-law cast again, the repetitive clicking of the line as it unreeled and stretched fifteen, twenty feet from us. "Way the wind's moving this water, kind of looks like we've launched out from land," he said. "Always appreciated that particular illusion."

I said I had as well and bit into another tamale. I was killing time, was aware of as much, waiting there for Lafayette to ever give the word to head out or, if he never did, for some explanation why to arrive at me.

Sometime later, most of the hot dogs gone and nothing to show for them, I joked that it was too bad we didn't have the organ with us. That if we planned to stick around out here, we could've changed our strategy some. Maybe have given his lung a go.

STUBBORN AS A FENCE POST

From a squat position, Bo Rutherford gripped the fence post between his legs with both hands and chucked the six-foot-length of bodock wood into the yard before him. The post hobbled up its trajectory before it performed a mule-kick midair and nose-dived into the ground behind the storage shed. The yard was still soft with thaw and the post carved a slab of sod from the earth. The red clay beneath the grass like a wound. As if the earth was coughing blood. Rutherford wasn't sure at all what to make of that. Rutherford hadn't been sure what to make of much lately.

This was late February, two weeks after the ice storm. The post was a felled limb that had succumbed to the inches of ice that had coated it. Six months later, during the first weekend in August, the town of Bodock would hold its annual Bodock Festival in honor of the bois d'arc tree the town was colloquially named for. The Chickasaw had found earliest use for the bois d'arc in Mississippi, borrowing from their Osage neighbors's use of the wood for durable bow staves. Early European pioneers with their black powder and muskets found more use for the tree as fence posts, the decay-resistant wood said to last longer than the hole it was set in. Modern Bodockians flung six-foot lengths of the wood into history during the World Bodock Fence Post Tossing Championship.

Rutherford had discovered the felled limb in the backyard a few days ago. The limb was just over six-feet long, about the length of a competition post. At first, he'd flung the post around the backyard because he had nothing else to fill the afternoons now that he didn't have a baseball team to practice. Then he did some research on the competition, snuck into the fieldhouse, borrowed the chalk machine with the set of keys he hadn't surrendered upon being fired as head coach of the Bodock Warriors, and chalked off two lines twenty-feet apart—the measure of last year's winning toss—in the swatch of grass behind the aluminum shed. He didn't bother unclipping the tape measurer from his belt now to determine how short the post had come up. The sod the post had kicked up lay several feet away from the line. Instead of repairing the divot, Rutherford kicked the grass clump into the chain-link fence at the back of the property.

Over the fence rattling, he heard Norah say, "What you doing home?"

His wife stood on the concrete patio. A striped tank top framed her wide, soft shoulders beneath an unzipped windbreaker. The end of February proved warm enough for her tan legs to ooze like firm caramel from the cutoff jean shorts her tank top was tucked into. He wondered why she'd come home on her lunch break to change. Something else different about her he couldn't quite run down.

Rutherford wiped his hands on his cargo shorts and put his arms out to hug her. She didn't move. He said, "Could ask you the same damn thing."

"Principal called the shop wondering where you was. Why ain't you called in for a substitute?"

Rutherford shrugged. "Forgot."

"You aiming to get your ass fired?"

Rutherford shrugged. "The fuck I care?"

She walked over to him then and handed him an envelope, its flap torn open. Printed in blue ink was the Bodock High School return address. Inside the envelope was a formal letter detailing the terms of his revised teaching contract. He had until Monday to sign and return the contract to the central office. But the only reason Rutherford had taught "Mississippi History" one semester and "Bodock History" the other semester of the school year to twelve-year-olds for the six periods before baseball each day was because coaches were required to teach. Wasn't his fault he'd inherited lofty expectations because the previous coach had already ascended into the ranks of state-level legend even before retirement by leading thirteen of his sixteen squads to the playoffs and three of those on to state championship titles. Wasn't his fault the boys he'd coached in his three-year tenure lacked the ambition, the drive. They wanted pussy and good grades and Rutherford wouldn't deny them either. But they didn't even want to chance titing-up on a renegade ground ball in the event it messed up their pretty boy faces. He'd needed more than three years to get the lazy shits to see that regret would outlive their youth. They'd been as soft as the damn wet ground before Rutherford but without the scars.

He said, "You opened my mail."

"Thought it was your paycheck."

"Could of told you it wasn't."

She crossed her arms across her chest and the tan flesh of her cleavage folded over the pale outline of the swim top she wore when she laid on the suntan bed.

"Obviously," she said.

She held back the envelope from Rutherford, pulled the papers from it, located the contract. "Sign this right now and run it up to the school. We got a mortgage."

"I'm kind of busy."

"So sign it and I'll run it up there."

"If I'm contractually obligated to Bodock, I ain't gonna be able to take another coaching position somewhere else."

"You got another coaching gig lined up elsewhere?"

Rutherford wished Norah knew something about it. He'd turned thirty-eight that year. At that same age, his old man had collapsed dead on a scrimmage field in Pensacola. Even before his dismissal, Rutherford had spent waking nights with the denim curtains drawn over their windows and Sunbeam crumbs collected in his chest hairs and every light in the house off in anxious expectation of the hereditary heart disease that would surely seize him in his La-Z-Boy. Sometimes he felt its presence in his chest. The pain hung from his sternum like several weighted donuts hitters used on deck to increase bat speed.

Rutherford shrugged. "Working on it."

"Jesus."

"At least I got goals."

"They ain't never included me. I see that now." Norah crammed the forms into the envelope and slapped the package on the gas grill on her way back to the house. "I'm going up to Eriksson's."

"In that?"

Norah stopped at the door and picked at the ends of her hair. Rutherford realized then her hair was short and cropped around her face. It looked all right enough but he preferred her hair long, past the shoulders. During the summer, sunlight would draw out fainter brown strands of hair like vines spiraling down tree trunks. He'd often look forward during long bus rides home from one more disappointed division loss to burying his face in those curls, getting lost in them woods.

"You took the morning off, got your hair done," he said. "See, I pay you attention, baby."

"Bo." Norah forced a smile. "I went to the beauty shop two days ago." She shook the sliding patio door down its track and turned back around once she was inside to close the door. "Going to work now. I'm going to change then I'm going to work and I ain't exactly sure when I'll be home."

Thirty minutes later, Rutherford heard her car start and the chassis whine and the brakes squeal as she backed down the incline of the drive. He felt pretty shitty about how Norah was leaving but he hadn't worked up the nerve to apologize before she headed out. He figured at worst she'd go into Eriksson Fitness Equipment and be back by her usual five-thirty, give him plenty of time to work up a good apology, formulate some kind of satisfactory response to his current employment crisis.

Until then he chucked hell out of the fence post from one end of the yard to the other. He'd never taught geometry but he experimented with different degrees of release points until he'd find one that launched the post so that it seemed to go the distance. But each time the post landed short of the line like so many moon-shot fly balls he'd sent sailing with promise to left-center that spring at the farm league in Birmingham, only to have the shots die like all his major league dreams at the warning track or in the glove of some future minor leaguer.

Even after six, he explained away her tardiness. She must have been swamped with managing employees' paychecks at the end of the week and wanted to catch up on mailing off checks to local steel suppliers and invoices to the regional high schools and small colleges Art Eriksson supplied with weight lifting equipment so she wouldn't have to go in on Saturday. Wasn't until he heard the house phone ringing impossibly loud from the backyard and looked at the digital Timex on his wrist that read three minutes after seven that he became worried. The ringing sounded so close, as if Norah had run a line out to the shed. The call cut off in the middle of the second ring. Around him crickets fiddled. He thought it could've been Norah checking in or a high school in sudden desperate need of a baseball coach and decided to wait in the house for one of them to call back.

Inside, Rutherford didn't find the cordless phone docked on the port attached to the wall in the kitchen. Reckoned Norah set it down somewhere. Was probably dead by now anyway. He took a seat in the La-Z-Boy next to the phone in the living room and helped himself to the Styrofoam box his loving wife must have left him in the fridge: a double order of six barbecue chicken tacos from Mi Pueblo. They frequented the Tex-Mex place even though Rutherford had to be cautious of what he ordered on account of his reflux. She had even written DINNER on the box in blue Sharpie, the capital I dotted with a heart. The series of small gestures broke his own heart a little. Working on his fourth taco, he had become too distracted with thoughts of what Norah was doing for dinner to note the mound of diced jalapeños and fiery tomatillo salsa buried beneath the shredded chicken. He pictured poor beautiful Norah sitting alone at Mi Pueblo, nibbling on complimentary nachos smothered in house-made salsa or queso. Norah kept a tight body, took advantage of working for a company that specialized in manufacturing weight-lifting equipment.

His mouth and sinuses began to pulse with heat and guilt and his eyes pooled tears of jalapeño sadness. Bodock was small with only so many places to look for her. He imagined a scene from a movie, bursting in to rescue Norah from her loneliness. Rutherford abandoned the fifth taco and left the tray on the side table and picked up his keys on the kitchen counter.

On his way out the door, he ran into Gray Sherman on their doorstep. Gray's arm was raised, anticipating the knock.

"Hello, neighbor," Gray said. They lived in Happy Hollow, a neighborhood dropped down in several acres of cleared-out bottom just off Main Street. Gray lived in the cove at the end of the street half a mile away. Cul-de-sac, Gray insisted as he did now, his arm still cocked as if refusing to give up on the knock just yet. "It's me, Gray Sherman, from the cul-de-sac."

Gray was wearing a pair of jeans cut off at the thigh and a faded Bodock Warrior Track-and-Field T-shirt. The small surface area of his upper lip only allowed a thin mustache. The rest of him favored towards skinny, too. Gray had gone to high school with Norah and had been a considerate enough queer to Rutherford even though Rutherford didn't know a single other homosexual to compare Gray to. He owned a little sandwich-and-soup diner on Main Street and a floral shop next door. Called them Sherman's Chowder & Flowers. The same men who joked that Gray jacked off into the homemade mayonnaise could still be seen in there buying roses for their wives on the occasions of birthdays and anniversaries, Valentine's Day and the habitual fuck-up.

"Um, sorry, Gray. Norah's out." He wondered whether to ask about some flowers to take to Norah now. "On my way to meet her."

Gray retired his arm. "You mean she ain't here?"

Rutherford shrugged.

"That's strange. I called a little while ago but the line was cut off. Sounded like someone answered and hung up." Gray gestured at his house in the cul-de-sac. "Her car's parked in front of my house. I walked down here to see if everything was aight—"

"Huh?"

Gray said, "What's that?"

"About her car."

Gray held his hands up in defense. "Oh, it's aight. I mean, she can leave it there all she wants. It ain't hurting nothing. Least I can do. Probably the car just went dead, right?"

Rutherford shrugged off his own worry. "Probably."

"Probably she was just making the loop or something so she could park in front of y'all's house facing with traffic and it just went dead in front of my house. Not that I mind it being there, like I said. Happens all the time. Well, not all the time. But it definitely could happen. Is definitely in the range of possible things to happen, you know." Gray furrowed his brow. "But you said you was fixing to go meet her."

Rutherford didn't respond. The street lamps ignited in the dying light, their electric hum as they pitched shadows off parked cars and piles of pine branches hemmed with needles and bare oak limbs that had been collected at the edge of yards after the storm and spilled out into the street.

"Coach?"

"Huh?"

"You going to meet her. That's what you said, right?"

"I meant at work," Rutherford said. "That's what I meant. I meant I figured she was still at work, was going to surprise her there. Take her to Mi Pueblo."

"Know what? Bet she tried to call you on her way home and y'all's phone was acting up like it did me."

"Might of. Been in the backyard all evening."

"Well see there. Probably the car died and she walked home to change and get a jog in before it got too dark. You know how fit that woman likes to be. Ever since high school when we was on the track-and-field team."

"Norah ran track?"

"And field." Gray pointed at his shirt. "Both of us did. Well, I was on the boys' squad, she on the girls', obviously." Gray sighed, wiped his forehead. "Some winter weather, huh? Oh well. Bet you just missed Norah is all. You probably just didn't hear her come in then is all. Probably gonna be in here soon and y'all'll still have time to eat. Y'all should come by my shop tomorrow for lunch." Gray laughed. "It's kind of funny you know. Norah's car parked there in front of my house of all places."

"What do you mean?"

"Well, if it was in front of any other man's house, you'd have to worry about folks talking. But I'm the resident gay man on the block." Gray gave Rutherford a friendly punch on the arm. "See y'all tomorrow. Don't forget to tell her to call me when she gets in, let me know everything's all right. Sure that it is."

Rutherford stepped back inside the house. He tried not to think about his wife having an affair. But the thought had already been planted by the gay florist. Maybe it had been there before that. But Norah wouldn't be dumb enough to park right in front of the man's house she was having an affair with, Rutherford thought. She would park in front of an old homosexual friend's house as if paying a visit, then sneak off through backyards to rendezvous with her nearby lover.

Rutherford felt a kick in his chest that dropped him to the carpet. A tremor of pain shot through his chest again. His mind perused its limited medical dictionary before landing on palpitation. All he could imagine right at that moment was Norah beneath some gentleman friend, her gorgeous legs parted and the man's body perpendicular to hers. Her areolas under the man's microscopic gaze and her tan flesh the receptacle of his sweat and other more despicable vehicles of DNA. Previously Rutherford had enjoyed the stares Norah commanded from other men. His players couldn't help stealing glances at her in the bleachers during all those home games and even some away ones or when she made some unexpected visit to the field house or practice. Until about five minutes ago, Rutherford had been gracious that her job offered her a free gym membership, something he reaped the benefits of without ever leaving his bed, much less ever stepping foot in Art Eriksson's gym. Art Eriksson had competed on the semi-pro bodybuilding circuit in the Sixties, had even taken Mr. Mississippi in 1968 and 1969. Art was in his fifties now but his body still held remnants of its former glory: chest-thick and his upper abdomen protruding with dense muscles and the elastic band of the sleeves of his every polo shirt slit to accommodate the musculature of his biceps and triceps. Art saw Norah almost every day, lived a few streets over. Art had found every success he wanted in life and Rutherford was convinced that Art now found his nude wife under him and his own jackassery had sent Norah there.

When he heard the patio door open, he was sprawled on the carpet. Legs splayed, hands clutching the exponentiating knot in his chest. He saw Norah standing above him.

"I'm dying, Norah."

"You ain't dying."

"Thought it'd been heart disease," he grunted. "Might still be. If it is it'd be that and my heart breaking with grief simultaneously. Where have you been? Did you have a good time with Art?"

"Who?" Norah said. "Get up. You ain't having a heart attack. You just got a bad case of indigestion."

"Not this time." He noted Norah's hair and the same clothes she was wearing earlier now sweat-matted and clinging to her figure. The glisten of her deep cleavage under the ceiling fan light he feared had been on display for Art all day. "Please tell me you didn't go to work in that."

"Didn't go in to work," she said. In her hand was the cordless phone. Grass clippings clung to her bare ankles and feet. "Been in the shed all afternoon." She glanced toward the recliner. "See you ate them tacos already."

"Not all of em." He propped himself up on his elbows. The pain in his chest had lessened but was still present. "What was you doing in the shed?"

"Watching you practice."

"Huh?"

Norah leaned back against the plaid couch "I had about every intention of going to work and staying the night at the Bodock Inn on account of the ass you was being. But after I packed a duffel bag, I realized something. I shouldn't be the one spending all evening watching *In the Heat of the Night* on a thirteen-inch television worrying and waiting for Bo Rutherford to come around. So I hatched a plan to corner you into signing the contract and kicked the duffel bag under the bed and picked up dinner at Mi Pueblo and parked in front of Gray's place and snuck up to the house. I wasn't sure where to hide until you was done with dinner so I took a seat on the riding lawn mower and watched you practice from the back window of the shed."

"Let me get this straight." Rutherford leaned his weight on his left elbow. "You basically poisoned me—"

"Poisoned you?"

"—'cause you couldn't think of no better way to get me to sign the contract?"

"If you call giving you spicy food 'poisoning you.' Doubt anyone else would. Judge Ford sure as shit certainly wouldn't"

"You know how crazy that sounds?"

"Is it really all that much crazier than not telling your wife you was thinking about quitting your job?"

The air conditioner kicked on. The ceiling fan whirled.

"That Gray guy came by," Rutherford said. "Said to call and let him know everything was all right."

"Guess I ought to go move the car."

Norah closed the lid on the tacos and returned them to the refrigerator, grabbed two beers and took a bottle of antacid from the cabinet above the fridge. She squatted over him, her jean shorts creased into her hip cleavage. "Sorry again." She dropped a Tums into Rutherford's mouth, popped open a beer and handed it to him. Then she opened hers, drained the neck out of it. "It was insane. I just thought if I cornered you while you was down I could get you to sign the contract."

Rutherford crunched on the medicine. "I'll sign the contract." He swallowed. "Shit."

"That ain't the point, Bo." She swatted him on the side of the head. "I was being selfish. Not any more selfish than you was." She stood. Her knee fired off a quick succession of pops, the thick scar from her previous injury elongating as her leg straightened. "I really was fixing to leave you for a while, Bo. Hated watching you obsess over something trivial like throwing a damn stick—"

"'Preciate that."

"—and me not being to think of a damn thing to do to help. You got to let me in, Bo."

Tears accumulated in the corner of Norah's green eyes and Rutherford was at a loss. He knew he had been at a loss for a while now. He had at least as many losses in his life as he had in his failure as a baseball coach. He would've appreciated a win. Norah swiped a thumb below her eye. Her tricep was not yet the loose sling of flesh of middle age. He imagined those arms docking a pole hard into a vault while in mid-sprint or flinging some shot put into a gravel pit. His mind wrapped around an idea.

"What's that track event where you spin around with that shot put thing on the chain or whatever the hell it is?"

"You mean field event." She dabbed below her other eye, rubbed her finger against her shirt. "The hammer throw. Why?"

"That's the one. You do that one?"

"Ain't a high school event. Neither was javelin. Too dangerous."

"You do any events where you spun?"

"I threw discus."

Rutherford gave a half-grin. "You think that'd work throwing a fence post?"

Norah looked out the patio door at the fence post leaning against the grill. She inhaled deep and sighed like surrendering. "Perhaps. You want me to show you?"

"Yeah, baby."

She unfolded the contract. "Sign this."

"Norah. I'm a coach. Ain't a history teacher."

"I know you want to coach. I want to not lose our house. And if you want me to help with the fence post thing you got to sign this contract."

Rutherford mulled it over. He pulled himself to his feet. Joints echoing Norah's. "Aight," he said. "Aight. I'll sign it after we practice."

"Nice try," she said and reached for the Sharpie on the dining room table.

For the remainder of the evening, Norah coached Rutherford beneath the motion-detector floodlight mounted on the side of the shed. Norah suggested they focus on the three-quarters-turn throw first. She told him to stand with his right shoulder facing the throwing area, like so. Hold the fence post out in front with both hands like a baseball bat. Slide left foot behind you, pivot on your right foot, until you've gone 180 degrees. She mocked released the post as she planted her left foot and followed through the momentum of the spin with her right foot. All this in slow motion. Said, Nothing to it, and told him to give it a try. But Rutherford had grown potbellied and clumsy. His feet would not cooperate and tripped over each other. He released the post and followed his own momentum to the ground where he landed on his back. The post landed over the fence.

She laughed. "Close."

He flipped her the bird. She turned and favored her right leg when she hopped the fence. The bottom half of each of her butt cheeks compressed from beneath her cut-offs. He imagined her twenty years earlier in track shorts jumping hurdles. After she retrieved the post, she guided Rutherford through the process a couple of times. Thirty minutes later his tosses improved on accuracy and distance. Fifteen minutes after that fatigue took over.

"Let's call it a day," Norah said. "We'll get up early and practice in the morning. Then you're taking me to breakfast."

In the morning, they drove into downtown Bodock and ate pancakes and fried tenderloin and biscuits with white gravy. From the front window they could see the vacant grass lot between the Piggly Wiggly and the old Cummings Drug Store where the competition would be held in August beneath the second largest bodock tree in the state. Just across the street the old Civil War cannon and the granite pedestal holding the statue of Col. Claygardner, the founder of the county, who fought a skirmish near Bodock against a fraction of Grant's men who had followed him down from Shiloh after one of Claygardner's trips smuggling moonshine and whiskey and arms into Memphis. The skirmish had no effect on the outcome of the war and Claygardner died later fighting in east Tenneessee for some asinine reason only his friend and former slave Beauregard knew about.

Rutherford hurled one last throw that bested any of his previous ones. A similar toss would be good enough to take second place come August to some former All-American bruiser who played ball under Bear Bryant in his final year of coaching. Inspired by his rejuvenated confidence, he convinced Norah's body to follow his to the ground. He still wasn't sure what to make of things and didn't think he could see himself coaching some little league team sponsored by

Sherman's Chowder & Flowers, which would be the only option available it seemed if he stayed in Bodock. But maybe Norah would give him an all-state short stop one day. And gravity was working in his favor now. On the ground the air wrapped around them like a lukewarm bath. An early spring chorus of crickets warmed up. The floodlight above them blinking.

HEARTWORMS

ALL THE BOY WANTED was a gun to put his dog out of its misery. His grandfather had told him once that most of God's creatures were not made to suffer. Most of God's creatures included gut-shot deer and broke-leg horses and terminal cases of most dog breeds. Chad, twelve, owned a dog that was one of those breeds, a rat terrier he'd received for his second Christmas. Now the worms in Lady's heart had retreated to her lungs where they swelled her black-brown-spotted white fur like a helium nozzle had been plugged into her.

Chad had his fingers locked into chain links in the fence. He rested his head against the patterned metal, which dented a pentagon into the thin flesh of his forehead. Most of the afternoon had been burned away watching Lady struggle to her feet, wobble across the pallet of pine needles covering the pen, and whimper at the boy's high tops. She started with a cough of some persistence a couple of months ago. Then sacrifices of blind, gnawed-at moles that she would dig up around the yard were no longer left on the back stoop of their house. Sprints toward realms unknown ceased.

"Just gettin old," his old man had said.

But then her belly inflated this week and kept on swelling, her fur stretched taut around her ribcage, her backbone defined as knuckles.

"Heart damn worms," he said. "Nothin we can do about it. Not a damn thing."

Today was Saturday. He'd been out of school since Wednesday because of an ice storm that had dropped acres of timber and knocked power out across the county. The temperature had risen and the frequency of limbs splitting from their trees had lessened by now so that it was safer to venture out. So the first thing this morning, the boy had unlatched the gate and offered Lady the chance to run around. The dog would have none of it. The boy changed out her water and gave her fresh dry food. But all day he avoided touching her, resisted scratching her fur behind her unclipped ears and her hind leg. She stared up at him with eyes that couldn't comprehend his betrayal. But he just couldn't push past the thought that she might explode heartworms all over him.

Later, when the sun had flattened out across the horizon, he found his old man dozing in the blue corduroy recliner. The footrest kicked up, a sitcom muted on the television. He was a small-shouldered man and thin except for a small paunch of gut his unbuttoned jeans accommodated. A Mountain Dew sweated onto the end table. The laminate surface curled away from one of the corners and a Gulfport coaster sat next to the can.

He nudged his old man's shoulder. "Pops."

He watched his father's slack-jawed, stubbled chin work its mouth into words. "Huh."

"Was wondering," the boy said.

"Some Dinty Moore in the cabinet you can heat up." His old

man thumped the coke can. The can rang hollow. "Get me another Dew."

The boy went to the kitchen. "They ain't any in the fridge."

"Try the one in the garage."

In the carport fridge, Mountain Dews shared space with his mother's Old Milwaukees. Cans of either divided the shelves and filled the storage in the doors. Chad took a Mountain Dew back to his father. His father cracked it open, drained a good bit of it, and flipped some channels on the television. Taxidermy flew feathered around the living room and a deer peered its antlered noggin out from the wood-paneled walls. His father didn't hunt now and Chad had previously had little interest in the sport except for the prospect now that his father had shot a gun before and may still have that gun somewhere in the house.

"Pops."

"Huh."

"Was wondering if you could teach me how to hunt?"

"Hunt what?"

"Deer, I guess."

"Too late this season."

"What's in season?"

"Work's got me too busy anyway."

"Can teach myself then if you just get me a gun."

His father pulled on the Mountain Dew again then produced a can of Grizzly from his back pocket. He packed the can against his palm before he snatched a plug that he folded impressively quick into his lip, spitting some strands of the snuff from his lip into the empty can.

"What's the sudden interest?"

Chad betrayed his intentions by looking towards the backyard.

"This got anything to do with that dog of yours?"

"Sir?"

"Listen to me. Leave that dog alone. I ain't got time this week to dig a grave."

"But she won't run around or dig up moles. We should of took her to Dr. Svens."

"Ain't fixing to pay a vet for something I can handle my damn self."

Later that night, Chad microwaved some beef stew and watched his father snore from the recliner until he was convinced his old man was out until morning. His mother worked at a twelve-hour overnight shift at the hospital in Tupelo on Saturdays and two other nights during the week, so she wouldn't be home.

Chad snuck through their bedroom into the closet. He looked around and behind his parents' clothes. Chad had a perfectly fine air rifle his grandfather had left on their doorstep last year for his birthday. He knew little about guns except that he needed something that could do more than fart out BBs.

At the bottom of one of the drawers he found what he had learned—from a creased *Playboy* a classmate had stolen from his father—was a thong. That find surprised him. He had known for about a year now from locker-room talk in P.E. how he had been conceived in a sort of general sense. A boner rubbed somewhere between a woman's legs. The rest was magic, he'd guessed. But Chad could not remember a night his father had not fallen asleep on the recliner and not still been there snoring the next morning. Still, at least once his old man must've felt inspired enough to peel himself off the recliner and visit Chad's mother in bed. Or perhaps she had taken the initiative, put on this thong, and met him on that ratty old corduroy recliner just the one time they conjured him up.

An hour later, he concluded his search and decided that if his father still possessed a rifle or a shotgun, he kept it locked up and dormant as his pecker.

The next day was Sunday, which meant church and pan-fried pork chops afterward at his grandparents' house. His grandparents lived in a small rancher on three acres. Along the east end of the property was the railroad that his grandfather, Hambone, had worked for. Between the house and the tracks sat the barn with its thin fiberglass walls where horses were raised and shod and broken to subsidize his earnings at the rail yard. When Hambone was made supervisor, he continued the side enterprise out of habit and hobby.

In the kitchen, Granny slipped the last batch of thin battered chops into the skillet on the stove. The chops rejoiced when they hit that hot grease. Hambone rode into the dining room from the den, his six-foot-five frame hunched over a motorized scooter. He wore a polyester button-down and light starched khakis and a hem of the khakis caught on the mouth of a work boot. He shook Chad's hand again like he had in the fellowship hall at First Baptist in front of all the other old timers and coffee drinkers. His paw swallowed Chad's and whipped his thin arm around like a horse would its tail.

At the table were deviled eggs, mashed potatoes, brown gravy. On a plate lined with paper towels, fried chops spread their grease like slick colorless blood. The way Granny's bony fingers clutched the hardboiled egg half when she served Chad reminded him of Lady's rib cage stretched out across her firm swollen belly.

"Eat up, boy," Hambone said. "Chad here's puny as a rail pin.

Y'all ain't feeding him?"

"He gets fed," Chad's father said. He wore khakis and a casual khaki wind jacket over a polo shirt and held a plastic bottle of Mountain Dew while sitting next to Granny. Chad's mother had slept in that morning after leaving three empty beer cans on the counter after her shift.

"Don't seem y'all are doing a good job of fattening up this foal."

"Got a high metabolism, I guess."

"Hell. He's about to hit the spurt and his bones ain't got any fat to stretch with."

About all of Chad's classmates at school had hit the spurt and had filled out and boasted of hairs trailing from belly buttons down around their pecker and balls, which was all put on display pissing into the trough in the restrooms at Bodock Junior High. Chad always retreated to a stall to do his business.

After lunch, Hambone excused himself to digest his food lying down. Granny slurped coffee while she cleared the table and washed the dishes.

"Saw where schools wasn't gonna be open tomorrow," Granny said.

"They don't know when they're gonna get the power fixed."

"What're y'all gonna do with Chad?"

"Sheila's off work."

Granny hummed. "Your father wants to know if Chad can sit with him tomorrow." Chad's father had moved from the table to a stool near the counter and spit into the emptied Mountain Dew bottle before twisting the green cap back on. "What for?"

"I got to work."

"I mean why's he need someone here?"

"Well, I guess cause he's gotta sit in this dusty house alone all day while I'm at work. He can't get around anywhere or drive. Ain't got any neighbors but them blacks packed into them government houses over across the tracks. He likes to spend his days out in the barn, but he can't get there and then inside all by himself. He needs someone to hold the door so he can drive up and down the ramp. He thought it might be good to have Chad around during the day, get his mind off wondering when his next heart attack gonna come."

His father removed the cap again and spat twice into the bottle before twisting the cap back on. "What if something happens?"

"He ain't like he was with you. He don't drink no more."

"Meant like a heart attack."

"I gotta take a leak," Chad said to no one.

Hambone was occupying the hall bathroom, but Chad didn't really have to go anyway. Was just worried about being here tomorrow. Chad knew to call 911 if Hambone had a heart attack but didn't know what one looked like. But it wasn't just that. His father had often joked about getting his ass whipped with a limb from the bodock in the backyard until his legs bled. Chad's own father had only ever popped him with his hand a couple of times. That never hurt much.

Chad wandered past the hall bathroom but stopped when he got to the open door to his grandparents' bedroom at the end of the hall. The maroon comforter on the king bed was faded and stained and turned back from depressed pillows. Chunky blue carpet on the floor. A wheelchair Hambone had abandoned for the scooter leaned folded in a corner and the walker he hadn't managed for some time stood beside a nightstand covered with papers and torn-open envelopes and a Bible. A handgun of some caliber weighed down a stack of papers.

Chad hung his head back out the doorjamb and looked down the hallway to the kitchen. Could still hear them talking. Hambone still in the bathroom. He thought he had enough time to catch a quick glimpse of the gun. Even had the thought he could pocket it before Hambone got out of the bathroom. But he had no clue what kind of gun that was or if it'd be any account in ending Lady's misery. If there was a better gun to use. He walked quickly over to it. Its metal was black and it had a wood-grained handle. He reached out his hand then paused. Still heard no movement. He recognized the design as a revolver because of westerns and the spinning chamber. The revolver surprised him with its heft. He imagined such a heavy gun would do the trick. Tried not to imagine the blood that would spread like oil or grease, the pine straw soaking it up like paper towels.

"That's a Colt .45"

Chad startled at the voice that boomed behind him and dropped the Colt on the ground.

"Careful there, boy." Hambone drove the scooter around the bed. Chad had never appreciated how quiet the machine whispered along on its battery power until it had snuck up on him. Hambone leaned over to retrieve the Colt. The waft of Old Spice and sweat and the rot of Hambone's labored breath reached Chad. In the last half decade Hambone had suffered three heart attacks and an open-heart surgery. Had a hip replaced with an artificial one. Slipped some discs and had the operations to fix them. Still he had a head full of gray hair greased into a part. Hambone said, "Damn good way to blow your ankle clean off your foot. Good thing it ain't loaded though."

Some dust motes floated about. Hambone stooped over in the chair, inspecting the revolver and then Chad. Mumbled something to himself. He seemed to be going over an important thing in his mind and didn't speak for a few minutes. Chad feared his grandfather was contemplating whether he would report Chad. His father would put this together with his warning last night and would perhaps hire Hambone to administer a bodock limb continuously across his ass.

"My son ain't never taught you about guns?"

"No sir."

"About how to shoot?"

"Um, no sir."

"Hell then. Let's learn you how."

Chad got dropped off just before eight the next morning. Granny had already left to calculate her teller drawer at the Peoples Bank. His father had lost the argument with his mother that evening about dropping Chad off. He was running late to work now and didn't walk Chad to the door. Chad hung around on the stoop of the carport before he mustered the courage to go in. Inside, he walked by the washer and dryer in the mudroom into the kitchen that opened into the dining room. The scooter was pulled up parallel to the dining table and Hambone sat sideways in the seat eating leftover fried pork chops and biscuits Granny woke up early to knead.

"Help yourself," Hambone said. Chad cut open a biscuit over a clean plate and buttered one side of the biscuit and then the other after Hambone told him he needed to fatten up some. Scooped some Welch's grape jelly onto his biscuit with a spoon left in the plastic jar. Over the jelly he placed two slices of cheese already carved out of the wheel of red wax and slapped a fried pork chop between the dressed biscuit.

Chad walked the plate over to the table. He was not used to

having company when he ate. Most mornings he sat on the couch and spooned Fruit Loops or Fruity Pebbles or ate pancake and sausage on a stick, a breakfast version of a corn dog that came frozen in a Jimmy Dean box. He could never get the sausage fully thawed in the microwave. This pork was cold, too, but Hambone said that was the only way to eat anything that had been fried and leftover. Hambone wore worked-in khakis and a clean button-down white shirt, the collar stained brown with long-ago sweat. The shirt held short sleeves and his rail-tie forearms held liver spots. A gold medical bracelet on his wrist. He slurped at his steaming mug.

"You want some coffee?"

Chad shrugged. "Never had any before."

"Gonna be a day of firsts for you. There's a cup hanging on a peg over the Bunn over there. Pour you some whole milk in the cup first then the coffee. Stir in some sugar after that."

After breakfast, Hambone retrieved the gun from the bedroom and brought it and a holster to the kitchen. The gun closet, which had originally been intended as a pantry, was the first door on the right off the dining room.

Hambone jiggled the handle. "Shit. Granny done locked it again."

Chad tongued at a hunk of pork caught between molars. "Where's the key?"

"Don't know."

"Where's the last place you had it?"

"Knew that then the damn thing wouldn't be lost."

Chad shrugged. "That's what my mom always asks when I lose something."

"Sounds like something her drunk ass would say."

Chad didn't know how to respond. It was true that she often said those exact words with an Old Milwaukee in her hand or her head still under a pillow come lunchtime and Chad in need or want of something.

"All right," Hambone said. "Here's you another lesson. No matter who it is or whether their opinion's valid, anyone ever say something like that about your mother you punch them in the goddamn face. Understood?"

Chad nodded and cornered the pork abrasion against his gums.

"You know how to throw a punch?"

Chad shook his head. "No sir."

"I'll learn you that another day. Hell. Where's that goddamn key."

Chad dislodged the pork in his teeth. With nowhere to spit, he was forced to swallow it. He had the thought that they would get nowhere today without a key and felt like kicking the door down. He looked at the small round hole in the door knob. They made slender keys for it but such a key wasn't necessary to open it.

"Hambone," Chad said. "I can get this door unlocked."

"How?"

"Need a coat hanger."

Hambone squinted an eye at the possibility. "There's some empty ones hanging in that back bedroom."

Cobwebs coated the corners of the retired bedroom. A large spider crawled across the ceiling and the pillow cases were brown and dirty. Chad retrieved a metal hanger from the closet and carried it back down the hall, unwrapping the coiled neck into a straight rod before inserting the straighter end into the hole. He fiddled the hanger around until he'd located the lever to the lock, which he depressed and held down while he twisted the door knob. The door creaked open.

"Well sumbitch," Hambone said out the side of an impressed smirk. The closet proved too small for both of them so he pointed

Chad's attention toward the popcorn ceiling. "The cartridges gonna be up there in one of them boxes on the top shelf. There's a step stool right there."

The closet held all kinds of old guns coated in varying degrees of dust that spoke of the duration of their disuse. Longer guns were braced upright in a rack affixed against the wall. Some wide barreled and narrow ones and some of the narrow barrels held scopes. Lined on the lower shelf were pistols. Like cousins they resembled the one Hambone kept on his nightstand. Chad climbed to the top shelf and chose a box and reached it down for his grandfather to inspect.

"Dust off the box," Hambone said. So Chad did. Dust motes snowed toward the carpet. Hambone waved the air clear in front of his face and said, "Nah. Them are twenty-two cartridges. Get the box next to em down."

Chad returned the box to its dustless indentation among the exoskeletons of long dried-out insect carcasses littering the shelf. He wondered how Hambone got the bullets down on his own when the door was unlocked. Chad chose the correct box next and when he stepped off the stool he pointed at the longest of the thin barreled guns. The breech of the gun held some kind of cool scope. "Kind of gun is that?"

"Thirty-aught-six."

"What about that one?"

"Twelve gauge."

"What's a twelve gauge?"

"A shotgun."

"What about the thirty, uh, six?"

"Thirty-aught. It's a rifle."

"What's the difference?"

"One has a rifled barrel. Spins the bullet around, makes it travel further. Don't explode until on impact." Hambone mimicked the flight of a rifle cartridge by spinning the index finger of one hand toward Chad. When the index finger reached his grandson's chest Hambone demonstrated the detonation of the cartridge by spreading all of his fingers out. "The other fires shells filled with metal bearings. Ain't got the range of a rifle but the shells explode when fired and the bearings spread out as they're discharged and cover a wider target at a closer distance."

This time Hambone positioned his fingers like a shadow puppet, slowly spreading out his palm and fingers as he moved his hand toward Chad. "You can use either hunting. The shotgun's good for killing ducks and birds, small game like rabbits and squirrels. A twenty-two rifle is good for rabbits and squirrels also. Can still use a shotgun for deer. Use birdshot for winged game and buckshot for hunting deer."

"What's birdshot and buckshot?"

Chad thought he might be asking too many questions, the coffee coursing through him, turning him jittery and hyper. But Hambone didn't seem annoyed. He rested his arms on the handlebars of the scooter and explained how birdshot-grade bearings were smaller than buckshot-grade bearings so they didn't fuck up the bird meat too much you couldn't eat it.

"Could use a slug in the shotgun as well," Hambone said. Chad started to ask what a slug was but Hambone went on: "Ought to get on down to the barn to shoot. Fixin to burn away the rest of our day up here." Hambone mulled over something else and said, "Climb back up there and get the box of twelve-gauge birdshot. The thirty-aught-six might go right through the barn, hit one of them colored folks over in the project down there. But we can give the twelve gauge a try. Hopefully it ain't gonna kick the joint right out of that scrawny shoulder of yours."

On the way to the backyard Chad walked in front of the scooter. In a plastic Jitney Jungle grocery bag, he collected horse apples from the bodock tree littering the path so Hambone's scooter did not run up on one. They also needed the horse apples for targets. Hambone carried the pistol on his hip in the worn leather holster and the box of rounds in the cage affixed to the handlebars. The shotgun he cradled in the nook of his elbow. With his free hand he steered the scooter out to the backside of the barn in the bright sunlight. The battery-quiet motor like a sustained muffled fart. The sun had not yet burned off the morning chill.

"Go in the barn there and bring out some bales," Hambone said.

"How many?"

"However many you can bring out here until I say you ain't got to bring no more."

The hay was wet and molded and the rope holding each bale cut through the hay, spilling it on the dirt floor. Chad had to manage one bale at a time, which he heaved onto the ground against the exterior wall at the back of the barn. Once Chad had seen his grandfather hurl a damn horse right out of that barn. Not a pony. A full-grown walking horse too stubborn or not broken enough to yield to a bit. Hambone grabbed the horse around its neck and whipped the equine mass around, sent it stumbling to the dirt of the pen adjoining the barn. After the family had all left that afternoon, Hambone broke the horse's leg while trying to break its spirit down enough to follow his orders and had to put the beast down. Hambone himself couldn't ride a horse anymore so he'd sold them all off on account he couldn't even tend to them. Sure as hell couldn't toss one onto the ground now. Chad wondered whether Hambone would've already put his own self down like he had the walking horse that afternoon. But folks were different than animals.

When Chad had amassed ten bales, Hambone instructed him to build two stacks of four bales against the barn as a buffer so the bullets could not travel through the thin fiberglass wall. Stood two more bales in front of those stacks. On the shorter stack he placed three of the bodock balls from the plastic bag.

Hambone had parked the scooter about fifteen feet from the barn. There he showed Chad how to load the gun. He switched off the safety and flipped the safety latch that allowed the barreled magazine to swing away from the hammer and barrel. Hambone slipped a single bullet into one of the six holes in the round magazine. He handed the gun to Chad to load.

Hambone said, "The tapered end of the round should point away from you in the same direction you'd be aiming at."

Chad held the gun with his right hand while he filled the rest of the empty chambers with his left. He returned the gun to Hambone who showed his grandson how to cock the hammer, how to line up the sight at the end of the muzzle between the two sights over the breech. Hambone held the gun with both hands, saddled the scooter sideways, and allowed himself about a second to aim. The bullet tore through the horse apple on the far left. A section of the horse apple cleaved from the whole.

"Your bat," Hambone said.

In his effort to draw back the stubborn hammer, Chad accidentally pulled the trigger. The pistol cracked loudly and surprised him as dirt spat up from the ground in front of them. The pistol nearly kicked out of his hand.

"Keep your finger off the trigger until you're ready to fire."

Chad's first shot missed the hay bales completely and drew a hole in the side of the barn. Later, when he was returning the hay bales, he would notice the dot of light on the dirt floor, its tail following to the hole in the thin wall that already filtered daylight like translucent membrane. His next two shots landed in the short stack of hay bales. His sixth and final round grazed one of the horse apples, shaved off some yellow ridges, and spun the ball on the bale.

"All right. Not terrible. Reload and try again."

By the fourth shot of the second reload Chad had solidly nailed one of the horse apples. The horse apple exploded into thirds.

At twelve, they retired the hay bales to the barn. Chad raked up straw that had fallen out of the bales then collected the horse apple fragments, forty-five casings, and emptied twelve-gauge shells in the Jitney Jungle bag, which he chucked over the chain-link fence into the railyard like Hambone instructed instead of in the outside garbage cans.

Before preparing lunch, they put away the Colt and the twelve gauge. Chad's shoulder was still sore from the recoil of the shotgun. The first shot had kicked him to the ground. After the second round his shoulder had felt like it would about dislocate. While Hambone drove down the hall to return the Colt to his nightstand, Chad climbed the foot stool and realized he did not have the box of forty-five cartridges. When Hambone returned, Chad glanced at the empty basket on the handlebars and asked if Hambone had the cartridges.

"Think I might of left em in the barn."

"You need me to go get em?"

"Nah. We can get em tomorrow. About to get some lunch right

now. You done wore me out."

The cartridges down at the barn might have made for easy picking but there was no way to borrow the Colt without Hambone realizing it was gone. There was a whole closet of other guns here but no way for Chad to know which gun to try to sneak out.

Before Hambone could reverse out of the gun closet, Chad asked, "What if you need to put an animal out of its misery? What kind is best then?"

Hambone stopped to consider the question. "A handgun. Something small like a twenty-two."

Chad said, "I thought those was a rifle."

"They make em in revolvers too. Use the same long-range cartridges as the rifle."

Hambone waved Chad out of the closet so he could pick a pistol smaller than the Colt .45 from the lower shelf. "There's a twenty-two."

Chad took the pistol from Hambone's paw. "Can I have it?"

Hambone considered it. "You ain't quite ready to have a gun on your own. 'Specially not in town limits." He handed the gun to Chad despite his words. The revolver was much lighter than the Colt but the magazine mechanisms and hammer were similar.

"Hide it in your room," Hambone said. "Practice releasing the magazine and cocking the hammer. Clean it some. It's a good starter pistol."

"How do I clean it?"

"I'll show you after lunch."

"What about bullets?"

"Some wishful thinking there. But hell no."

For an hour after a lunch of store-bought pimento cheese sandwiches, Hambone taught Chad how to load and unload the twenty-two revolver with empty twenty-two shells that had already been discharged. When they were finished, Chad stowed away the twenty-two and the empty shells at the bottom of his backpack and the rest of the afternoon was burned away sitting in the den. Only a little daylight came through the window curtains. John Wayne howdy-partnering and hello-pilgrimming on the television.

Chad listened for several minutes after Hambone began snoring upright in the recliner. Then he retrieved the hanger again from the spare bedroom and picked the lock on the gun closet. Quietly he grabbed a handful of live twenty-two rounds from the dust-streaked box on the top shelf and packed those in his bag as well.

His mom was on a shift that evening and Pops was passed out on the couch. Chad went to his room and raised his shirt up in the tall mirror on the back of his bedroom door to inspect the proud bruise on his shoulder. He unpacked his bag, pulled the twenty-two from the bottom and the empty and live cartridges, and hid the empty cartridges in his closet in the pocket of an old winter coat he had outgrown where they clanked against a half-empty can of his father's snuff he was still mustering the courage to try.

He fed the live rounds into the revolver and slid the back door open and walked out to the dog pen. The gun was heavier loaded and gave him a sense of power that quickened his heart rate and unsettled his stomach. Lady lay halfway out of her dog house. Chad found himself praying she'd just died already. She struggled to her feet though when she heard him at the gate, her lungs wheezing as she hobbled toward him. The gate rattled the chain link behind him. He hid the twenty-two behind his back and took a knee in the moist pine needles.

"Hey girl," he said. The fence around their yard was chain-linked as well. Some neighbors had left their porch lights on but no one was out to watch. With his left hand, he began to search her head and neck for some tender efficient spot that would accept the bullet with the least pain. When he groped behind her unclipped ears, her hind leg kicked lazily at her swollen side. He rubbed behind her ear some more. Her leg nudged her flank again and she whimpered yearnings for him to continue. He massaged her head and muzzle and the tips of her floppy ears. Her leg was out of control. Chad laughed and kept at it until he realized he couldn't do this thing tonight. He imagined her head detonating as the horse apples had. That sounded pretty damn awful. Told himself a bullet in her neck or lungs or heart would just hurt her more.

Chad caught a stank of shit. Somewhere in the pen was a steaming turd pile, and the floodlight on the back of the house didn't light up the pen enough to risk finding and cleaning it up without smashing it beneath his shoes or the knee of his jeans. The worms had been making Lady constipated, so he decided this was a good sign. A bill of improving health. He decided she could sleep in his room tonight. On the floor instead of the bed, though. In the event she exploded heartworms.

Morning. A knock on his bedroom door awoke him. His father leaned in wearing a National Furniture T-shirt tucked into his blue jeans and an unbuttoned flannel shirt. White tennis shoes beneath the tapered cuff of his jeans. Lady raised her head.

"What's the dog doing in here?"

"I dunno." Chad found the remote on his nightstand and turned on the television. Tom and Jerry quietly beating the shit out of each other.

His father furrowed his brow at the dog's wheezing. "She don't look so good. Came down here to tell you Granny called on her way out the door. Said Hambone was still worn out from yesterday and was taking a raincheck on today."

Chad scratched biscuits and fried pork or bacon off his wish list and would have to settle for the bowl of Fruit Loops waiting on him upstairs. Pops said, "About to go into work. Need anything?" Chad shook his head. He had slept in his white briefs and was waiting for his father to leave before he crawled out of bed to throw on his jeans and a shirt. Pops made to turn then stopped, looking back at Chad. "Where the hell you get that bruise?"

Chad forced his eyes to stick to the television, fixed on Tom chasing Jerry with a wooden mallet. "Uh, what bruise?"

"Don't play dumb. The damn bruise on your shoulder."

Chad looked at his shoulder. Thought, *Shit*. Kept staring at his shoulder long enough for Tom to get his tail clamped in a mouse trap and three knots somehow pounded on his own head with his own mallet.

"Dunno."

"To hell with that. Hambone grab you?"

"No."

"He hit you?"

"No!"

Pops inhaled deeply and grabbed Chad hard by the shoulders as if trying to squeeze the answer out of him. He let go when he saw Chad wince at the bruise caught in his father's grip. He walked out of the room to the phone in the hallway. Chad could hear him speaking to himself through an intermittent series of rings, saying comeon-comeon-comeon-pickup-pickup-pickup-pickup. His father came back in the room. "Hambone ain't answering. Get dressed."

"Why?"

"'Cause I fucking said. Let Lady out, then meet me at the truck."

His father peeled the tires of the Ford Ranger off Main Street onto Gatlin Road. Antebellum homes suffering peeling paint and sagging foundations and other states of disrepair flanked either side of the street before easing into what his father often called the ghetto, a government project of identical detached homes, squat brick structures enclosed in chain-link fencing that encroached on the north end of Hambone's property.

His father's tires spit gravel like flakes of snuff when he wheeled into the driveway and braked hard behind Granny's empty space in the carport. He shut off the truck and pocketed the keys and grabbed the empty Mountain Dew can in the cup holder. "Come on. We're fixing to have us a little talk with Hambone then I'm gonna take your ass back home and be late for damn work again I guess."

Chad followed his father up the stoop and watched with the helplessness of the convicted as his father banged a fist against the security door. The door was metal and had been spray painted white instead of powder-coated. His father banged again, longer this time. The handle to the security door was unlocked and his father opened it and banged against the wood door behind it. No answer. His father stepped back and mulled something over before checking the key ring in his pocket and mumbling "Shit" to himself when he came up empty. But then he jolted as if he'd remembered some important thing and found a spare key on the sill of the mudroom window.

"Go wait by the truck."

"What for?"

"Because Hambone ain't answering. Quit asking fucking questions."

"You think Hambone had a heart attack?"

His father ignored him. He unlocked the door and opened it a little. "Stay out here."

If it was a heart attack, Chad was glad it hadn't happened on his watch. He felt sad and hoped that Hambone was just laid up in bed. He wanted Hambone able to get around to teaching him more stuff. How to drink coffee. How to throw a punch.

His father wasn't in the house long before Chad remembered the box of bullets Hambone had left down at the barn yesterday. He walked down there and in one of the stalls found Hambone lying flat on his back in the hay, his legs caught on the scooter where he'd fallen off his seat. The toes of his work boots pointed upwards. A wall of the stall carried liver spots of blood and the swoop of Hambone's gray hair mopped at the blood that spilled out of the stall. There was too much for the hay to soak it all. Daylight pointed to the spillage through the hole Chad had left in the fiberglass wall of the barn yesterday, the Colt death gripped now by paws that had swung rail ties like thin bodock switches. Chad heard his father yelling for him and for Hambone and he thought about Lady's leg in its ecstasy last night. Hambone's legs were still propped on the seat of the scooter. Legs that weren't broken like the walking horse's but that hadn't been of much more use to Hambone, either. Hambone had all those heart attacks, too. Granny told Pops that Hambone was just waiting until the next one came. Like he was carrying around leaking sticks of dynamite, biding his time until one blew his ass away. A heart full of worms just ready to explode.

FRISON THE BISON

For a week following the storm, Frison Ferguson has been out of work and without a customer's nightstand or medicine cabinet to raid for prescriptions. At present, Frison plugs away as a contract cable technician for Bodock Ridge Communications on a piece-rate basis. The ice storm had driven Bodockians into their homes without telephone or television and only the moans of trees arthritic with ice for entertainment. But now most power and phone lines have been knitted back across the city limits of Bodock, and this morning Frison's two-door Datsun lunges across the cursive county road leading from his trailer on the still-powerless outskirts of the county into town. His lineman frame fills the compact truck cab comically.

Out of a warehouse tucked in the back corner of the industrial park, the site manager doles out the days' assignments to a huddle of independent contractors whose coffees and cigarettes and breaths loft a collective vapor into the chilled air. Frison grabs his assignment sheets and notes the address of the earliest scheduled appointment, slings a new roll of RG-6 coax into the bed of the Datsun and drives across town to the first customer's house. There, he connects a new line to one of the six connections housed in the tap on the cable pole. He runs the line to the weather-proof box attached to the back wall of the house, fixes a fitting to the cable, and screws the fitting into the primary port of the cable splitter. Then he follows the only cable line from the splitter running into the house.

In the living room, he finds the customer stretched out in a recliner. Squares of builder-grade vinyl tiles cover the floor. Winter has turned mild and warm. Frison wipes the sweat from his slick freckled scalp, thinks, What fucking ice storm?

He nods at the blank television. "Where's your remote?"

"I got ya." The customer leans the recliner upright, shifts his coffee to his left hand. He wears red sweat pants and a sweatshirt with crimson stains. With his right hand, he pulls a remote from a pocket stitched to the side of the recliner and makes a show of fiddling with the device. Finally, the television screen flashes on. Some college-aged contestant on *The Price is Right* runs up to the stage. Bob Barker wraps an arm around her and explains the rules of the game to her big tits covered by the letters of her alma mater on her sweatshirt.

"Got you fixed up," Frison says and searches the paperwork on the clipboard for the customer's name. Frison hands the clipboard and a pen to the customer. "Just sign there, Barry."

Barry signs and returns the clipboard. Frison clips the pen to his chest pocket. Barry says, "Y'all ain't hiring is you? I been looking for some work, man."

"You run cable before?" Frison regrets asking the question. He doesn't like talking to customers or people in general and would rather bust ass through as many jobs as he can complete in a day and go home to his empty rental trailer and the pleasure of folding himself into his own sort of regret.

"Nah. I worked at the Video Shoppe for a few years though."

"They don't pay you for training."

"Don't guess that matters."

"You got a bathroom?"

"Yeah, man, just down the hall there."

The white tiles continue down the hallway, past the bedroom and into the bedroom Frison ducks into. The room is bare. No nightstand, no bed. He backtracks to the bathroom where he turns on the water and opens the medicine cabinet. He hopes for some Xanax or Lortab but all he finds are an old toothbrush, the bristles thread-worn, the neck caked with old toothpaste. Some matches and a plastic travel jar of petroleum jelly. A bottle of Ambien and some Viagra Barry obviously won in the divorce settlement.

He pockets a couple of tablets of Ambien. They're not his first choice, but this evening when the sun slips down too early, he will knock himself out under the yellow glow of a flashlight on the nightstand in his still-powerless trailer with a beer or three and the Ambien.

Too much free time, too much lonesome rope allowed too wide a range to wander, ain't ever good.

Frison had played left tackle for the Bodock Warriors before mowing players over for two seasons at the junior college team over in

Booneville. Everyone called him Frison the Bison. A damn Frigidaire with a ballerina's legs. One night on a drunken whim, he exposed himself in the cramped hallway of a house party to a co-ed he didn't know was fifteen and still enrolled at a local high school. Her father was a district judge and easily convinced himself and the presiding judge that Frison's was the first pecker his daughter had ever laid eyes on. Frison got nine months in county for exposing himself to a minor, lost any chance of signing with a D-1 school. Had already expended his two-year JUCO eligibility, his playing days over.

Frison can still pirouette across the topography of attic beams trailing cable thread through his belt loop with much grace and no fear of crashing through a customer's sheetrock ceiling.

On the prescription front, the next two jobs are a bust. But Frison makes good time. At one-thirty, he arrives on the last assignment, feeling pretty good about knocking the job out quickly, calling into the shop to pick up one last job or maybe tonight dancing under a cold shower and finally heading up to Flick's. He figures some of his old teammates might be up there, at least someone he went to school with. Often he's wondered if anyone had heard about what happened. Probably they have. Probably they would say something to him about it. They might just ask casually or, if they've had enough to drink, give him shit about it. It would be a bad idea to put himself into that sort of situation, which is what he reminds himself of every time he feels optimistic about stretching back out into the larger world. So he'll probably just nurse a six pack driving county roads, pop the Ambien halfway through the last longneck before pulling into his dump of a rental hoisted on cinderblocks above an exposed crawlspace of purring raccoons and clicking possums. At night, mice and baby possums would sometimes wake him squealing in the jaws of a copperhead.

The doorbell echoes with silence. Frison booms a series of knocks through the house to no answer. Frison rubs his shoulders and the neck guard of muscle and leans to peer in the windows. The boards of the porch moan like ice-heavy trees beneath his weight.

The cable company would've notified the customers yesterday by phone about the appointment. Frison returns to his truck, straps on the tool belt. His gut laps over the worn straps. Beneath his unzipped hoodie is the blue BRC uniform shirt. The shirt is half-buttoned and reveals a glimpse of the yellow-feathered headdress of the Bodock Warriors emblem on a black undershirt. He unloads the yellow ladder from the rack in the truck bed into the brown unkept grass. The gray-bricked antebellum is an intersection of Italianate and Gothic styles, which is something Frison remembers from a school field trip once, the house once owned by a wealthy Scottish family before the Civil War bankrupted them and scattered the enslaved they had forced to work their property. The house had a name: Lochness? Lochinvar? The abode sits on a slow-rise knoll isolated by undeveloped acreage on either side and falls within city limits, so power should've already been restored. Frison reasons the doorbell must have ground out at some point before or during the storm. Could be the customers are out running errands or around back disposing of timber debris in some back gully.

Walking around the side of the house, Frison thinks he hears voices like from a television muffled by the exterior wall. But at the back of the house, Frison discovers a bois d'arc tree branch has arm-tackled the power and phone lines sometime in the last day or so: the pulp at the break of the branch is not weathered gray but bright orange. The lines run from a utility pole that materializes through a brush line a hundred or so diagonal yards from the house. Next to the utility pole stands the squatter cable pole. Between two long rows of raised garden beds a long length of coax lags from the pole through the deep grass of the lawn. Frison sets down the ladder and the spool of coax and tries the backdoor. Nothing doing. Frison can abandon the job, call quits on the day, lose the fifty dollars he pockets for service calls. Instead, he figures he'll go ahead and get working on the assignment. No worries if the customers don't show. Would not be the first time he has forged a signature to close a job.

Again Frison connects a new line of RG-6 from the tap on the cable pole to the three-way splitter in the cable box affixed to the house. He strips the insulation off the end of the coax to reveal the copper wire of the conductor before compressing a fitting around the stripped coax with a pair of crimpers and screwing the fitting into the main port of the splitter. From the splitter drop three other lines of cable. Each line enters the house through three holes drilled into the frame of a basement window, snaking along the basement ceiling before running up through the floorboards and into a television in some separate room of the house. He's certain the home is without power, but just to make sure, Frison uncaps one of the cable lines from the splitter and licks the end but doesn't get that mild shock on his tongue that would tell him the line is alive and feeding into a plugged-in television.

Frison zip-ties closed the cable box and knocks on the backdoor just to make sure no one's home. No one answers, so he signs the paperwork against the side of the house. Folds the form back into his pocket.

Frison hobbles back to the truck wagging the ladder and coax spool when something shatters through the basement window on the side of the house. The ivy skirt of a live oak quivers where the object landed. A muffled bark of a voice follows. The ladder he carries clangs to the ground. The tools in his belt chime as Frison eases toward the empty space where the basement window pane had been held. The chill of a breeze scratches low branches against the roof. The side of the house hasn't seen a rake and Frison's size-fourteen steel-toes rile up much racket trudging through the swamp of foliage. Frison doesn't hear any voice now over the mud burping beneath his steps.

When he reaches the basement window, Frison leans between two skeletal hedges and a second item hurls through the shattered pane and slips through the hedges and between his legs, shattering on the stone perimeter of the border bed.

"What the shit." Frison squeezes through the hedges and lowers a knee to the wet ground at the base of the house, careful to steer clear of the direct path of hurled objects.

A woman's voice says, "Would watch out for them jars if I was you."

The lid of a hurdled mason jar at Frison's feet holds dentures of serrated glass. A piece gnaws at his knee but does not puncture the Carhartts. He regrets that he hadn't called it quits earlier and for a long moment Frison still considers just leaving. The voice doesn't know he's from BRC. He could be a meter reader or a burglar for all the voice knows. No damn way to trace him back as the cable technician who abandoned her in the basement. But is it worth the risk? The only jobs out there for someone who has to register as a sex offender are those that don't require a background check. Cable installation is by far the best he's come by.

He peers into the broken window but can't make out much

beyond the shafts of light the basement windows aim into the cellar.

"I can see you up there," she says. "What was you doing behind our house?"

"Come to fix your cable."

"You're late."

Frison hasn't sighted the source of the voice and feels foolish and contempt for it as he explains the doorbell, the attempts at knocking.

"Electricity went out again this morning. Came down here to start up the generator. Slipped down them damn fool narrow cellar stairs and got myself stranded down here. Backdoor's unlocked. Don't worry yourself with knocking."

The backdoor is not unlocked. Frison returns to the window.

"Backdoor's locked," he says.

"Just break the window and let yourself in."

"You can't make it up the stairs?"

"Wouldn't still be down here if I could."

"Passed a store down the road a piece. I can go back there, call y'all some help."

"Somebody's gonna have to break something to get in here. Might as well be you."

"Ma'am—"

"Please," she says. "I ain't been able to check on my husband for a few hours." A moment goes by. "Please."

Frison thinks her husband should be damn sick or dead not to answer the door, much less fetch his wife out of the basement. Frison considers again not having left and what sort of medications a man that kind of sick would take. Considers also the space of the rectangular window frame, no snugger than the tightest threshold of any crawl space he has fit into. Frison tells the woman to move back and he kicks the rest of the glass from the window pane with his steel toe, wraps his hoodie around his fist and rakes the pane for shards. The window nestles six feet above the basement door. Frison removes his uniform shirt and lays it across the pane. Then he skims in feet first, belly down. His bloated torso catches but he breathes deep, sucks in, and slips through like a gourd-headed, breeched newborn, feet lighting the floor a half-moment after he releases his grip on the window pane.

The voice belongs to an old woman. She sits hunched over on a plastic Borden's milk crate flipped over in a corner of the basement. Somewhere an indoor generator hums and more natural light tapers down the narrow cellar stairs. Loose-strung coax sags from the beams. Two cables slant route to the right side of the house and a third fly-patterns towards the front. Frison shakes out his hoodie and dusts his hand across the fabric for shards before offering it to the woman's shoulders.

"I'm Gladys Eutuban," she says and pulls the hoodie around her, offers her hand to Frison. "I came down to the basement this morning to switch on the battery generator. Didn't want Beau to suffocate. About broke my own fool neck too."

"Too?"

"My husband is Beauregard Eutuban." Eutuban had at one time owned half the town, the furniture plant where Frison had worked the midnight shift, and Eutuban Lumber & Quarry. Last summer, Beauregard was running dogs near twilight out in the woods behind his house with Colonel Gardner when his four-wheeler spilled over on a hill steeper than he'd initially gauged. Broke his neck.

"I remember the four-wheeler still growling upside down," Gladys explains as Frison hauls her up the cellar stairs. "Its headlamps losing themselves in the dark by the time paramedics arrived back in there."

The stairs lack any railing or brace other than the cinder block wall to the right going up the stairs. Mrs. Eutuban had slipped on her way back up the stairs and grabbed at nothing but damp cold air. She'd half-landed on her knee cap and her right wrist and the dysfunction of both had not allowed her to find the balance or leverage needed to even sit and lift her way up, one step at a time.

Frison drops her in a chair at a table in a nook of the kitchen.

"Been meaning for years to get at him to affix a railing," she says.

On the table stand wobbled stacks of *Better Homes and Gardens* and *Southern Living* and *Bon Appetit*. She is somewhere in her late sixties and petite and her frame loses itself in Frison's XXL hoodie. Out of the basement, her red hair still burns like a match. Her skin glows pale.

"Where you keep the plastic bags?"

Frison searches the upper cabinets around the sink for any prescriptions he can grab on his way out, but Mrs. Eutuban directs him to the cabinet beneath the sink. Hanging on the door is a plastic grocery bag stuffed with other wadded-up grocery bags. Frison double-bags two and opens the powerless freezer. The ice tray is a jagged terrain of melted and refrozen ice cubes. Frison manages to break away a handful and herds the pieces around a fifth of vodka and a fifth of gin in the tray. He kneels at Mrs. Eututban's feet. The gray slacks Mrs. Eutuban wears disguise the swelling. In high school, a similar injury had inflicted his own knee when he landed on the face mask of a rival. Frison can recall to some degree how to treat the injury but feels invasive hiking up her slacks to bare her knee to the ice pack. He pinches the material at the bend of the knee, pulls the fabric around the joint. Her knee has ripened to the size of a baseball. He rests the bag on her knee and she rests her hand on his to assume responsibility of the ice pack. Her soft hand over his paw like a blanket outgrown.

"Pressure hurt?" he asks.

"A little."

"What about to move it?"

She nods.

"Might of gotten yourself a slight patella fracture."

"Speak English."

"You cracked your kneecap. Ain't too bad though."

"You know a lot about knee injuries."

"Played football."

"My husband played for Bodock as well."

Frison furrows his brow.

"Your shirt," she says. Frison glances down. His uniform button-down is back at the hedge bed and the black undershirt holds pockets of sweat around the arms and beneath pectorals now in soft decline. "Probably remembers you. Used to never miss a game Friday nights. His memory's sound if his body ain't."

Frison has never returned to the Hollow for a game, but he remembers a time when he'd looked forward to the idolatry reserved for alumni come back to scout out the next crop of players and marvel at the cheerleaders and bask in that stadium worship. He tells her she should be able to get around on the knee as long as she keeps it straight. He tells her she'll need to get a doctor to scope it out and asks if she has any athletic tape to brace the knee.

She laughs, "God no." Her otherwise thin frame exaggerates her knee. Her wrist is purple as a pomegranate but not as swollen.

"You wrist ain't swolled. Probably just sprained."

"I ain't worried about my wrist."

"You got a bathroom I can use before I get going?"

"My husband's who concerns me. He's up in the front room. He probably hadn't far to go on the ventilator even before the power left us." She adds, "Bronchitis."

"Huh. I can call y'all a doctor on the way out."

"Yes, well. Certainly you got more work to get to today. But I'm afraid my current condition entails me employing you just a little while longer. I'll compensate you for your time. Y'all can take cash right?"

"Like a tip?"

"If you need to call it that."

Frison chews his jaw over the offer. Then he hunches under her left arm, drapes that arm around his neck, and shuffles her off down the hall to the front room. He insists on parking her in the Victorian chair.

"Stand me up at the head of the bed."

She braces her operable left wrist on the bedside commode frame and her whole body juts toward her good leg like an offensive lineman responding to an audible. The living room curtain allows enough light to chisel from the dimness the foot of the bed Frison had made out from the porch and the form of a man lying in the bed. Thin legs run beneath a fleece blanket like newly laid PVC pipe buried in hurried, too-shallow ditches. Machines hum. Display screens glow red digits across a slew of pill bottles stacked across a TV tray near the bed.

"Open them curtains if you would," Mrs. Eutuban says.

In the dull light, a gray five o'clock shadow stitches across her husband's dark skin. In a corner a length of cable snakes up through the floorboard and into the back of an old wood-paneled Zenith.

"Most mornings I get around to shaving him," she says. Her husband's eyes are slit but unconscious. His chest wheezes. The walls are busy with various Bodock Warrior baseball and football and basketball jerseys in colors and designs too retro for Frison to have ever worn. Every morning and every other afternoon a home health nurse comes to check her husband's vitals, Mrs. Eutuban explains. Change his bed linens, move him to his bedside commode. Perform some light physical therapy. "They say recovery at his age is unlikely in any sense of the word," Mrs. Eutuban whispers, careful to shield her lips from her sleeping husband. The sleeve of Frison's hoodie falls from her purple-wrist hand. "But I guess they think rehab gives us both something to do."

A hose runs from a machine on the footboard of the bed to an alternating pressure mattress that helps Mrs. Eutuban manage the rotation of her husband's dead weight like ripening produce every hour and a half to prevent bedsores. The mattress engraves the bed sheet with low, rolling ridges. A pattern of wood ducks marches across the fabric. Mrs. Eutuban folds back her husband's blanket to appraise his left thigh, careful to keep his crotch covered. She repeats the process for his right leg before continuing to examine the rest of his extremities for pockets of rot. "No use waking him to check his ass and back," she says.

"Why's that?" Frison asks before he can stop himself.

"He's got a sore on his sacrum. Like at the base of his spine. It's chewed about to the bone."

"Shit."

"Yeah, well. At least he's paralyzed so he ain't got to feel it." She pulls the sheet back over her husband's torso. "Most days he's a pretty cooperative eater. Other days it's all I can do to encourage him to chew and swallow."

The whole thing makes Frison feel pretty shitty, but it doesn't stop him from shopping the small pharmacy on the TV tray once she quits looking in his direction long enough. On a table next to the tray, some picture frames and a pair of dentures get Frison's attention. The frames hold wedding photos and other occasions that evidence a life lived satisfactorily. If a lifetime demands one pivotal, dumbass choice, Eutuban at least waited until he was on a four-wheeler in his twilight to commit his. Frison looks over his shoulder, reckoning to find Mrs. Eutuban watching this curious intruder. But she's busied herself with another task and Frison reaches across a remote control, twists towards the light of the window the labels on the translucent-orange pill bottles. He settles on a bottle with a medication name typed on the label of some type of painkiller or tranquilizer that has eased his anxiety before.

"Who is you?"

Frison drops the hand gripping the bottle and seizes up as if holding an aluminum ladder that has brushed a power line.

Eutuban says, "Come closer." Frison cuts his eyes to Mrs. Eutuban. Her stenciled eyebrows arch with concern. The room silences itself except for the quiet labor of the ventilator and other machines gauging whether Mr. Eutuban is alive or ensuring that he remains so. Frison bends to Mr. Eutuban. The stale sour of the man's dehydrated mouth. "You a big sumbitch boy. Where is Gladys? Where's my wife, man?"

"Right here, Beau," she says. She hobbles to the head of the bed and caresses his hand before lifting his arm to examine its underside and reconfiguring the arm's position.

"Where'd you head off to?"

"Told you to fix a railing on them basement steps. Fell and about broke my neck too. Then who would take care of us."

"Who's that?"

"This is—"

"Frison," Frison says. He contemplates telling them his last name in the event Eutuban will recognize him as Frison the Bison Ferguson instead of the nineteen-year-old who flashed his pecker at a fifteen-year-old girl. Perhaps he would ask him about his playing time, busting heads down there in the Hollow. That one play in the North Half Championship game where Frison stood up that middle linebacker with his right arm, clotheslined that blitzing corner's ass right into the turf with his other arm, giving Ben McWhirter an extra half-second to let his receiver complete his fly route and score the touchdown that brought home the North Half Championship.

But Eutuban hacks a wretched chorus of coughs, and before Frison can give his full name, Mrs. Eutuban says, "He helped me out of the basement. He's here to fix the cable."

Mr. Eutuban nods his head back several times. "Come to bring me my *Jeopardy!*," he says before his eyelids drape closed again.

"You all right," Mrs. Eutuban assures her husband and swabs the corners of his mouth with a handkerchief folded over the bed railing. "He sleeps much these days," she says to Frison. "Waking up disorients him. We've watched *Jeopardy!* every afternoon for years. Before the accident we drank martinis too. He thinks Mr. Trebek is a hoot. I think he's smug. I like the trivia though. I'm gonna need you to help me make my way to the hall bathroom to empty his catheter bag once I've got it unfastened."

"You need help?"

"Probably already disclosed more of my husband than he'd like without handing off his piss sack to a stranger. I'll need to get cleaned up myself as well. Then you can be on your way."

Mrs. Eutuban propels herself to the foot of the other side of the bed. She leans on the bed with the elbow attached to her injured wrist. With her good hand she works to detach the catheter bag. Extinguished of conversation for now, she hums through the task.

"Them are the triazolam, right?"

Frison wheels back towards Eutuban, who is wide-eyed and awake again and nods best he can at the bottle still clutched in Frison's hand. "Recognize how them blue pills look almost purple in that bottle."

"Oh. Just curious what you was taking, sir. Thought they might be painkillers. Had an injury myself once."

"What kind?"

"Football."

Eutuban's mouth gulp words out of the air like a bream in the hot bottom of an aluminum boat.

"Beau," Mrs. Eutuban says. She grips her husband's urine bag at her waist with both hands like a purse, glancing between her husband and Frison and her husband's painkillers in Frison's hand.

"It's all right, man." He nods at the bottle Frison still grips, offers Frison a toothless grin. "Ain't for me to judge. Whatever pain you got, you got more years with yours than I got with mine."

Eutuban diverts his eyes until Frison packs the bottle in his pocket.

"There you go, man. What time is it?"

Frison glances at the digital Timex. His fat wrist strains the rubber wristband. Some time goes by before he can make sense of the shifting bars forming squared numerals. "Bout half past three."

"Hell," Mr. Eutuban coughs. "My *Jeopardy!* is about to come on."

Frison admits then that he went ahead and fixed the cable already and that the television ought to be working. Mrs. Eutuban has Frison rush her and the urine bag to the hall bathroom. When she exits, she carries the bag in one hand and swipes the corner of her eye with the other. They return to the front room and she switches on the set with the remote on the TV tray. A horizon of light on the screen. Frison holds his breath, waiting, praying for a picture to pull itself from the abyss of black static. Eutuban asks if his wife needs to sign anything for the young man. On the television screen the line of light implodes to a small ball out of which erupts an image. Frison says no and wonders if he should warn them about running the television and respirator on the same limited-power generator. But the television is already set to the local station and the familiar DOO-doo-doo-doo theme plays. "This is *Jeopardy!*" the Eutubans chant along with the announcer. By the end of the first commercial break, they all have martinis dirtied with olive juice. Frison doesn't know if his own is gin or vodka but either way the occasion marks his first martini. Mr. Eutuban sips his from a straw staked in a martini glass that Mrs. Eutuban holds up just below her husband's deflated chin. It's all too much for Frison. Something inflates within him like a gameday pigskin.

TWENTY MILE

THAT NIGHT AN ICE storm hit Twenty Mile but only the bois d'arc anchored in front of the bait shop froze. Sleet packed the tree's limbs and the limbs converged into a pair of boughs that plaited around the trunk and drove into the dry red clay. Horse apples glazed with ice dangled from the bois d'arc and the bug zapper hummed blue light against the glaze of ice. Otherwise the heat remained oppressive and the cicadas sang out beyond the loblolly pines and live oaks that crowded the bottom.

The others lay passed out in the shop, but Beauregard Eutuban, who was of Haitian descent, rocked on the concrete porch, watching the phenomenon unfold before him, a bottomless pickle jar of bourbon sweating into the cracks of his pale palms. Twenty Mile was a province of ghosts plopped down in a twenty-mile bottom.

Beauregard had figured that news out quickly once he'd climbed out of his own grave and walked a stretch of Twenty Mile Road before seeing his old friend and former master Colonel Leon Claygardner, whom Beauregard himself had buried, living out of a canvas tent in the shade of a bois d'arc tree.

Col. Claygardner had scared the tent from a Union sergeant near Murfreesboro on his way home after catching an artillery shell in his chin at Campbell's Station in '63. He'd picked the spot under the tree because it reminded of his deceased parents. While alive, the Colonel had given Beauregard his freedom papers long before Emancipation, and that alone kept Beauregard for the next century and change in this afterlife with his old friend. Beauregard helped frame Claygardner's bait shop with hickory and they used loblolly for the walls and the newfound dead would arrive and either stay a while or head down the rest of Twenty Mile for whatever came next.

Beauregard dropped his feet off an overturned milk crate, scattering playing cards onto the porch. He and Claygardner played gin rummy or bridge throughout the day but retired those for the thoughtless game of war when the last vestiges of the day would fall behind the bois d'arc. The games and companionship were an amenity to be sure. But what had really kept Beauregard here was this solitude on this porch between midnight and sunrise that Twenty Mile had afforded him for going on one hundred and seventeen years now. Each evening after his fellow Twenty Milers turned in, Beauregard would rock on the porch and drink and imagine the rest of his son's life, a life Beauregard had not had the blessing to witness. Some nights he imagined Beauregard Eutuban Jr. as the mayor of some small town in upper Illinois or a doctor practicing in Chicago. The owner of his own small business. He would have a good wife. A family to raise. Enslaved to no one.

Tonight, however, that solitude had been agitated. He had been watching the icy phenomenon unfold across the bois d'arc for a good two hours before he'd stood up on the porch, the blue Sunday suit he had been buried in draped down his long skinny legs to just above his ankles, and drained the last finger from the pickle jar. His trance broke from the bois d'arc long enough to watch the vessel refill with whisky, some strange magic he still did not understand nor question, before he stepped off the porch to better observe whatever had plagued the tree. After he'd made his way to the bois d'arc, he watched the tree cautiously before scraping a block of ice from its bark, which he dropped into his drink.

He reckoned he should've been happier he had ice for his bourbon now, but the last century seemed to have caught up with him overnight. Earlier in the evening, he'd had difficulty for the first time since his arrival into Twenty Mile imagining Junior as the owner of a dry goods store and its surrounding block of properties. Thought he had just been distracted by the tree, but he realized now that he could no longer recall what his son looked like. Couldn't recall his son's mother either. Beauregard tried to conjure up grandchildren and great-grandchildren but had no memories to go from. The picture Beauregard summoned from his memory now wasn't of his boy. A hundred years had slowly evolved Junior's face into a hodgepodge of memories and false memories that Beauregard couldn't recognize.

If he'd just thought to have been buried with a tintype of his boy.

Nothing deteriorated here except, it seemed to him now, his mind.

The sun breached the horizon and found Beauregard still awake on the porch. Ominous memories Beauregard forgot he had forgotten but not why he had forgotten them encroached upon his thoughts now. His attempts to distract, such as trying to figure what was going on with that tree, were only half successful. Claygardner—for whom the sudden disappearance of his parents had left him an orphan when he was twelve—had insisted the tree looked like his parents hugging. But Beauregard could see now that was foolish. They were clearly fighting or fornicating. Robins and mockingbirds joined a dove mourning the new day and the first rays of light had lit the belly of a cloud that hung just over the bois d'arc where the thaw of the tree met the ubiquitous muggy heat of Twenty Mile. The sun would soon bake the place as had been its way for the duration of Beauregard's residency here.

Usually at this time, Jose McCullough, the half-Guatemalan proprietor of the shop, was up fixing breakfast. Before Twenty Mile, Jose had been the sous chef at Mi Pueblo, the only Mexican restaurant in Bodock. He'd insisted on breakfast every morning to Claygardner's approval and Beauregard listened for the chef's racket in the kitchen. Nothing stirred behind him. He drained his glass again and instead heard the tennis shoes of their resident angler approaching from the path at the rear of the bait shop that cut down to the pond.

"Morning, Bobbie," Beauregard said.

Bobbie tipped her orange University of Tennessee cap. She was heavy hipped and her large breasts would have toppled a taller, skinnier woman. "Fell asleep. By that I mean I was passed out." Bobbie set a kitty litter bucket half-full of catfish and pond water down on the porch. "What's your excuse being up this early?"

"Contemplating."

"Uh huh." Bobbie nodded towards the bait shop. "Mi Pueblo got coffee brewed?"

"Didn't know he was up."

"Out back filling firewood into those empty grease drums. Got em arranged around that garden of his." Jose had sown the garden from seeds he carried with him when his yellow pickup turned to a pat of soft butter against the grille of an eighteen-wheeler, which had landed him here. "He think his tomatillos're gonna catch cold in this heat or something?"

"Tree froze last night."

Every night Bobbie retired after dinner to go night fishing. She regarded the tree for the first time that morning. "Huh. Hell, see that now."

This being some locale nestled between their past life and—their best-case scenario—the purgatory of a forgiving God, Bobbie didn't question the bois d'arc suddenly freezing up in a climate that nudged at triple-digit temperatures any more than her fellow Twenty Milers had last night. Bobbie yanked a slick catfish from the bucket and plopped the specimen on the stump set off to the right of the porch. The catfish's white belly bellowed out from beneath the fish. A cleaver was lodged in the stump. Bobbie took the filet knife beside the cleaver and shaved a collar just above the gills.

Beauregard asked, "How come you ain't never gone on?"

Bobbie carved off the fins and flipped the catfish over and stenciled a line with the filet knife down the length of the fish's belly. "Gone on where?"

Beauregard nodded towards the back eleven miles of Twenty Mile Road.

"Huh." Bobbie gutted the fish and plopped its entrails on the porch and began on the next one. Later she would nail each fish to the side of the stump where she would peel off its skin. She had lived her whole life in Bodock and about knew everyone, which meant she knew of no woman there who shared her desires who would probably ever come down that road. So Bobbie had settled for her other love. "Fishing ain't never been better. This life or the previous one or, hell, the next life for all I know."

"You think Jose gonna ever move on?"

"You thinking about moving on?"

The only way into Twenty Mile was Twenty Mile Road. Most folks who died around Bodock eventually headed this way. That much they all knew. The bait shop sat somewhere around mile nine, and when confronted with the truth regarding their own mortality, the first instinct of most newcomers who arrived while still in denial of their circumstances was to sprint back down Twenty Mile Road the way they'd come. Claygardner kept newcomers from returning to Bodock to roam as a specter among the living by a trap door that vivisected the incoming road about a quarter mile from Twenty Mile. The door was rigged so that its release didn't trigger on the way into Twenty Mile but would drop a would-be escapee right into an eight-foot ditch. No such physical obstacle kept Twenty Milers from continuing on to whatever destination lay beyond the twentieth mile. No such physical obstacle could. Claygardner had tried them all to little success in the interest of increasing the population of his fledgling ghost town.

"I been here hundred twenty years," Beauregard said.

"Huh," Bobbie said as she wedged the cleaver from the stump and hacked the tail off a third catfish still pulsing with life. The slick beast drained the last of itself down the tributaries of the barked stump. The angler dropped the tail on the stump for Jose to fry later. Bobbie said she had been convinced she was going to tuck tail the hell out of Twenty Mile in Jose's yellow pickup when he first arrived, after the Bodock Post misattributed to Jose a crime of bestiality and

Bodock all but ran Jose—instead of Josh McCullough, the actual culprit—from its borders. But before she braved wherever she would arrive after crossing the threshold of the twentieth mile, Bobbie had decided to tangle fishing line with the elusive catfish one last time. That evening she caught the fifty-pound flathead that had, Bobbie deduced, bullied inferior catfish from taking bait.

"Since then caught damn near the equivalent of a bushel each day. Got myself a quiet stamp for fishing and no reason for nothing else. I'm happier than a lone prick in a well-staffed brothel."

To Claygardner, Twenty Mile was a secondhand Bodock, another attempt to build a burgeoning town of his own in what seemed the infinite acreage of an afterlife, all beneath the shade of his parents. Jose had been given the keys to a rundown, barely functional kitchen in a place he would never be run away from. Beauregard had—what? Glasses of whiskey that refilled at his volition and decades to rehash a family history he hadn't lived to see?

But now, dark reminiscences that Beauregard had tethered to his unconscious knocked at his waking thoughts, free to fill the void of the slipping memories of Junior and his wife and all the grand offspring he had never seen.

For the first time, Beauregard found himself contemplating his departure from Twenty Mile.

Around noon, a flowing gown approached Twenty Mile. The promise of a woman of splendid curvature shrouded in a loose summer dress or a leg-slitted evening gown of deep cleavage gathered the Twenty Milers on the porch only to witness a bald rotund man trudge the last tenth of a mile to the edge of the concrete porch. The man bore clammy skin and a thick beard overwhelmed with gray hair. To the left of the porch a fly buzzed the coordinates of the rotting innards of catfish to its colleagues. The ice held tight to the bois d'arc and appeared as if the cold flora were breathing into the sweltering air.

The blue patterned garment the newcomer wore kept the front of him modest. The back of him was left exposed. Strands of back sweat carved tributaries in his dust-caked skin before converging into the crack of his ass. The humidity had all the inhabitants of Twenty Mile in a perpetual state of nut soup or swamp crotch, as it were, but the newcomer's garment did allow the enviable luxury of a breeze.

The newcomer panted. "Back there. Looked like. Y'all's tree. Was on. Fire. Don't. So much. Up close."

The Twenty Milers watched the newcomer catch his breath.

"Been meanin to ask an expert once he came along what had afflicted my tree," Claygardner said. "What was you thinking, Beauregard?"

Beauregard said, "Ain't nothin, Colonel. Just caught a cold. Tree be aight."

"That a hospital gown?" Bobbie asked.

"Yes," the newcomer said.

"Well," Bobbie said, looking around, seeing if anyone else wore the same glaring grin of epiphany. "That'd about explain it."

The newcomer said, "Explain what?" and asked the Twenty Milers to pardon him while he reached behind and held the gown closed. The newcomer scanned the population of Twenty Mile and chuckled. Col. Claygardner wore a straw slouch hat and his gray double-breasted shell jacket held the yellow facings and insignia of mounted infantry that he had stitched to his sleeves himself. Two stars on his collar and the arsenal belt that slouched across his gaunt hips held an empty holster. His facial hair grew down from his ears but stopped even with his lips because of a distilling accident at the age of twenty. Jose had on his Mi Pueblo chef coat and baggy checkered pants and a pair of grease-stained Nikes. "I must have stepped off into some sort of deep-fried collective unconscious. Are y'all all Southern archetypes? The Confederate, the slave, the Mexican immigrant."

"Guatemalan," Jose said. "Natural-born American."

The newcomer asked Bobbie, "Are you supposed to be some kinda lesbian Bill Dance?"

They invited the man into the bait shop for nourishment. Claygardner sat facing the door at his usual lopsided table where he crossed his legs and lapped his wide-brimmed hat over his knee. The blades of the ceiling fan creaked around their axle like a mudbogged wagon wheel and Beauregard had to push back against some old memory nudging into view.

Jose got started on the coffee to the satisfaction of Bobbie, still butchering the catfish, before disappearing behind the curtain to fire up the kitchen. For lunch, Jose fried over-easy huevos and catfish, served both with a dollop of lime-cilantro mayonnaise. The newcomer introduced himself as Harold Fitch. Fitch had a wife of fifteen years that he "made love to" every Friday and two kids who attended Bodock Junior High, where Fitch served as school counselor to the tumultuously hormonal student body. Last thing Fitch remembered was reclining on an oral surgeon's chair and counting down from one hundred. It was an outpatient surgery but all four wisdom teeth needed to be cut from his gums rather than pulled. The surgeon knocked him out something good. Beauregard was unfamiliar with wisdom teeth. Bobbie explained they were the appendices of the mouth.

"Got no teeth left, myself," Claygardner said, his sock puppet mouth sunk down his face. "Wise or otherwise."

No one asked but Claygardner retold for Fitch the time he fended off Ambrose Burnside during the Yankee's Knoxville Campaign in '63 because the bastard northerner had plagiarized the distinctive architecture of Claygardner's beard. When Claygardner finished the story, Fitch confessed that he had once sported a pair of sideburns in his more fashion-foolish days.

"A pair of what?" Claygardner asked incredulously.

"Sideburns," the newcomer said.

Claygardner slapped his slouch hat against the table and tugged at the handlebars of hair on his own jaw, irate that the bastards in charge of naming things had named this fashion after that double-chinned son of a bitch.

"Man brings nothing but terrible news. Let's send him back to Bodock, Beauregard." But Claygardner instead produced a pack of cards from a pouch in his hat. The cards from last night still lay scattered on the porch but there was always a new pack each afternoon. "Then we can get back to our game. Damn noon and we ain't played a hand yet."

The sound of Claygardner's voice now conjured some déjà vu of resentment for his old friend. He tried to stop himself but couldn't reign in the sudden contempt, the origin of which he hadn't the coordinates for yet.

"Was a shame," he said, "you trekking your flat ass clear cross Tennessee just so you could tickle yo nuts over Ambrose's beard."

"Huh?" Col. Claygardner asked.

"I mean, you ask nice," Beauregard said. "He mighta met you halfway."

Fitch asked, "What exact level of my unconscious have I stepped into?"

Beauregard had let himself go too far and invited Fitch out on the porch. There he said, "Don't mind the colonel. He just ill about that tree. Don't want to lose the shade it provide."

"I guess that makes a kind of sense," Fitch said but sounded uncertain. "An ice storm was supposed to land in Bodock the day after my procedure. I guess my unconscious projected the knowledge of that storm onto the tree?"

Beauregard didn't know exactly what Fitch was saying but could tell the man would have a hell of a time resigning himself to his fate. He'd need some help acclimating so Beauregard invited him to sit, and when he did, Fitch did not concern himself or his modesty. His balls clung to a pasty thigh like a clapper welded to its bell. He set his drink behind him on the concrete porch.

Beauregard asked, "What do a counselor do exactly?"

Fitch perked up at the opportunity to discuss the subject of himself. He crossed his legs and sipped his rotgut and caressed his beard before he explained that he counseled students on both general and specific instances of typical adolescent issues: bullying, puberty in general, low self-esteem stemming from acne or sudden weight gain due to hormonal imbalance, profanity as a declaration of maturity, general lackadaisicalness, fondling the female form, the male form, the self-form, i.e., masturbating in bathroom stalls or locker rooms. Fitch threw in that he possessed a BA in psychology but had had to settle for a master's in counseling.

Fitch's head dropped and he looked where the hospital gown covered his chest like he could still feel the regret of that decision in his heart.

"My pacemaker," Fitch said.

"What's a pacemaker?"

"Got a bum ticker," Fitch said, pointed at his sternum. "A pacemaker's a device that keeps my heart from quitting suddenly—"

"Know what, man?" Beauregard said, hightailing toward any change in subject. "Got a dilemma you might counsel me on."

"Are you thinking about taking off?"

Beauregard coughed on his bourbon. "How did you know?"

Fitch's smirk loosened into a shit-eating grin and fondled his smart gray beard again. "That surly Confederate man owns you right? As the archetypal slave it's only natural you'd be led to believe yourself property. Therefore, to leave your owner would be to commit the Judeo-Christian sin of theft. Perhaps you even feel indebted to the Confederate for placing a roof over your head and food at your table. The clinical term is Stockholm Syndrome."

But Beauregard was only half listening. The memory of the moment when Beauregard realized that Claygardner had lied about freeing him had arisen from a dark corner of his memory. The moment had come only a year after the War had begun. Beauregard and Claygardner had been smuggling goods and whiskey for profit into Memphis. On one trip to the Bluff, their wagon got stuck in some mud and they were digging their way out when a lynch mob seeking enslaved fugitives approached. The spokesperson had asked for papers on Beauregard but not the stolen mount he was riding and Beauregard remembered thinking they were in a heap of trouble because for years Claygardner had assured Beauregard that his papers were in safe keeping in a lockbox at the Gum Pond Bank, which wouldn't do them much good, staring down those white hoods now. Without the authentic documentation that Beauregard was free, they'd have to blow themselves through that lynch mob best they could. Or at least die trying. But then Claygardner held up a hand in a truce. Draped back his overcoat slow-like. And instead of pulling a pistol, he handed over the papers still claiming his ownership of Beauregard.

"Since this is my own unconscious," Fitch said, "your dilemma must be the projection of some guilt of my own. I applied for a job at a rival high school recently and included in my resume an acceptance into, and a significant amount of coursework completed towards, a second degree from Yale. Really I've only finished one psychology distant-learning correspondence course." Fitch shit-grinned his glass. "Not worried about confessing that to you, either, cause you're a figment of my imagination."

To Beauregard's left the neglected guts of Bobbie's catfish breathed their stench into the air. The bois d'arc still lofting fog in the immediate atmosphere that recalled for Beauregard every load of dirt that had filled and been slung from his spade digging Claygardner's grave beneath the family bois d'arc tree. The hatred that Beauregard had forgotten until right now on this very porch that he had carried with him ever since his oldest pal had forged his freedom papers.

He had a thought right then to say fuck it. Why remain in Bodock if all memories faded like the autumn leaves he had not seen in over a century?

Before he left, he wanted to remember why Claygardner had denied Beauregard his liberty for twenty-something years. Wanted to ask the son of a bitch right to his only friend's face. Before he left, he needed to know.

On the porch, Fitch blasted a fart unobstructed by clothing so that his ass cheeks flapped against the concrete. Fitch said the two of them should, for the foreseeable future at least, concentrate on his problems, this being his unconscious and all. He would be waking up soon anyway. Then Beauregard would cease to exist. Until then Fitch had to take a piss and was pretty certain a catheter would not have been implanted for an outpatient surgery. As such, he'd urinate all down the dental chair.

"Obviously I'm not wearing a diaper," he said and pointed at the piss-boner pitched beneath his gown. "Perhaps I should just walk it off around the shop."

Dusk that evening punched cold back into the tree. Beauregard and Bobbie bookended the porch, bourbons in tow. More newcomers kicked dust now in the dirt lot in front of the shop. They'd arrived throughout the afternoon: Monroe Brown, from complications due to stroke, and Colonel Gardner still dressed in Trebark camouflage and whose heart pumped for the last time somewhere between his house and his tree stand a couple days before the forecasted ice storm was to hit Bodock. Also Baldwyn Galloway, a Civil War reenactor struck down on foot by an eighteen wheeler. Claygardner took to the Civil War reenactor and, in between retelling his war experience, marveled at the way Baldwyn could make up his face with pale red dirt and could distort his body to resemble a battlefield casualty. After one of his postmortem positions, Baldwyn suggested they ought to recreate tomorrow afternoon the whole of Claygardner's Civil War narrative.

Each of the newcomers had said upon arrival that their deaths seemed obvious. Baldwyn regarded his mortality as a small payment to stand beside the idol he had for years worked his way up the ranks of his reenactment company to emulate. Fitch heard none of their discussions and wobbled on the porch in a stupor more drunken than any anesthesia could achieve. Red dust clung to an area of the gown where he had ended up pissing himself. Some of the flies from Bobbie's catfish remains decided to end it all in the electric blue of the bug zapper.

Dusk froze any thaw that had occurred that afternoon, and the thaw caulked the wrinkles of the tree's branches, swelling the bois d'arc like something arthritic. An hour later, Claygardner was inspecting the pistol Baldwyn used for reenactments—to Claygardner's disappointment, the piece was not the .44 Colt Army Revolver he had carried, but a U.S. Aston single-shot smoothbore horse pistol—when one of the lower limbs of the bois d'arc gave and collapsed and trembled against the ground.

Claygardner moaned and moved fast toward the bois d'arc. He picked up the limb and tried to fix it but abandoned the strategy when he couldn't get the branch to stay on the trunk. He diverted his efforts to holding up the other branches before they could be felled too. The front brim of his slouch hat bent against the bark so that it appeared he was hugging the tree. The newcomers stood unsure what remedy to administer as Claygardner's tears froze his sideburns against the bark.

Bobbie waved Beauregard over. He ambled around a swaying Fitch. "This shit's fixing to get too awkward," Bobbie said. "Ought to do something."

"What for?"

"Look at him. He's embarrassing himself."

"Ain't my problem."

"Y'all pals, ain't you?"

Beauregard didn't know how to answer that.

Bobbie had been a truck driver and many of the goods she'd been hauling—a second-hand fryer, a diesel generator—powered the baitshop. The daylight-sensor floodlight that she had installed in a corner of the porch awning clicked on just above Beauregard's head as he finally figured on a way to save the tree.

But he refused to be the one to do it.

Beauregard walked Bobbie to the back of the shop. Fitch was the only one to notice Beauregard slipping off and mumbled affirmation of his self-proclaimed genius. He wondered aloud why he had ever let his wife convince him of marriage and children and settling for his doughy life. Here before them was a savant, Fitch slurred, and slumped to the porch.

At the garden, Beauregard instructed Bobbie to balance one of the barrels on the rim of its base. The barrel began a drunken roll to the front of the bait shop. The wood Jose had chopped rumbled about the barrels.

"What in hell are y'all doing?" Jose asked Bobbie.

Beauregard stepped in. "No ice is gone plague your garden, man." As evidence he pointed to many of the vines and stalks already sagging not with ice but by their respective fruit. "So you mind rolling another barrel around to the front?"

The newcomers offered their hands when they saw what the resident Twenty Milers were up to. Claygardner was moved to tears and worked flame back into the barrels until all five were lit and standing vigil around the tree. Beauregard had moved to the back of the crowd that waited in silence until ice dripped from the branches. Jose had retreated into the shop to prepare a victory feast. The small flood of customers who followed the excitement indoors found that Jose had laid out for them chorizo corn tacos made from venison Colonel Gardner had on his person and garnishes of tomatillo salsa and cilantro. Accompanying the tacos was guacamole with avocados and tomatoes and red onions and limes from the garden, and on the side was elote with mayonnaise and chili powder and a squeeze of lime lathered over the corn cob. Bobbie pardoned herself from a sit-down supper and took hers to spend the evening alone on the pond banks. Beauregard did not know how to move his feet beyond the perimeter of light spilling from the bait shop porch.

Claygardner had hung back in the dirt lot as well while the rest of Twenty Mile retired to supper. "Finally got us two more skilled in card playing. Gardner and Monroe's both experienced in bridge and poker. Can finally extend our repertoire."

When Beauregard didn't respond, Claygardner said to his back, "Heard you been contemplating this morning."

Beauregard faced Claygardner. "Bobbie got a mouth like a damn catfish."

"The Angler?" Claygardner asked. "Hell, Fitch told me. Said himself was a liber-tay-rian? Whatever the hell that is. Concerned with rightful property and whatnot. Who else did you not confide in besides me?"

Beauregard took a minute finding the words: "Well, couple more card games just gonna mean a couple more ways I could wipe your ass each morning."

"Mean you ain't tired yet of cleaning another man's shit chute?"

Beauregard shrugged. "What's friends for if not to deny another his freedom and then lie about it?"

"Emancipation was gonna free you anyway."

"Twenty-five fuckin years after you lied to me about it," Beauregard said. "Fuck you, Leon. Just cause you convinced that your parents turned into trees instead of facing the fact they left you don't mean I or any other sumbitch on God's creation gotta stick around and be your therapy group."

"What's a therapy group?"

"Something the newcomer said." Beauregard walked out into the dirt some more before he stopped and pointed at the gnarled bois d'arc. "You know it look like they fuckin, right?"

"Wish I could not allow it. Believe me when I say I do regret not authenticating your official release from slavery while alive and that, if I had some similar something to keep you here now, I'd gladly repeat the mistake."

Beauregard didn't know what to say to that. Was he supposed to feel remorse just because Claygardner had staked here in Twenty Mile just to watch all manner of folks decide they didn't see in this place what Claygardner did? Beauregard had despised all of them but despised himself now for any sympathy he held for his centuries-old companion and for allowing himself to endure—or for being complacent to whatever power had been the agent in him enduring—the betrayal by burying the knowledge of it so that he could without guilt accept what Twenty Mile offered him.

"How'd you do it?" Beauregard asked. "How'd you block my memory?"

Before Claygardner could answer, it occurred to Beauregard that he'd never see his old pal again. He hoped this memory wouldn't follow him where he was going. He hoped no memory followed him.

"Never mind," Beauregard said. "I don't wanna know."

"Aight. Shit, you ought to know, you leave it seems I'm fixing to get a replacement to beat me in cards for the next century or so anyway."

"Come again?"

Claygardner nodded at the bait shop. "Monroe in there said he worked his entire life selling furniture for a man that looked like you. Same name as yours too. Said that Eutuban owned a lumberyard and a quarry and a furniture plant. Lot of land."

"No shit."

"Guess your kinfolk made it in Bodock after all."

The muscles in his neck fisted around his Adam's apple. If he left, he might miss his kin. But what if he stuck around and discovered the news was a lie? Even if true, was this just another play to get Beauregard to stay? He was done with this horseshit and looked for distraction. His eyes landed on Fitch. Beauregard studied the form until another idea blessed him. Beauregard told Claygardner to hold on a minute and walked into the bait shop to borrow a disposable razor from Jose's shaving kit. Beauregard returned with a bowl of cold water and shaved Fitch's chin. He left the sideburns curving up into his mustache in the Ambrose fashion. Then he aided Fitch to his feet and leaned him against a four-by-four column and gave Claygardner the word like so many pranks he and Claygardner had pulled over the years on those newcomers they didn't like or that had just possessed the misfortune of stumbling into Twenty Mile during yet another streak of boredom. Claygardner drew the blank-loaded pistol he hadn't returned to Baldwyn.

"You know I never gave a damn about Ambrose's whiskers, right?" Claygardner said.

"Right."

"I was just et up with guilt."

Beauregard nodded and let the colonel keep his lie and dignity. Wasn't like he was gonna get this whip-cracker to change his mind after all these years or admit being full of shit. He watched Claygardner aim at Fitch through the belching flames of two oil barrels. Claygardner yelled to the counselor, "Ya dead, son! Welcome to hell!"

The lids of Fitch's eyes lifted then widened with recognition. Claygardner cocked the hammer, pulled the trigger. The pistol pissed fire and farted much smoke into the holdout of cold air that still fought for territory around the bois d'arc. Fitch slipped backward onto the porch and landed on his back. From there he reached behind him where he felt the pile of catfish guts his head had landed in.

"Oh shit! Oh shit!" Fitch yelled and took off like some blue-caped near-nude banshee back towards Bodock. He screamed about the slaveowner having blown his goddamn genius brains out. A cloud of gravel dust chased behind him.

Beauregard had already aimed himself in the opposite direction toward mile marker ten and didn't turn to see the entertainment bring the newcomers back onto the porch, whisky-handed and jaws still gnawing mouthfuls of their intermitted feast.

OFFERINGS

NOAL CLAY HAD BEEN awake for the last hour when he heard the tail end of something of interest on the police scanner. He propped himself up on his elbow but the transmission had already moved on so he unspooled his legs from the wagon-wheel quilt—he had slept on the rug again—and retrieved his thick-framed glasses from the coffee table. While he waited for the scanner to loop back around, he watched the gray dawn creep through the window and grant shape to the room: the sectional couch where his navy hoodie and jeans lay. White socks permanently stained by the red clay dirt. The leather accent chair and ottoman where he used to read *Field and Stream* or *Rolling Stone* or *McMurtry* while Jacqueline leaned into the corner of the sectional couch, annotating recipes in a cookbook buried in the collapsed lap of her linen skirt. Pale legs exposed, freckles on her thighs marching from somewhere beneath the skirt. An old-fashioned sweating through the napkin-wrapped glass in both their hands. Toys scattered on the rug. Dash asleep in his room.

The house was empty now.

He stood and made for the side table where the scanner sat, his lower back hurting like the hell it did every morning, a herniated disc in the L3/L4 region that throbbed and radiated to his hips and down his thigh like there was nothing there between the joints or discs. Just bone grinding bone, rubbing together, blazing up a dull, persistent agony. He pulled himself onto the couch, dug around in his hoodie, mashed one of the two 10-mg Vicodins out of the gum wrapper foil that Carol had pushed into his front pocket last night at Flick's Bar.

After he worked up some saliva, he swallowed the pill.

The scanner landed back on the frequency of the Claygardner County Sheriff's Department. A deputy radioed that they were on their way, but the scanner jumped frequencies before the deputy gave the destination. Noal turned the dial back to the sheriff's frequency, where he recognized Sheriff Patrick Morton responding that he was already at the property. That he'd be waiting for them on Country Road 209 at Colonel Gardner's gate.

Shit.

Noal dragged on his jeans and pulled the Carhartt over broad shoulders, wrapped the foil back around the other pill and stuck it in his pocket. In the entry way, he pulled on the work boots he'd kicked off at the door after lurching in sometime around two this morning and holstered the .357 Ruger revolver he kept on top of the phone book in a drawer of the hutch. He watched the answering machine next to the phone long enough to know the light wasn't blinking with a new message. In the phone book, Noal found the dispatch line of the Claygardner County Sheriff's Department. Carol was on duty like she'd said she would be.

"Sheriff left about thirty minutes ago."

"He say what his business was out there?" Noal asked.

"I don't know if I can tell you that, Noal. But Patrick, I mean, Sheriff Morton didn't say. All he said was they was headed out to Colonel Gardner's land. Over."

"They?"

"The Rivera twins."

What the shit? "They out on the colonel's land or mine?"

"Why'd they be on your land, Noal?"

The Colonel had forty-three acres on the west end of the county that bumped up against some family land of Noal's. Far back as he could remember the Clays and the Gardners in one dispute or another over the property line. Wasn't unusual for the Colonel to trespass on Clay land. He didn't know what business Morton and his sheriff's department had with the Colonel but they could all be standing on his land right damn now.

"Noal? Just how long you stay at Flick's last night after I left, hun?"

"Didn't shut it down," Noal said and hung up.

Hunkered in the middle of Claygardner County, Bodock was a small town of about three thousand burrowed in North Mississippi hill country, carved out of a ridge that cut a divide from north to south right down the middle of the county. Flat lands scattered on either side of the ridge. Stitching it all together was Highway 6 on which Noal hauled ass west across in the single cab pickup while Dwight Yoakam crooned on the radio about love lost in Bakersfield. During the next music break the deejay read from a report about some arctic front from Canada that had paired up with a wet weather system before sweeping through Oklahoma, spitting ice all along the way.

Twelve minutes later at the Thaxton marker, Noal steered the GMC north on tertiary county roads. Another ridge on this end of the county lifted the broken pavement over knolls and dropped it into ravines where trees draped curtains of moss and kudzu. On CR 211, Noal slowed to a crawl as he came up on the hunting trail that led to his twenty acres and the cabin where Noal and Dash had spent a weekend after the boy's fourth birthday, just the two of them, before the wreck in late October that busted his back and claimed their son's life.

Jacqueline had estranged herself to the cabin going past two months now.

And just as Noal feared, from the road, down the short trail that led from pavement to haypatch, was parked nearly half of the Claygardner Sheriff Department. Noal wheeled the GMC into the cold red mud and its tires slid over the ruts churned by the trucks that came before him that morning as he cussed the cheapcantankerousstubbronsonuvabitch and killed the volume on the radio so that only the defogger vents could be heard, whistling their lukewarm air.

When the tires found traction again, the old GMC lunged forward, the chassis warped from the wreck moaning and creaking in the effort. He parked it where Sheriff Morton's tan Bronco with the department shield emblazoned on the door sat next to a four-wheel-drive Mazda without any departmental identification. Thirty yards from the trucks, a body was slumped over in a tree stand ten feet above the ground at the perimeter of the clearing. Its head resting on the rifle support in front of him, arms dangling like limp pipes from which the very life of him had leaked out. Beneath the body, an aluminum ladder leaned shiny against the gray pine. Sheriff Patrick Morton and two deputies, twins Hal and Whit Rivera, stared up at the hunter perched above them as if in admiration. As if the corpse were now the mounted trophy.

Noal could tell from there that the body they were staring at had once belonged to Colonel Hines Gardner.

Morton turned to say something to the twins before heading Noal's way. In the rearview mirror, Noal tried with no success to pat his shock of buckeye-brown hair down on his head. Flecks of gray sprouted in his sideburns and more gray speckled his beard that had grown shaggy and misshapen in the last months and Noal brushed the coarse whiskers over the firm scar that ran underneath his jaw. To cover of the scar what the beard could not, he'd borrowed one of Jacqueline's turtleneck dickies. He holstered his gun, shut the truck door, and met Sheriff Morton halfway across the haypatch. They shook hands and Noal stole a glance at the stand of trees on the other side of the patch that hid the hollow from view, a blind of oak and old growth pine that, so long as the deputies hadn't searched the whole property yet, would have disguised well enough the trail that sloped to the cabin and Jacqueline.

"Nice turtleneck," Morton said. "You tryin to be the great white Shaft or something?"

Morton wore his brown sheriff jacket a size too small and tailored so that it hugged the distinguishable curve of his biceps and the barrel of his chest and cut a V from his shoulders through his torso. In high school, Morton would often push a date back two hours or cancel altogether if he'd been too busy all day to make it to the gym. The elastic band of the jacket rode above a pair of khaki uniform pants holding a leg crease so sharp it could have shaven the tight, short goatee framing his thin mouth. His thick bushel of black hair was parted neat and shiny to one side.

"Why're you dressed like you're highway patrol?"

Morton chuckled. "Sorry about all this."

"And what's there to be sorry about exactly?"

"Got a citizen calling in this morning that they saw someone hunting out here—out of season, as it was—when they was driving by. Caller said they sat there for a while and the body hadn't moved none. Was just slumped over, probably drunk, which was a dangerous position to be in in a tree stand."

"You know who called?" Noal asked.

Morton shook his head. "Call was anonymous. We came out here to have a look." He wore the expression of someone who knew he was in over his head. For a few years now, he'd happily served as Chief Deputy of the Claygardner Sheriff Department under Larry Presley. About a month ago, Morton found himself in the role of interim sheriff once Presley pulled a stunt similar to his first cousin once-removed and suffered a stroke on the toilet of his RV. "We didn't know it was your land."

Noal nodded at the colonel, an orange brushstroke halfway up the tree like a happy little mistake in a landscape painting by that hippie on public television. "Colonel sure as shit knew."

Morton headed back to the investigation and said over his shoulder, "We'll get him down and outta here quick as we can, Noal."

But Noal was already following Morton to the Colonel's corpse with a pair of latex gloves he'd dug from his tackle box of investigative equipment he'd accrued over his eight years of service. He kept the kit in the truck bed even though he was going on three months suspension now from the Tupelo Police Department in Lee County, which neighbored Claygardner County to the east. The truck bed was covered by a camper shell and Noal had to move some shit around including a mostly empty half case of Coors Original to get to the tackle box. The case only had one beer left in it, which—once he'd found and pulled on the gloves—Noal stuck in the glove compartment for later.

"What's he think he's fixin to do?" one of the twin deputies asked, nodding at Noal.

"It's his land," Morton said.

"I mean with the gloves."

"He's a cop."

"Not on our payroll he ain't."

Morton said, "Noal, you remember Whit from high school." Then Morton pointed to the twin on the left. "And his twin brother, Hal, there's our chief investigator now."

The twins had been full-grown freshmen when Noal and Morton were seniors. Fought with each other only half as often as anyone else. Whit more trouble than Hal, but Hal always backing his brother's play. Didn't want to get on their bad side or you'd get a kidney punch from one of them while facing off against the other, find yourself pissing blood for the next forty-eight hours. They were nearly identical in their wide shoulders and husky torsos and stick-thin legs, Whit carrying a good bit more weight. Both had on Carhartt ducks and pecan ostrich work boots. Hal wore a white long sleeve beneath his uniform black polo. Whit, an employee sweatshirt from Faxon Feed Mill, his father-in-law's agri-supply store where he worked security the three days a week he didn't serve as a deputy for Claygardner County. Both twins wore chin beards and dark curly hair they inherited from their Mexican father.

The twin named Hal said, "So this your land, Noal? Maybe you can shed some light on this for us then."

Noal said, "Shed some light on what?"

"What the Colonel was doing out here on your property."

"Looks like he died hunting on land he was too damn stubborn to accept wasn't his anymore." Noal looked at Morton. "You can check the deed and court records."

"You lookin to press charges?" Hal asked.

"On a deceased man?" Noal said. "What I want is y'all to drag his ass down from there."

"You get a lot of coyotes out here?"

Noal shook his head, shrugged, and held his hands up incredulously. "You mean like folks smuggling immigrants over the border?"

"No, like animal coyotes?"

"How would I know? You see a deer cam out here?"

"What about panthers, wild dogs," Hal asked, "anything of that nature?"

"You think the Colonel died 'cause a cougar treed him up there?"

"We got a deer out here need to figure out what happened to it."

Noal shook his head. "What damn deer?"

They led him out into the field beneath a sky swollen with gray clouds. Out of habit Noal counted his strides, rounded off about a hundred yards to the deer carcass. The deer at first looked as if it had been run through a dull wood chipper. The overnight chill had preserved it some but the meat had started to ripen. The animal's back was broken and its entrails spilt on the ground. The tendons of its hips severed, hind legs hanging from their split joints like a Thanksgiving turkey. Meat from its hindquarters and backbone had been torn out. Tufts of fur crowded the animal, pieces that might've fit into patches of visible flesh had its skin not been ripped back and turned inside out.

Noal scratched the back of his head. "Huh. Well hell."

Whit said, "What you think got hold of it? I'm thinking cougar or maybe some of them fighting pits them boys let run wild all over Black Zion."

Noal shook his head at the stupidity of that slur. "White folks'll do the same."

"To the deer?"

"With pit bulls."

"What about coyotes?" Morton asked.

"Could've been," Noal said. But the way the deerskin had been ripped back reminded Noal more of a black bear. Not that they'd had any bears in this neck for decades. He looked in the immediate vicinity of the deer. Around the carcass the ground was rutted but if coyotes or a bear or the chupacabra had gotten at this thing, the prints of their paws had been erased by the muddle of boot prints from the deputies. So he widened the perimeter, where he did find some coyote markings, but then coyotes roamed through there all the time. The wild canines were overpopulated and traveled freely about anywhere east of the Mississippi. That last night spent at the cabin Noal and Dash had spied their reflective eyes like orbs floating along the nocturnal haypatch. These prints could've been from yesterday or a week ago.

Morton told Noal how they'd walked the field but only found a couple prints besides their own. "Figured yours and the Colonel's," Morton said but Noal wasn't really listening. He scanned the side of the deer farthest from the Colonel but saw no dried blood on the ground or coughed out against the pine saplings by a long-range cartridge. Morton must have noticed and said, "You can see a little blood trail there. We're thinking the Colonel shot the deer when it first came out into the field maybe right over there. No, not the grove but the treeline west of there. North then, whatever. Wasn't a clean shot but good enough the deer didn't make it far before keeling over."

Back at the Colonel, Noal didn't spy an empty casing on the ground.

Morton said, "Whit, if you can get the deer."

"I ain't on the clock right now, chief," Whit said. "I gotta get on to Faxon."

"How you fixing to get there?" Hal said. "You rode with me."

Whit huffed and grabbed a pair of gloves and a heavy-duty garbage bag from the Bronco and gathered up the deer. The others removed the Colonel from the tree. While Hal was up on the ladder and Morton stood down below waiting to receive the corpse, Noal's gloved hands retrieved the wood stock, bolt-action .270 rifle that lay on the soft ground beneath the Colonel. But the cartridge that skipped out of the chamber when he eased back the bolt was live and so hadn't been fired. He reckoned one of them could've already collected the spent shell for evidence. But Noal wasn't about to risk asking. If there were no empty shell, it'd mean the Colonel hadn't shot the deer. And if the deputies weren't aware of that fact already, they sure as hell would be if Noal asked them to produce the evidence.

Noal pocketed the live shell instead of returning it to the chamber of the rifle. Then he cleaned his glasses with his untucked shirt, looked in the direction of the cabin, and got a bad feeling about how the deer came to be shot and butchered.

Hal also served as coroner for the county and retrieved a body bag from the Mazda to set the Colonel in. Noal pushed his hands against his hips and arched his spine. He'd been taking his current dose of Vicodin 10-mg for about ten weeks now and had slowly grown tolerant so that his back felt bearable but coiled. The muscles around the lumbar hard and knotted. His hips managed all right long as he didn't stand still for any stretch of time. Which meant they hurt just standing around like this.

"What're you putting down for cause of death?" Noal asked as the coroner filled out the paperwork on the hood of the Mazda.

Hal looked at Morton. The sheriff nodded back.

"Gotta wait on a autopsy."

"Taxpayers would appreciate it if you just put being old."

"You don't think we owe a decorated World War II veteran, his family and friends and community the closure of an exact cause of death?" Hal asked.

"All I'm saying's that it could've been a stroke or cardiac arrest or any other typical shit that gets people who are old. I'd be willing to bet he had prostate cancer too but that ain't probably why he's dangling halfway up one of my fucking trees."

"Whatever we gonna do, brother, let's get it done quick," Whit said. "I'm late for work. Ol' Faxon gonna dock my pay as is." Then laughing: "Ain't gonna fire me though cause his daughter like this dick too much."

"If y'all send this body down to Jackson," Noal said, "it's gonna bring attention to the fact that the Colonel was going senile and was found trespassing and poaching on someone else's land when he kicked the bucket."

"We can keep that part out of the Post," Morton said. "Say we found him on his own land or something."

Hal said, "That good with you, Noal?"

Noal could see he wasn't talking them out an autopsy. "If it gets all y'all the shit off my land quicker, I'm fine with never mentioning he was here."

Morton said, "There we go then."

Hal nodded and said he was glad they were all on the same page. "I can go check up at his house after I've driven the body over to Batesville. Rule out foul play while we wait for confirmation from the medical examiner."

"Foul play?"

Hal said they'd removed a leather tri-fold wallet from the Colonel's back pocket. There was a Veterans Health Administration card, a Medicaid card, a Social Security benefits card, and a driver's license, all with the name and photographic identification of Colonel Hines Gardner. "But there wasn't no cash or credit cards."

"Maybe because he knows there ain't anywhere to spend money on my land."

"I'll handle searching the house," Morton said.

"There's still the problem of the deer," Whit said. "Maybe set up a watch out here or something. Get gaming and fishing in on this. Might be a wild predator needing relocating"

Noal began to protest, but Morton held up a reassuring hand and smirked. "Hal, please inform your brother that I said I'll drive by the house on my way out. Doubt whatever animal or ailment gave the Colonel a heart attack will return to the scene of the crime though."

The twins began the extraction of the body. Whit left the cloth gloves the Colonel had been wearing on the corpse's hands but wrapped them in plastic and rubber-banded the bags above the coat cuff while Hal did the same to the Colonel's boots. They sealed off the heavy plastic body bag and set the bag beneath a tarp in the bed of the Mazda and lifted the tailgate closed.

"You drop me off at Faxon first?" Whit asked his brother. "I'll pick up my truck at the station later."

"That's the opposite direction from where I'm headed, brother,"

Hal said. "I gotta get this body to Batesville so they can haul it down to Jackson. Morton'll have to give you a lift."

After Hal left and Whit was sitting in the Bronco, Morton pulled Noal aside and said, "You hear anything about this ice storm?"

"Caught something of it on the radio this morning."

Morton nodded. "Supposed to move into Arkansas late tonight. Already hit Missouri pretty hard. A couple inches of ice or something like that. Some power and telephones out. Supposed to gather steam before it hits here. I dunno if we're ready for it if it gets as bad as they say it's supposed to." Then, Morton said more quietly: "You heard from Jacqueline?"

Shaking his head, Noal looked down to keep from glancing in the direction of the cabin. "Still with her folks."

"She blamin you or something? 'Cause, I mean, it's…I can't imagine. You know. But I was at the scene. Hal was too. Both of us saw it wasn't your fault. Said as much in the report that it couldn't of been avoided."

"I really don't want to discuss it, Morton."

"Aight. Look, don't worry about us sitting anyone up out here. Hal gets a bit overambitious sometimes. Thinks we got a force of thirty men when we're a good bit shy of about maybe a third of that. Like I said, I'm gonna go check up at the house but I figure that'll be about the last you hear of this."

"All right," Noal said but again he wasn't really listening. "Sounds good. Had enough of folks dicking around on my land for one day."

Two weeks after the funeral, Noal had talked his police chief into letting him return to work. It was too soon but he needed the distraction from his thoughts and guilt and from trailing around the house behind Jacqueline, not knowing what else to do but fetch her bowls of Campbell's soup that had gone cold and the depleted bottles of red wine and other artifacts of a grief that lacked vocabulary. If he stumbled on Jacqueline somewhere in the house, she would respond with one-word answers before just exiting the room without warning.

He felt her blame and believed he deserved it, even though all she knew was that their son had unbuckled the straps of his car seat. Their curious boy, unrestrained and unbuckled at the moment of impact. But one week after he went back to work, three weeks after the funeral, Noal snapped at her reticence and threw a Coors bottle at the wall where it shattered into a nova of beer against the plaster. He blocked her departure from the room, yelled at her beautiful, withdrawn face. Wanting some reaction to verify she hadn't permanently checked out but got nothing for his effort.

So he told her the truth about that night. About the accident and the mistake he'd made that ended their son's life. What really happened in the moments before the long black Lincoln with its headlights off had grown like a shadow across the road into the oncoming lane. Told her no, Dash hadn't released himself from the confines of his car seat. Noal had put him up front with him to let Dash stand in his lap and help him steer. Noal was right there to watch him. What was the harm in it? The lie about the car seat had just slipped out of Noal on the EMT ride through sobs and tears and screams that were a loud enough siren on their own to announce to any passersby what formidable grief and guilt was being delivered to the hospital.

And he regretted the revelation the moment the tremors of her broken heart rumbled up to her face.

The next day, Jacqueline left, her 1982 Peugeot 505 still parked in the carport, a note beneath the wiper instructing only that she had taken a Greyhound to her parents' house in Natchez for the Thanksgiving holiday. Noal didn't call or chase after her.

A week after she left, Noal received a call from her father, an accomplished trial lawyer and mountain climber who'd once summited Denali. A man Noal generally respected. "Sport," he said over the phone, the old fashioneds he'd taught Jacqueline how to make slurring his speech. "Jacqueline wanted me to call you, let you know she was doing all right. Well, not all right. You know what I mean." Noal had asked him what he was expected to do, Mr. Portier in that deep Delta accent saying, "Shit, sport. This is new territory for all of us." Did he know when she was coming back? "Eventually's about all I know."

Three more weeks skulked by. Noal was placed on unpaid leave and eventually suspended after an incident that he imagined Tupelo PD had probably described in his file as a mental breakdown. Then with Christmas on the doorstep he tried to renovate but in the quiet spaces of the house he heard and saw Dash creaking down the hallway or calling for Noal while he stood in the noise-canceling vacuum of a shower. Walking the hall, he'd catch a glimpse in his periphery of Dash playing in his bedroom, their towheaded boy cross-legged building a castle or the monolithic Faxon Feed Store out of blocks of different shapes and colors and the square kind with numbers and letters on the sides.

Hard to endure that alone, so Noal surrendered the house to its ghosts and retreated to the cabin to get his mind on something else. Maybe get some renovating done out there instead. But mostly to do some drinking. He drove through the cattle gate off the county road and on a whim parked in the haypatch and cracked open a beer. Whitetail were in the tail end of their rut so he took a walk across the property with the .270 Weatherby magnum he kept shelved with a Browning Auto-5 twelve gauge in the rack on the back glass of the GMC. At the grove of trees across the haypatch, Noal hopped the wire gate at the trailhead and, not far down the trail that led through the woods about a hundred yards to the cabin, he saw Jacqueline rocking on the porch. Which seized his heart. He had to contain the gasp that would've broken the still silence of the woods. Noal eased to a knee, emptied the Weatherby and cleared the cartridge from the chamber before he looked for her in the rifle scope. Her fair skin even paler in the cold. Her whole face bearing both the hope and despair of longing. He wanted to go to her. But the wound below his jaw was fresh then, the gash less than a week old and healing but still flesh torn and red and new-bruise purple. He hadn't yet grown the beard to cover the laceration, so he resigned himself to their empty house in Bodock. Faced a lonesome there you only get when all the sounds of a child had filled a place once and then just didn't anymore.

But before he stood, something through the scope caught his eye. Strewn across the moat of pine needles and beneath the bodock tree that regularly lobbed horse apples at the cabin roof lay the poorly butchered corpses of quail and mourning doves and squirrels. Their feathers and fur littered the terrain and rib cages stripped of flesh pointing upwards like hungry sinful hands. And so for these last two months, he'd been bringing her supplies and food he left in a cooler at the mouth of the gated trail leading to the cabin. He had nowhere else to hunt but on this land so the protein was always just some ground chuck or pork shoulder from the store. Boxes of groceries and ingredients she'd never been without: onions, garlic, basil, parsley, thyme, olive oil, red wine vinegar. A miscellany of spices. After some thought, he'd affixed a bell to a tree near the gate to let her know she had supplies waiting. Kept the days random so she couldn't predict when to meet him there. With each new week of beard growth, telling himself next week, next week. Next week he would walk the supplies all the way to the cabin door.

He'd also hung a notepad in a Ziploc bag to a nail in the fence post where she would write a grocery and supply list and leave mail for Noal to send to her parents. Once earlier on, she'd used the pad to explain why she couldn't return to the house, that memories were ghosts that could haunt or console. Her parents knew where she was but could Noal not tell anyone else.

Then, two weeks ago, she'd asked when she could see him.

After Morton cleared off the land, Noal drove back into town and gathered some things from the house. Since he'd heard the weather forecast this morning, the airwaves hadn't shut up about this front that would land in North Mississippi sometime early Thursday morning, bringing with it the threat of utility outages and shutting down schools, factories, roads. He reckoned the warnings were probably at least half hyperbolic, but at the house he filled a sack with batteries and matches and candles, grabbed a couple gallons of water they kept in the utility room, and set a tank of propane in the truck bed for the cabin stove.

Before he left, he sat on the toilet and tried, going on the third day in a row now, for a bowel movement without much success. The daily hydrocodone stopping him up. He swallowed a couple of stool softeners and thought he should probably eat an apple or something, but they didn't have any fruit where he stopped at the Butcher Block on Main Street, so he grabbed a dough burger and fries and a large sweet tea to go instead. Drove his lunch back out to the haypatch where he sat in the truck now, working up the nerve to go check on Jacqueline. It was well past time. He had dropped off groceries just Sunday and couldn't figure why Jacqueline would feel the need to shoot a damn deer or even how she had done it except with the .22 magnum that stayed at the cabin. The rifle had no more stopping power than the cabin had a phone, so how she would've made the call to dispatch to report a dead man in a tree stand was beyond Noal as well. Morton had said the deer was shot a few hundred yards from where it keeled over, so Jacqueline could've hit the deer with the .22 and tracked it where it fell, at which point she discovered the Colonel dead in the tree stand. Got herself spooked then. But then she still would've had to find a phone, and it didn't explain why the Colonel was there in the first place except that he might have really been going senile.

What he needed to do was get some clarification from Jacqueline.

All he had to do was work up the nerve to walk down there. After all this time.

He sipped on the tea that drank like syrup. The Styrofoam squawked fitting back into the cup holder and the radio deejay made an obvious joke about the day's forecast, the mercury still hovering in the mid-sixties and muggy. Too warm in February even for Mississippi. Two states over, though, a severe cold front was dragging behind the wind from the west that whipped sudden gusts against his truck now. Noal watched the tall grass of the haypatch bend to the gale. He had meant to bush hog the edges of the patch, maybe cut a deer path through the center of the field and hunt the patch and the surrounding acreage. Teach Dash all those things his father had never taught him, that Noal's paternal grandmother Granny Lou had had to instruct him on instead. Wake Dash early, get set up in the tree stand or tripod and watch the sun rise. Drink coffee in the morning. Beer in the afternoon. Catch some large-racked buck strut its shit out into that field.

Jacqueline had said from their very first date that she would never move back to Mississippi. But then he sold her on the idea of not renewing the rent on their one-bedroom Midtown apartment. Noal got a job with the Tupelo Police Department, his experience with Memphis PD meaning he'd fast-track to detective in three years. Jacqueline got the three-bedroom brick rancher Noal had grown up in, a blank slate for her tendency toward mid-century modern décor, the house bought and paid for already, the only inheritance of any value that his late father had left him. Tear down the dusty curtains. Let the large panes of glass light the house. Without a mortgage, she could stay at home until Dash entered kindergarten. Maybe I could open up a yoga studio, bring wellness to Bodock, she'd half-joked to Noal.

Noal was too bloated to finish the burger and crumbled the foil wrapper around half of the sandwich and dropped it in the grease-spotted paper bag. Drained the last of the tea. He smoked a bowl of tobacco in the pipe that Jacqueline had bought him for their first Christmas after Dash was born to curb his cigarette habit. Then he packed another bowl right after the first one and remembered the beer from the toolbox he'd stuck in the glove compartment. He swallowed the day's second Vicodin, the last in his bottle, and nursed the lukewarm Banquet well into an hour as he shifted in the seat, trying to get comfortable. While his pain was becoming more insistent at the current dose, he appreciated that he could take a pill now and not feel mentally impaired for at least an hour afterwards. His first month of taking Percocet then the Vicodin he'd feel just downright loopy, his lucidity a casualty before the drugs could round out in his bloodstream and his every thought or movement didn't feel as encumbered as if he were underwater. It was the same reason he'd only smoked pot a few times and not since he was twenty-one. He'd done plenty of stupid shit drunk but he appreciated the illusion of control that alcohol afforded. Everything else just reminding him of his own powerlessness.

But now he only had one beer on him so that, by the time he took the last pull, collapsed the aluminum can in his hand, he'd resigned himself to the knowledge that, without more liquid courage, he was still too chickenshit to go down to the cabin. It was only a few after four but he needed more Vicodin before tomorrow and the sunlight had nearly flamed out behind the tall tree line. His thoughts drifting to the last time he and Jacqueline had spoken more than two meaningful words to each other, the night before the funeral when Jacqueline curled up on the far side of their bed and Noal had put as much distance between his wife and his guilt as the mattress would allow.

"My womb is empty," Jacqueline had said. "My heart is emptier and heavier. It's like I have a fist pressed against my ribcage that I..."

She'd not been able to say Dash's name and Noal hadn't understood how something could be emptier and weigh more simultaneously. The antiphysics of goddamn life. Not unlike their union, which now seemed easier to preserve in their separation than if Noal were to walk up there and face the truth that he'd been hiding from behind the scar on his neck all this time: that they couldn't survive this.

He positioned the empty beer can on his knee. The sun had slipped behind the trees. He needed at least to get a note to her, ask her about the deer before this Colonel situation got out of hand. The cabin crouched in a holler so Jacqueline would not have seen the men and her own husband in the haypatch. But their voices had probably carried to her. She'd be on alert tonight, watching the path as its sloped from the field down to the porch.

And he had done run out of time on today.

On the radio, another deejay from another hour of empty talking heads reported a prediction of two-to-three inches of ice. But Noal had until tomorrow to drop off the sack of supplies. Had a couple days more probably before the Colonel's autopsy. Could figure things out before then.

Last night at Flick's, Carol told him she wouldn't be home until after dark and asked if he could come winterize her outdoor faucets. Carol handled his supply of Vicodin so he cranked the truck and headed back to town.

That afternoon, Noal had stopped back at the house and made a collection of old towels and plastic grocery bags and duct tape on the table in the breakfast nook before heading out to Carol's. He also had the thought he should probably wrap the spigots around his own house as well before the ice storm landed but figured he could get that done sometime tomorrow. Before he moved the supplies out to the truck, he saw the light on the answering machine blink. Noal played the message and rang back the Tupelo Police Department. A secretary patched him through to the police chief.

They made some small talk then Chief Gary Donaldson said, "So Bubba says you ain't never been by to talk to him."

"Meant to, Chief. Just never could work it."

He heard the chief clear his throat away from the phone. "In the last ten weeks?"

Noal could already see where the conversation was headed. He felt the need for a smoke and elected for the pack of Vantages he kept in the drawer of the hutch next to the Ruger.

"Think it's just I've got a difficult time, Chief, accepting the credibility of a psychologist named Bubba."

"Bubba's a helluva head doctor. He worked Eubanks through his PTSD after that hostage situation a couple years ago."

Noal hadn't thought through where to ash so he opened the door to the carport that faced the hutch and stretched the phone out so he could stand on the bricked stoop. "Yeah. I ain't never been witness to his miracles but I've heard all about em."

"And he talked Merv down from continuing to cross-dress after he came out from a year of undercover busting that prostitution ring."

"The folks at the Church of Christ were complaining or something."

"About had him excommunicated."

"That's Catholics do that, Chief."

"You know what the hell I mean, Noal."

"Yessir."

A pause on the line. Papers rustled on the other end. "Look, Noal. Only way you're coming back is if you log sessions with a psychologist. You can do in-house with Bubba or go independent. Don't matter."

"Not sure I need a psychologist, Chief."

"You do for a bunch of legitimate reasons I can't begin to understand. But I also need you to for bureaucratic purposes. I gotta file paperwork showing you're mentally and physically rehabilitated before I can clear you for duty. Guess you ain't been to PT nowhere neither."

"I do some crunches and push-ups around the house. Ten each for every adult beverage I consume."

"Yeah? How's that working out for you?"

"It's cut down on the drinking."

"Dammit, look, Noal." Some more papers rustled. Chief Donaldson cleared his throat. "Until you get your smartass to cooperate, I ain't got a choice but to let you go. Simple as that."

"My suspension-without-pay become too much of a financial burden to y'all?"

"You know what? Fuck you, Noal. This is for your own damn good. You can't just come back in here after the stunt you pulled, no matter the circumstances. And you're pissin me off now 'cause now I gotta find someone who can replace you. Which is doable I guess but—and I don't mean to inflate that head of yours any more than it is—but you're a good cop. But I mean, I get it. I can't begin to understand it but I get it. No one should have to bury their —"

Now Noal steered the GMC up Highway 9 before cutting west over to Harmony Loop where he arrived at Carol's doublewide a little after six. Her 1980 Pontiac Phoenix wasn't here and he figured she was running errands or filling in for the other dispatcher. Noal pulled to the side of the driveway so she could move around him. Holding a Maglite in the crook of his neck, he wrapped a towel around the water spigot in the front flowerbed, duct-taped the towel, covered it with a plastic grocery bag from Piggly Wiggly that he packaged tight and duct-taped as well.

He was repeating this for the spigot at the back when he heard her car honk. He finished up and met Carol on the square wooden porch at the front of the trailer. In her hands were two plastic grocery bags. Pinned beneath one of her arms a small paper bag with the red wax cap of a Maker's Mark bottle sticking out.

"Had to drive to the county line on my lunch break to get it," she said.

"Didn't have to do that."

"It's a thank-you for taking care of the pipes," Carol said.

Despite a shitty marriage on the front end of her twenties and pulling sixty-hour weeks to get by after her divorce from Eric Ward, Carol was still rural beautiful in her wide brown eyes, the narrow gap between her front teeth, and her pageboy haircut, short around the nape. They'd been a couple once—or rather several times—through their junior and senior years of high school.

"Looks pretty ghetto, Noal."

"Guess it's better than a burst water line."

Carol crooked her head like taking it in from another angle. "Maybe. I guess the hedges'll keep it covered."

Noal took the grocery bags so Carol could unlock the door and followed Carol into the kitchen, kicking off his wet boots before he treaded across the carpet.

"Go get you a shower," Carol said. "I can still smell the bar on you from last night and everything you done did today."

Carol bent to retrieve a nonstick skillet from the drawer beneath the oven. Noal had been over here about twice a week since just before Thanksgiving, after TPD suspended him, and each time Noal and Carol would just sit out back in aluminum-frame lawn chairs and work through the six-pack he brought. Then Carol would sit and keep him company through the slow haul of his nightly pint, smoking their cigarettes to nubs. Not one of those times had he crashed at her place though. Not one of those times had she asked either. But even taking a shower under another woman's roof seemed to cross some line.

"I'll get a shower when I get home."

"You'll get home hungry then."

"Carol, I ain't fixing to take a shower over here."

She was smiling at him with her lips tight, defiant and stubborn-like. "I ain't fixing to sit down and eat with you smelling like you do."

Noal didn't want to be a dick about it, so he carried a beer with him into the bathroom, which he couldn't finish before the shower had run cold. After he stepped out and realized that his dirty clothes had been lifted from the bathroom floor, he put on his fogged-over glasses and wrapped a pink towel around his waist and another around his neck and carried what was left of his beer toward the smell of sautéing beef in the kitchen. "Where'd you put em?"

Carol emptied the contents of the Hamburger Helper into the nonstick pan. "You mean your clothes?"

"Yes I mean my damn clothes."

"I threw em in the washer real quick."

"You got my clothes while I was in the shower?"

"Wouldn't make much point for you to just put dirty clothes back on." Carol did her wink thing again. "I didn't look, hun. Promise. That privacy glass blurs most everything anyway."

"Ain't about to eat in a towel."

"You wasn't this modest in high school."

"I wasn't married in high school either."

Carol didn't speak. Then she looked at the towel around his waist and the one around his scarred neck and Noal saw the recognition break across her face. She'd been the one who found him, thirty-six hours after his indefinite suspension had been delivered as a punctuation of a long line of shit lost: his dead four-year-old son and his estranged wife he had not heard from in weeks, whom he hadn't stumbled on yet out at the cabin, and now his job, the only thing distracting him from the albatross of truth that hung around his neck all day.

"I wasn't thinking, Noal. I'm sorry." Carol handed him the Maker's she'd poured for him and the wooden spoon. "Stir this while I get you something to wear."

Noal stood at the stove while she laid out some of her ex-husband's things on the bed. Star linebacker Eric Ward had ballooned in weight once a bum knee ended his football career and he didn't have tire-runs and forty-yard sprints to offset all the beer he started drinking so he would feel drunk and manly enough to take his frustration out on all the body parts Carol could cover with clothes. It'd been out of his jurisdiction and after the fact when Noal found out, but even now he wasn't beyond following the former-glory super chunk home from the bar and beating him senseless on the false testimony that Eric Ward had been drunk and disorderly and resisting arrest. Carol had kept some of the more comfortable clothes he'd outgrown so after dinner in the living room Noal sat in the recliner in sweat pants and a Mossy Oak turtleneck that Eric had worn hunting. Noal was working on a second bourbon, this time pouring it himself, the thick clear plastic cup colored mostly brown and floating a single eroding ice cube. At the end of *Wheel of Fortune*, the dryer dinged and the television segued to the Memphis news. Noal carried his clothes to the bedroom to change but kept the camouflage turtleneck and folded Jacqueline's white dickey into an inside pocket of the Carhartt hoodie.

Dressed, he poured a third bourbon in the kitchen where some Pavlovian urge for a cigarette afflicted him. Carol nursed a High Life on the couch and watched the television and on his return to the living room, he caught a glimpse of her soft back where her sweatshirt had ridden up from the band of her pants. Her body full-figured everywhere but her tits, which were small enough to still appear as perky as they'd been in high school. Noal could feel a drunk coming on now and saw her naked body pressed against his as they had been on his three-wheeler and sometimes in the back of his father's Galaxie and, on rare occasions when he got up the money, in a cheap motel over in Tupelo or Oxford.

He doubled-back to the kitchen for distraction and got to cleaning up. The news resumed and he turned around as the camera cut to Dick Rice in a too-tight corduroy sports coat and a gray part of hair. He listened to the meteorologist report with a severity Noal assumed was meant to convey the impending calamity, a low-pressure system that had developed in the northwest corner of the Gulf of Mexico, which would bring heavy precipitation northward across Mississippi all day tomorrow. Meanwhile the cold front currently moving through Arkansas would land in Memphis and then creep on into North Mississippi by midmorning on Wednesday. Temperatures would begin dropping into the upper twenties by Wednesday afternoon, turning the heavy precipitation from the low-pressure front down on the coast into freezing rain. Maybe as much as five inches of it.

"As far as ice is concerned," the meteorologist said, "a perfect storm."

The camera returned to the anchors and Noal directed his attention back on the chore of the dishes. Hamburger Helper wasn't something Jacqueline would ever cook but it was a step up from the canned meals and potted meat and saltines he'd been surviving on the last few months. After slopping the scraps off the dishes into the garbage and rinsing away the traces of ground beef and congealed sauce and instant mashed potatoes, Noal stacked the dinnerware on the counter to his right and ran a sink full of suds. He heard one of the anchors deliver a report that a writer must have pieced together in a hurry on how best to endure the storm, what supplies to stock up on. Ice, water, milk, bread, canned food. Charcoal or propane or both. Batteries.

Carol's reflection joined his in the dark window above the sink. She freshened up his drink on the counter before returning the frosty pint to the freezer. "Did you hear me?"

"Hear what?" This close he caught a whiff of coconut suntan lotion from the Video Shoppe–and-tanning salon where Carol must have gone after work, not having to wait for a late dispatcher to show up for her shift after all. The scent reminded Noal of the honeymoon weekend he'd spent with Jacqueline at her parents' place in Dauphin Island, a two-and-a-half-day buzz of Mexican beer and margaritas made with fresh-squeezed limes and pot he scored from a friend in the criminal justice program at Memphis State University. He figured Jacqueline knew to leave the sink faucet dripping. Wondered if she knew about the outdoor spigot off the house. If it froze and ruptured she would be without water for days.

"I said I was joking about you cleaning up."

"Oh. All right." He wiped a hand on his jeans, shook free a Vantage, and set the pack on the counter next to his wallet and keys and the empty bottle the ER doctor had prescribed after the accident, a thirty-day supply that the same damn doctor had denied refill requests for, directing Noal instead to consult his PCP. Noal lit his cigarette. "You got that Vicodin?"

Carol pulled the flip-top sandwich bag from a drawer and counted out four 10-mg pills, a two-day supply. Noal would take one in the morning and one after lunch for the next two days. Drink bourbon in the evenings until he fell asleep.

"Don't take one tonight," Carol said.

"I ain't."

"You've had too much to drink."

"I know, Carol."

Noal scrubbed a dish clean, set it with the others on a towel to dry. His back getting tight and knotted so he kneaded at what felt like ball bearings gathered in the skeletal muscle around his spine.

"Why don't you go sit down and rest," Carol said. "I can take over."

"Might need to up my dosage," Noal said.

"I dunno if my contact can get a different milligram."

"That'd mean I'd need you to get more each week."

"I could see about getting from him every week instead of every other," Carol said. "I can ask him."

Noal handed her the towel over his shoulder to dry with but got back to scrubbing the dishes. "Your supplier say anything about muscle relaxers?"

"He'll let me know Thursday whether he could get em."

Noal nodded, impatient for the relaxers but not wanting to push it. "They say what kind?"

"I don't think so."

"Lorzone?"

"Maybe."

"Not that it matters."

"Maybe we ought to figure out while I got you here how I'm gonna get the pills to you on Thursday," Carol said, "in case this storm does knock the phones out. You wanna just run by here? I could give you a couple of the Vicodin then and the relaxers."

"Storm's supposed to hit Wednesday night," Noal said. "What if I can't get over here Thursday?"

Carol thought about it. "I guess I could give you another day's

ROBERT BUSBY • 229

worth to get you through Friday. That would make six." Carol mulled something else over. "But no more. You'll have to find a way to get over here Friday or Saturday."

"Fair enough."

"Wouldn't matter if it wasn't," she said and counted out two more pills from the plastic bag and dropped them into the old Percocet bottle. Two pills remained in her stash. She'd insisted at the beginning on only giving him a two-day supply for reasons obvious to Noal. Any number of ways he could kill himself but still he wouldn't dare overdose on pills that she had procured for him. The two-day supply also meant he'd have to come around every couple of days so she could make sure he was still breathing. She wouldn't tell him where or how she got illegal pharmaceuticals, and while he respected her enough not to ask, he'd worked his share of narcotics cases in Tupelo and always overpaid her for them.

"Crazy about that deer, huh?" she said.

"What deer?"

"What deer. One something got a hold of out on your land."

Noal ran a finger of water in a coffee cup and tapped his cigarette against the rim.

"What'd you hear?"

Carol spilled what Morton had told her at the station that afternoon.

"And the Colonel dead? God bless him," Carol said. "Heard you told Whit it was the Chupacabra's cousin or something. He was up in arms cause he thought you was being racist, his old man being Mexican and all."

"I think it was Jacqueline," Noal said.

"What was Jacqueline?"

Noal thought he'd just see how the admission would feel in his mouth, not expecting the words to have slipped out but feeling like he'd unloaded part of a burden so he kept going.

"Who might've shot the deer."

Carol nodded. "Okay, Noal. Maybe you ought to go on and sit down now. Maybe ought to leave that drink in here too."

"Not lying, Carol," Noal said, unable to stop now, needing just to get that confession out of him, shuck that knowledge off on someone else, test their reaction to measure how fucking crazy he was. "She's out there."

"Out where?"

"At the cabin. Not two hundred yards as the crow flies from where the damn Colonel died."

Carol took in the news by lighting one of the Vantages. "Since when, Noal?"

Noal used his knuckles to count the months backwards. "Two months."

"Two months?" Carol said.

"Near about."

"The fuck, Noal?"

Noal told Carol about most of it then, how Jacqueline had stayed gone for a month with her folks in Jackson before he stumbled on her at the cabin. The incident with the corpses of small game shot with the .22. How he brought her supplies every week.

"What's she doing out there?"

"I dunno. I didn't put her out there."

"You ain't talked to her?"

"I leave the stuff at the mouth of the trail."

"Why don't you walk it up to her?"

Noal aimed the cigarette at his riptorn neck before he dropped the butt in the glass. The filter hissed when it met the water.

"You need to unload this on someone more qualified than me. Like that therapist your chief wants you to see. You know? You heard from Tupelo yet?"

Noal nodded but shrugged when he saw Carol wanting more.

"They fired you?"

"Ain't fixing to talk about it."

"Maybe if you did talk about it though they'd change their minds?"

"I talk to you. Ain't you got a degree in psychology or something?"

"I got a semester of Intro at Itawamba Junior College before I up and married Eric. And you don't talk with me. We see each other a total of four times a week. You've hung out here two times a week since November but you ain't never mentioned the accident to me once."

"Maybe you ain't the one I mention it to."

"Who else you talk to besides me, Noal? Not your wife, apparently."

Noal was rinsing the nonstick skillet and slammed it harder than he meant to into the stainless steel sink. The islets of suds that had not drained splayed out across his hoodie and onto the counter. "She fucking left me, Carol."

In the space in which Carol gave him to calm down, he searched for something to do while he humbled himself enough to look up at her. In the window he watched the reflection of sports highlights on the television behind them but not really paying attention to what was said. He retrieved the sponge from the drain, set it sagging with water on the back rim of the sink. Swallowed down the throbbing ache in his jaw and the back of this throat.

"I'm sorry about that."

"You wasn't at fault, hun," Carol said.

"What if I was," Noal said but kept that admission to himself. Jacqueline the only other soul in the world who bore the burden of that truth. The burden of knowing that someone you loved could be at that great a fault.

Carol put her hand on his shoulder. He resisted at first but let her turn him from the sink. Took a moment to bring her into focus. Brown eyes wide as planets staring at him. That small gap between her front teeth.

"Probably shouldn't drive home," Carol said.

Noal lit another smoke. "There enough room in your bed?"

Three months of coming over here and on any occasion drunk enough but never loosening enough to actually proposition his old high school flame. He feared her moment of hesitation, the look of consideration on Carol's face now. Noal himself drunk enough that if she said yes, he wasn't sure he could decline her company.

But she shook her head. "You don't need nothing else to feel guilty about, hun. I can make you a pallet on the couch. Or you can take the bed and I'll take the couch. I don't know what's best for your back, old man."

Noal tapped his cigarette against the sink but no ash broke off. Already sobering up now. Already ashamed of himself. "'Preciate it. Couch'll be fine."

Later, as soon as he heard her sawing logs from the bedroom, he snuck out the back door, circled around to his truck, and wound his way back home.

Pounding on the front door the next morning, Noal having slept on the thin rug again, his hips and back aching something terrible against the hard floor. His head throbbed with withdrawal. He found the bottle in the pocket of his hoodie and popped a Vicodin into his palm, but he couldn't work up any spit, so his throat muscled down the pill. The house was cold, the temperature having dropped during the night. He had slept in yesterday's clothes and pulled the afghan over his shoulders and stood slow. The clock read 9:08. Someone pounded the door again. Noal turned the deadbolt, left the security chain attached, and squinted cockeyed at the sliver of the outside world gone cold and gray.

"Yeah. Come around to the carport," he told Sheriff Morton.

There was some coffee in the Bunn pot, Noal didn't know from when, but no islets of mold were in there so he reckoned it wouldn't kill him and filled a stained white mug with it. Nuked the cup for a minute and then one more to be sure. Meanwhile over his hoodie he threw on the brown Carhartt vest hanging from a peg above the hutch and then tested the coffee, which tasted like shit and burned his tongue but he swilled half of it and took the cup out into the open-aired carport where the atmosphere smelled cleansed by the cold and the rain that were both still falling. The temperature not freezing yet, but the mercury was headed in that direction. Morton stood just inside the empty carport, his black raincoat dripping water onto the concrete. The sleeves of the raincoat held reflective stripes and its chest wore the word SHERIFF across it. A tube of a newspaper in Morton's hand like he was about to swat something. Behind the sheriff was Noal's GMC parked drunkenly in the driveway behind Jacqueline's Peugeot. Morton's Bronco idled in the street behind it. Noal felt for the pack of Vantages in the hoodie and offered Morton one but the sheriff declined.

"This soon," Noal said, picking up the coffee off the hood of the Peugeot, the Vantage squeezed between his lips. "Don't guess you're here about the autopsy."

"Not entirely. Hal said they was doing that on Friday."

"You and Whit find anything at the Colonel's yesterday?"

Morton gulped some tea from the Snapple he pulled from the deputy jacket beneath his raincoat. Morton was without most vices and abstained from alcohol, Coca-Cola, cussing.

"You mean Whit-less? Nah. We ain't find anything."

"So what're you over here for?"

Morton cleared his throat. "That .270 of Colonel's was a bolt action, right? So a shell's got to be shucked out? So if he shot the deer, he's got to of manually ejected it before he died. But the shell wasn't on him or in the gun. And if he died before the deer was shot, well then. Maybe it had to be someone else."

"You sure Whit didn't do something with the shell and just forgot?"

Morton snorted. "Nah. Hal said he checked the gun himself before putting it in evidence."

"So what're you thinking?"

Morton shrugged. "When's last time you went out and checked on things out at that cabin of yours?"

"Last week."

"Obviously no one squatting out there?"

"They ducked out when I tried to charge them back rent. What're you getting at?"

Morton slipped the newspaper beneath his arm, cracked his knuckles. "You hear about that meth lab exploded inside the county several months ago? Maybe a year now?"

Noal took another drink of the coffee but decided against the rest and slung what was left out of the mug over the car hood into the rain. "Y'all never identified the body, right?"

"Well, we thought the fire was so hot it melted his teeth. But then we realized he didn't have none."

"Dentures?"

Morton shook his head. "Someone pulled em."

"So it wasn't an accident? No one-man operation?"

"We never found who it was though."

"Sure they're still cooking?"

"Yeah." Morton slapped the newspaper against his palm. "We've followed a couple leads since then. We even run up on their cook sites but always after they done blown out. I had me a idea last night, though. Given the way that deer looked, like some retard on speed might of gotten hold of it, you know? You ain't been out to your cabin since last week?"

"Can assure you, Morton. Ain't nobody cooking crank out there."

"You positive?"

Noal squeezed the coals off the end of the cigarette and stuck the butt behind his ear for later, trying to think of some way or distraction to get Morton off this line of thought.

Morton pulled from the Snapple again. "Would make me feel better to go out and have another look. Just to be sure. I'd of done it already but I didn't want to go welcoming myself on your land again unless you was with me."

The coffee along with the morning cigarette had settled in Noal's bowels and he didn't want to miss the opportunity. And he needed some time to think of a plan.

"Gotta take a shit. You head on out there and I'll meet you at the gate."

At the haypatch, they parked their trucks near yesterday's tracks and the two of them split the acreage in search of a shell or footprints they might've missed. Morton paced the field and Noal returned to the tree where the Colonel had set up and eased himself to a knee and combed the area there well, brushing clumps of damp leaves and pine needles away in a delicate manner, not wanting to send the theoretical shell flying farther into the woods.

Noal scanned the patch and through the overcast and rain found Morton nearing the grove of trees that hid the cabin. Noal cupped his hand around his mouth and yelled so that Morton stopped and turned and Noal could wave him back with his right arm.

With Noal's left arm, using his body as a shield, he pulled an empty shell from his pocket. The cartridge was the Winchester he had shucked from the colonel's bolt-action yesterday. On his way out here, Noal had pulled off on a back road and fired the cartridge through the Weatherby .270 he kept racked on the back glass of his truck toward the ground in an uninhabited stretch of woods.

Noal placed the empty casing on the ground, covered it with underbrush, and drove the casing into the ground with his knee.

When Morton reached him, he inspected the dirt clogging the casing. "Where was it?"

"Pressed into the ground here. Saw something flash when I was raking through the brush. Probably one of y'all stepped on it without realizing it. Course I was out here too and should've spotted it myself."

Morton scratched his head. At what Noal couldn't guess. Then the interim sheriff chuckled. "No offense, but for a quick minute there, I might of hoped there was a meth lab or something out at your place. Special election's in a month. I gotta break a big case if I'm fixing to be elected sheriff."

"Real sorry I couldn't be more of a help, Morton."

ROBERT BUSBY · 237

Around three that afternoon, Noal finished prepping the exterior of the house for the storm: insulating the spigots, caulking where the windows let in drafts, dragging Jacqueline's ferns inside from what had otherwise been a mild winter. After he showered, he filled the tub with water in case a pipe burst and went around the house, leaving all the faucets dripping. On his way out to the cabin, he stopped at the Piggly Wiggly. Beneath the camper shell in the truck bed, he still had the two gallons of water and the propane tank and sack of supplies he'd gathered from the house yesterday. But if the storm actually made good on all these weathermen's omens, then who knew when the grocery store would be open again in time to drop off more food for Jacqueline.

Noal grabbed a cart from one of the corrals in the parking lot. Inside he weaved through the mass of folks hectic and eager to get home and holed up before the roads got bad. He collected the non-perishables first: another gallon of water, beef jerky, dried apricots and cranberries, pecans, almonds, canned soup, beans, beets, tomatoes, Jif peanut butter, jelly, wheat bread, bagels, paper towels, paper plates. But then he remembered the working gas stove and how Jacqueline would still be able to cook. So he set a carton of eggs and a few bags of Romaine into the buggy. A head of mustard greens, a green mesh of lemons, balsamic vinaigrette, another gallon tin of olive oil, a bag of rice, two Boston butts at the butcher, and a couple loaves of French bread in the bakery. On the pharmaceutical aisle he picked up a bottle of stool softener and some Miralax.

"Ever see anything like this?" the owner, George Kemp, yelled over the constant jingle of the handbell tied to the door hinge and the incessant chirping chorus of items scanned. George had turned old, had a turkey neck and jowls that hung from his gourd-shaped head. He'd hired Noal over twenty years ago as a bagger even before Noal was of legal age to work. Noal held the position through junior high and high school and some summers home from college. Noal watched a woman at the next lane unpack five cases of toilet paper from her buggy and four gallons of two-percent milk.

"Not since the last winter storm caused everyone to go batshit crazy. Do nothing but sit on the toilet and drink milk for three days straight."

George chuckled and rung up another item. "Good for business anyway. Heard Colonel's left us."

Noal nodded, not sure what shape the news had taken through the rumor mill of Bodock. But George didn't say anything else about it and got to examining a loaf of French bread, holding it up to Noal as if maybe he might not have known it was in the buggy. "We out of sandwich bread?"

"Not sure, George."

"Hell." After George looked toward the bakery aisle, he got on the PA and ordered someone to check. "Can't remember if we got another pallet in the back. Hope we do. Factories ain't even let out yet."

His old boss rolled the bottle of vinaigrette over the scanner, the glass clanking against the metal before George stood it with the rest of Noal's groceries. The grocery seemed short-staffed for the influx of shoppers so Noal shook out a paper bag, got to bagging groceries. He built a frame in the bag with the olive oil tin on one side, on the other side the peanut butter and jelly, the can of tomatoes, the Miralax. The bags of nuts, dried fruit, rice on the bottom. Lemons and eggs, loaf bread and lettuce toward the top. Started a new bag with the vinaigrette and cans of soup, beans, beets.

After a while, George said, "Well. Me and Dyanne, we still

praying for y'all."

Noal turned so he wouldn't have to look at the man when he told him he appreciated it. Maybe it was supposed to be a comfort, but all these sentiments ever accomplished now was to pull the memory of his boy and the reality of his absence from wherever Noal had compartmentalized it so he could keep busy until the finality of the day when he got drunk and numb and hopefully passed out before he had to face the truth of his dead son, alone like he did every night. But whose fault was that but his own? Noal looked out the large panes of glass streaked with rain at a parking lot gone blurry and packed with slow-moving cars ambling around pedestrians huddled beneath umbrellas slipping to and from the store. A dented minivan turned down the far end of the center lane of the lot, looking for a space. Heading away from the store was a woman with bags of groceries hooked on one arm and leading a young boy on the other. Beneath a light green umbrella, she wore red curls, a pair of high-waisted jeans, tennis shoes. A too-long leather bomber jacket that swayed against the shaggy blonde hair of the boy who came up to about her mid-thigh.

"That gonna be it, Noal? Hey, you aight, son?"

Noal shook from the trance, his gaze landing on George as the manager slid one Boston butt across the scanner where it bumped into the other shoulder which rested next to the gallon of water on the bagging platform. Noal wasn't sure what his old boss had asked him and looked back out at the lot. Through the wet glass the woman's movements seemed erratic, like she was treading over rocks on a riverbed. Noal was parked on that aisle and his mind fooled him for a moment into thinking they were heading for his truck. She stopped to dig in the purse on her shoulder for a set of keys. She had dropped the boy's hand but the boy had not moved from his mother's side in an obedience Dash had almost never demonstrated. Still, Noal could see the boy darting out into the lane. Out in front of the dented minivan distracted in its pursuit of a parking spot.

Noal tossed two twenties at the produce scale and grabbed a grocery bag and a loaf of French bread under one arm. He lurched down the lane, favoring his hip, keeping his hurting back straight as he could. The woman grabbed her son and pulled the boy against her leg, putting herself between her child and whoever this crazed man slipping toward them was.

"Get back," the woman yelled.

"Apologies," Noal said and held up his hands in surrender to the woman whose face was shocked with alarm. The driver of the minivan slowed to a stop and stared at Noal. Noal scowled at the driver. "Apologies. Sorry, ma'am. Didn't mean to scare your boy. Thought y'all was someone else."

Noal couldn't recall her name but, in a town this small, he recognized her. She furrowed her brow like she recognized him as well and then the shock in her face defused into something very near sympathy.

After she and her boy had climbed into their Taurus and reversed and pulled away, Noal stood holding his groceries there in the middle of the parking lot. Just getting wet. Embarrassed as hell. The minivan was still there waiting and it honked and the driver shrugged condescendingly at Noal. Noal flipped off the driver. The driver rolled down the window and pointed at the empty parking place.

"You're still in my way, bud."

After Noal slid the GMC out of the parking lot, he aimed down Oxford Street until it became Old Highway 6 and the store fronts surrendered to dense woods on either side of the road. At the haypatch, Noal parked on the end opposite the stand of pine and hardwood that hid the trail to the hollow and the cabin. The rain hung over the field in a mist. Small bits of ice peppered in now with the rain against the windshield, and his frustration in the parking lot had grown into an anxious urgency to deliver the groceries.

The sack of groceries sat on the driver's seat with a bottle of wine he'd pulled from the house. He opened the sack to see if there was room for the wine bottle and French bread in there and realized he'd only made it out with only one bag of groceries. He'd left the bag with the cans of soup and beets and vinaigrette still on the bagging station with the gallon water and the pork shoulders. He thought about going back but didn't feel up to showing his face after he'd made an ass of himself. Thought about what all he had at the house but he hadn't been to any grocery store for himself in months, instead purchasing his wares at gas stations late at night when the stores were less populated. He wouldn't have anything in the pantry but pork in a can and some hotdogs he would microwave and eat with white sandwich bread. Jacqueline always built a meal around a protein but he felt like she deserved better than any of what he could offer her.

The time was about five o'clock now. He'd missed lunch and his noon dose so he worked up some spit again, took a Vicodin, and tried to figure a plan to get her something before morning.

Around nine p.m., Noal finally saw movement across the field. A set of eyes hovering across the hay patch. The eyes would skip several times, cover twenty or thirty yards, then stop to oscillate in place, a deer just checking its surroundings, studying the strange metallic creature with four wheels in which Noal sat. Noal had already removed the .270 magnum from the rack behind him, slid out the bolt action, slipped a round from the buttstock shell holder into the chamber, and deposited three more cartridges into the magazine.

Noal couldn't see through the windshield where tiny webs of ice had already formed again from when he had last scraped the glass. So he rolled down the window without taking his eyes off the field and its quadruped inhabitant. He propped the rifle across his forearm and glassed the creature. In the scope saw the twitch of white tail like flame in a cave. He flicked off the safety but the deer launched off again, skipping toward the edge of the hay patch. Before it disappeared into the woods, the deer paused at the tree line and Noal switched on the spotlight mounted to the side mirror and watched the animal freeze just long enough for Noal to pull the animal into the sights, drape the crosshairs down the deer's flank, and squeeze the trigger, the barrel flinging fire into the darkness.

Noal shucked the spent shell from the .270 and pocketed the casing. Then he dropped the three cartridges from the magazine into his palm and filed them back into the shell holder, after which he cranked the truck and drove over to the animal. The buck was young. A spike. Noal had rushed the shot which had only broken the deer's shoulder but left it alive. The spike kicked its hind legs and grunted and slid across the cold ground. Noal fought against the memory of that late October night and, coming to in the cab a few moments after being knocked out cold from the collision, an alarm of horns still sounding on both vehicles, Dash's little body pinned between his and the steering wheel, not like the spike in some active death but already still, already lifeless, already slid on into the abyss or—when Noal could muster the optimism on better days—Heaven.

Noal opened the door and vomited that morning's biscuit then nothing but sour beer and bile and stomach acid onto the ground. The pool of sick breathed a cloud against the cold air as he stepped out into the falling sleet that rang heavy against the truck and the trees and the leaves that covered the ground this near the woods. Ice bit hard as BBs against his head. He carried the revolver to the deer and fired once into its lungs so as to ease the fear and panic that gleamed in the black holes of its eyes.

 After Noal holstered the Ruger, he grabbed the spike's hind legs, lifted it some, and guessed its weight at about ninety or a hundred pounds. He wasn't even fixing to fool with trying to get the animal on his shoulders. All he needed was to throw his back out. He walked to the gate of the cabin trail and dragged the cooler that stayed at the trailhead back to the truck, where he loaded the groceries, supplies, wine, and the gallons of water into the cooler. Also, he unpacked a tarp from the police kit in the back of his truck, closed the deer inside it, and ziptied some of the ringlets of the tarp together. Then he rigged the cooler into a sort of cargo sled by tying the tarped bundle to a handle of the cooler and securing the two tanks of propane onto the cooler with bungee cord from the truck. He tied a short length of rope to the free handle of the cooler, used the rope to drag the haul back to the gate where he removed the bodock fence post from its ground hole, drew the barbed wire to the other side of the path, and towed the cooler behind him.

 In front of the cabin, Noal kicked away rotting horse apples that had been deposited from the bois d'arc tree that autumn. Near the porch he left the stores he had dragged from the haypatch. The cabin windows held squares of light so that he figured Jacqueline was up or that this woman he had shared a dark bedroom with for the better part of a decade had taken to sleeping with a light on now. It'd been so long since he'd seen her. He didn't know who would answer the door and he feared most of the versions his mind conjured up now of the person he had married. The person he had turned her into. Before he could second guess being here, he dropped the rope and stepped up on the porch. He forgot about the floodlight that sparked on and he felt like that deer in the beam, his breath caught in his chest, some flight instinct, one last entertainment of the option to retreat except that his feet were nailed to the boards. He was here now. His exhaustion hit him. Inside was the red square of heat from the potbelly in the living room. A warm place to sleep.

He knocked on the door.

"Jacqueline, open up," Noal said. "It's me."

Felt like another two months standing there on the porch. He listened for movement inside, the creak of the floor, shoes against the wood. Her voice responding. But the storm drowned out everything.

Then his next worst fear flashed across his mind: that Jacqueline had been alive as recently as three days ago, when she moved the food and supplies he'd left at the gate on Sunday, but that she had sometime in the interim died. Noal scooped the keyring from his pocket while the possible causes of her death flickered across his psyche: either by her own hand or from natural causes or carbon monoxide poison or any of the other interminable ways a human life ends, all of them only ever as severe but never worse than the daily death of those that the dead leave behind.

Before he could single out the key to the cabin from the ring, the door cracked open to reveal a face between the door and the jamb. The face wore his old Pendleton hat and red curls fell from the faded felt against the fur coat taken from a black bear three generations of Clay ago. She stood silent for a long while, looking at him, and he wondered if she shared his disbelief at the space they occupied on the porch at that moment.

"Noal?" she said. She stood behind the opened door as if it were a shield so that the left half of her body was not seen, shaking her head as if in disbelief or trying to jog herself awake. Her sea-green eyes betrayed no anger, her thin lips stern but without emotion. "What are you doing here? I wasn't even certain if I heard knocking or not."

"Were you asleep?"

"What time is it?"

Noal read his watch. "Little after ten."

She shook her head. "What are you doing here?"

"Brought you some food."

"That doesn't tell me anything."

"Wanted to check on you. With this storm and all."

"I'm fine. Should I expect you back in another two months for the commencement of tornado season?"

"Jacqueline —"

She held up a hand. "Never mind. I don't want to have that talk yet."

Jacqueline had stepped from behind the door a little farther so that, when Noal glanced down, he saw in the grip of her other hand was the barrel of the twenty-two rifle, the buttstock resting on the floor. Noal thought again of what urgency had brought him here now: the deer, the Colonel, the storm. Tonight's deer. "There's something else we need to discuss."

"So you're coming inside then?"

He thought about what had kept him away: the wreck, the guilt, anger, shame. His neck. Concerns not as urgent as a storm or a crime but also more so.

"I've got to break down this deer first. Get it dressed before all the meat freezes."

"I'm still not even sure this is real. I'll make us some coffee. Maybe that will wake me up."

Noal cut the young buck free from the tarp. Steam rose from the two bullet holes in its flank where warm blood had pooled in the tarp. He stood still and settled his heavy breathing while the woods filled with falling glass. Slung over a low branch of the bois d'arc tree was a rope tied to a slender rod of iron rebar. The rebar was bent into a lazy W and hung about six feet from the ground, already sheened with a thin layer of ice, gyrating slightly on its tether. He squeezed the Maglite into the crook of his neck to illuminate the surgery. With a knife from his pocket, he made an incision between the two bones just above the knee joint of the animal's hind legs through which he threaded the rebar, hoisted the animal up, and tied the rope off around the tree trunk.

He'd been wearing gloves but folded the pair into a back pocket so he could feel the knife and the cuts and not screw up the meat. First, he made an incision through the hide of the animal from its hind legs to its rib cage and cut open its belly and felt the last vestiges of trapped warmth leaving the buck as he pulled its intestines out onto the ground. He lacked a hacksaw so he skinned the deer from its hind quarters down to its neck and had finished jerking and slicing the skin away from the fat and muscle when he heard the cabin door open again.

Jacqueline charging at him with the rifle.

"Whoa whoa," Noal said. He left the thick skin hanging over the spike's head like a hood. About ten feet from him, Jacqueline shouldered the twenty-two and got a good aim on him. From the porch light the blue denim of her leg leapt from the black fur of the coat. Her jeans were tucked into some green galoshes that he recognized had belonged to his granny.

"Where's your truck?" she asked.

"Lower the gun, Jacqueline."

"Your truck. Where is it?"

"Parked in the haypatch."

"Where are your keys?"

"In my pocket."

"Which one?"

She was pale-faced and freckled, so beautiful and stern and her dark eyes deep with grief and worry. He could see the crows' feet that seemed to have grown longer, stretching to her temples. "I ain't leaving, Jacqueline."

"What pocket are they in?"

Noal told her the left one. She removed the keys from his vest, stuck them in her back jeans pocket, and swung the small-game rifle at the bounty of the cooler in the yard. "That going inside?"

"I can get it when I'm done."

But Jacqueline was already hauling the cooler over to the porch. They each got a handle and lifted the cooler onto the creaking floorboards. "I'm ready for you to be done," she said.

"We ain't got anything else to eat," Noal said. "There ain't meat in that cooler. This storm's may end up bad too. Not sure we'll be able to get anything from the grocery store for a few days."

"How about I just stay outside here with you then."

"You'll freeze."

"Then I guess you better make it quick."

Noal released the propane tanks and looped the bungee cords through a handle of the cooler then returned to the deer. He'd planned to rough-bone the whole deer, let it age in the refrigerator, but he figured that could wait. He needed to remove the tenderloins first before they dried out in the air so while Jacqueline unloaded the cooler, he spun the animal until its back faced him and sliced along either side of the backbone to the top of its ribs and removed the backstrap by teasing the muscle away from the bone as he sliced. Then he butterflied the loin and stacked the cuts of venison in the refrigerator on the porch, pulled the deer higher toward the limb, and tied the pulley off again so no coyotes nor, in the unlikelihood that Whit was right about one damn thing for once, any other predators could get at it.

Inside he kicked off his boots. The cabin still had power for now: the small kitchen was lit and the only light in the living area a lamp that stood at the end of the leather couch. Much of the rest of the 700-square-foot abode hid in shadows. A couch, two rockers, and a circular wood coffee table huddled around a rug of Navajo design, all diamonds and stripes and shades of red. On the coffee table stood a stack of books that Noal had to move closer to see in the dim light: Foote's *Civil War* trilogy and his paperback *Shiloh* and all the Bronte clan. The baptismal Bible of his grandfather's opened to Ecclesiastes. He spotted a field guide, *All the Birds of North America*, Ormond's *Complete Book of Hunting*, and *Guide to Taxidermy* by Charles K. Reed, the last two reminding him again of the Colonel and yesterday's deer. Several yoga manuals and Jacqueline's mat beneath the coffee table, bungee cords holding its roll. An old Boys Scout manual and a Sears catalog from 1972. Several issues of *Gray's Sporting Journal* from the 1960s and all of last year's editions of *Bon Appetit*, including the ones that had continued to be mailed to the house, which he'd forwarded to her in the weekly stack of groceries and supplies.

Jacqueline had retreated into the kitchen and came out with a white tin cup.

"You read all these?"

"No. I had the time to though."

Noal wondered what all she'd been up to out here but he couldn't word the question so that it didn't feel foolish or naïve or inappropriate. She handed him the tin cup, the tail of a tea bag fluttering along its side.

"Thought it might be too late for coffee," she said.

"This is good," Noal said.

"I can still fix you a cup if you want."

"That's all right," Noal said. He'd never been much for hot tea but he took the mug in both hands, let his palms warm from working the cold meat. Steam breathed a fog over his glasses when he drank. "It's pretty good."

"It's chai," she said. "You bought it."

Jacqueline watched him drink. She had taken off the coat and hung her hands in the back pockets of her jeans, her arms angled at the elbows like wings.

"What?" he asked her.

"I just can't believe you're here," she said. "Or anyone's here. Do I sound different? I feel like I sound different now that there's someone else here to hear me speak. Are you okay, Noal?"

"Are you?"

She shrugged. "No. I don't know."

Noal didn't know what to say to that. Sleet beat against the aluminum roof and filled the cabin with white noise like from the machine that had helped Dash sleep. She stutter-started a couple of times to say something but never broke through the drone of the storm or, if her mind was like Noal's at that moment, the flood of thoughts. Which questions to ask or reserve for later. After a few sips he set the mug on the chest next to the door, a smear of deer blood on the white tin. He'd drawn up his sleeves but the cuffs of the hoodie were wet with blood as was the vest he wore over the hoodie.

Jacqueline moved to hug him.

"I'm nasty," he said but still she came forward. "I got blood all over me. You're fixing to get it on you."

"I don't care," she said. She wrapped her arms around his waist and he angled himself so that her head went to the side of his neck without the scar and he reckoned how long he could keep that gig up. When she let him go, she said she was going to clean up and retreated to the kitchen. Noal hung the vest then the hoodie on separate spare pegs on the coat rack on the wall but kept on the camouflage turtleneck. In the bathroom he ran a cold bath he had no intention of getting into, the tub just a reserve of water in case the pipes burst out here. Over the sink, he scrubbed his bloody hands clean, using some rubbing alcohol in the medicine cabinet to remove what the Dial bar couldn't and winced at a cut or scrape somewhere on his hand that he didn't know he had. He left the faucet dripping and the cabinets opened and, back in the single living area, squatted in front of the potbelly just outside the bathroom, rubbing his hands together nearly against the round iron side to get them warm and dry. He heard Jacqueline still cleaning up and from that vantage could just see her in the kitchen.

He reminded her to leave the water dripping in there.

"You didn't need to hike all this way to tell me that."

Noal smirked and shook his head and his hands prickled and

itched as they warmed. He stood, knees and ankles popping as he straightened from his squat. Finally still enough to acknowledge the ache in his back. He could go for a third dose of Vicodin but a quick search of both the vest and hoodie pockets confirmed that he'd left the bottle in the truck. He wouldn't ask her for his keys back so he'd have to make do until morning. He stretched his back and walked the tightness out around the room again, searching out other evidence of how Jacqueline had passed her time out here. Trying to reassure himself that she'd been okay in the cabin alone for so long.

"Did you work today?"

"Nah," Noal said. "I was, uh, off duty."

In the far corner of the room, opposite the potbelly, he saw something hanging from the wall. What looked like strange T-shirts or even small, dark onesies. He removed the small Maglite from his vest on the coat rack and moved over to the wall to inspect. Found not clothing but a few squirrel pelts and exactly one rabbit pelt nailed to the wall. Beneath the affixed skins was a wooden drying rack used for linens that had been folded out and which held a couple more fresh rabbit skins hung hair-side up on the rungs to dry out. Each skin retained its original contour, precise and reminiscent of the creature that had worn it.

Jacqueline said, "Work's going well though?"

Noal shrugged. "This is new," he said, pointing at what could pass for some pagan shrine.

"The tannery," Jacqueline said. "I had the idea from a game recipe book I found inscribed to your granny." Noal knew the one, a collection his grandfather and the men in his hunting camp had put together of recipes of their own devices or, more commonly, that had derived from their wives. "I set out to try out all the recipes except for the congealed quail-or-insert-other-meat salad. I've cooked a bunch of them and guess I became pretty good with the twenty-two rifle in the process. But I figured, with all the rabbit and squirrel, why not try my hand at tanning."

Noal rubbed the back of his hand along a squirrel pelt. The fur felt like a horsehair brush. He was reminded of when he first discovered Jacqueline at the cabin two months ago. But this wasn't madness, not of the variety that categorized those same desperate attempts she'd made at processing small game in order to procure food or even coming out here without telling anyone. It was the task-directed obsession of solitude. The madness of a craftsman in retreat, meticulously honing a skill. Were there so many hours in a day that given the space and solitude one could become a master of all things? What else was she to use her time for. How else to fill her days. Maybe she'd just been better than he'd been at speeding up the minutes of a day until they collected into hours that concluded one more planetary rotation closer to slipping off into the long sleep where memory couldn't follow. He was getting carried away and moved back to an earlier realization: the deer in the haypatch two days ago didn't look nearly as professionally done as these. But maybe it had been her first attempt at skinning game as large as a deer.

"A lot of venison dishes in that book," Noal said.

"I haven't had a chance to try those yet."

"But you've tried hunting deer?"

"Noal," Jacqueline said, standing now in the entryway to the kitchen on the opposite end of the cabin, which shared a wall as the bathroom. "I'm glad you're here but I'm ready for bed. We can talk tomorrow."

Jacqueline insisted on taking the couch. Said it was where she'd been sleeping anyway. That the loft trapped heat but got too cold once the fire died. So Noal climbed up there. The space didn't allow the height to stand so he had a time getting out of his clothes. The mattress, stretched from wall to wall, left no room for a nightstand, so he placed his glasses beneath a pillow and settled into the rough sheets that crinkled every loud inch his body moved.

Not three feet above his head, ice spat like machine gun fire against the aluminum roof. He was still awake an hour later when the power went out, and he could feel the sudden absence of electricity in the cabin, the silence of the refrigerator when it quit humming, the red digits vanishing from the face of the digital clock on a shelf braced between two roof beams in the loft.

And he wondered what it was he was doing here.

What sounded like a gunshot had woken Noal ten minutes earlier, after which he'd heard Jacqueline downstairs, moving in and out of the cabin, and last night had come back to him like the afterimage of a television screen. Now, wrapped beneath the quilted comforter, the heat of the potbelly that had risen and gathered in the loft overnight pushed away now by the invasion of a cold draft allowed in by the neglected fire, he sat cross-legged in bed facing out the singular circular window where every tree framed there shimmered in a glaze of ice. The whole woods seemed to droop beneath the weight of it. Each broken branch released in a crisp sharp note that splintered the woods, leaving its exposed pulp stark against all that white and gray and another orphaned limb scattered in the holler.

He climbed down out of the loft. Jacqueline was in the kitchen, but if she heard him moving about, she didn't acknowledge. She was standing at the gas range, a gargantuan brown Western Holly they'd removed from the house and stored out at the cabin during renovation. Noal had drilled two holes beneath the kitchen window and run a flexible gas line through each hole, one from the oven, one from the stove, to a pair of twenty-pound propane tanks that sat beneath the window outside. One of the stove eyes licked its blue flame against his granny's old skillet that already had fifty years of seasoning on it before Noal inherited it. Grease popped in the skillet beneath one of the venison tenderloins he'd harvested last night and water boiled in a nearby saucepan.

"Jacqueline?"

His wife jumped and, when she spun around, almost slung hot grease at him.

"Shit. You startled me."

"Sorry."

"It's okay." She stood looking for words. "It's been a while since I've heard someone else but myself speak in here."

Another pop of grease beneath the tenderloin that turned her attention back to the stove. She had on a pair of red ski socks over a pair of gray ones and the hem of the fisherman's sweater caught on a red toboggan hanging out the back pocket of her high-waist jeans. She glanced at her watch. "I thought you'd sleep later."

"You didn't hear me climbing down the ladder?"

"This cabin's always making noises." With a pair of tongs, she lifted the tenderloin and settled it on a plate layered with a paper towel. Then she looked between the plate and the skillet. "Apparently it's been a while since I cooked for anyone but myself either."

"That's all right."

"We can split it. I'll fry up a couple extra eggs."

Noal shrugged in agreement. "I can make us some coffee."

Jacqueline pointed at the saucepan already boiling water. "But add some more grounds to the press. I really don't know what I was thinking this morning. I mean, I knew you were lying up there in bed. But down here it just felt like a dream I'd had."

Noal added two scoops of grounds to the measurement in the French press and worked his way around her at the stove to shut off the eye below the saucepan of boiling water. He poured the water into the French press and then didn't know where to set the contraption so he wrapped a kitchen towel around the glass and held the press while the coffee steeped. Jacqueline cracked two eggs directly into the still-hot skillet, the egg whites cracking and quivering as they seared. The way she managed this kitchen, a million things going at once, reminded of the first time they met, back when she was tending bar at Murphy's in Midtown. He'd just graduated from the academy, barhopping and celebrating with his fellow recruits and had returned to Murphy's the next day at happy hour under the pretense of administering some hair of the dog but mostly hoping that he'd catch the curly, red-haired bartender he had only a hazy recollection of the night before. Her khaki safari shorts that afternoon squeezed pale legs for days as she popped longneck caps, poured drinks, whipped wisecracks right back at the hipsters and old sly perverts huddled around the bar. She recommended the sausage-and-cheese plate and Noal ordered it every day for a week, even coming in on his first few nights before he went on patrol during the twelve-to-eight graveyard in Binghampton, ordering a Dr. Pepper on those nights instead of bourbon or Pabsts until she finally asked him if he was planning a coronary or just hadn't worn out yet on casings of meat fat and sodium nitrate and processed cheese, Noal only able to offer what she'd later describe as his signature shy smirk, saying Nah to either question. So she asked him to help her close up. He didn't have a shift later so he was nursing a Pabst and told her yes. That was August and hot. Beads of sweat erupted like ripe transparent cotton bulbs around her neck and chest, gleaming there on her pale, freckled cleavage between the straps of her white tanktop.

You're a shitty stalker, she'd said later at her apartment.

Noal said he'd have to get MPD to teach him how to tail folks better.

What if I don't want you tailing anyone but me?

They were both twenty-three, Jacqueline having graduated from Rhodes College that May, and they moved in together two months after they met. Married seven months later on the beach behind her parents' place on Dauphin Island. Honeymooned there too and for six years gave themselves enough time to solve the equation of their shared selves before they invited Dash along for the ride. They'd made a good team, calling each other on their bullshit, most of the time with purpose, occasionally recklessly, Jacqueline always quicker to apologize than Noal and not always patient, but still extending more patience than he probably deserved, waiting for him to humble himself enough to offer an apology. In law enforcement terms, he felt he'd hit the lottery with the partner he'd been assigned by God or some other chief of fate. Left to his own devices he wasn't sure he would've had the judiciousness to see on the front end that there was no one better for him than Jacqueline to share a life, raise a human, make himself a better person. At Murphy's, he'd just thought she was hot. All that curled fire and freckles.

Before these last five months, they'd never been apart more than a few nights in their nine years of marriage. He feared the crashing of the fledgling heaven—or the illusion of some heaven no longer available to them—that was this moment in their kitchen in the middle of the woods.

Jacqueline dripped some water into the hot skillet. The water hissed and steamed and she caught the steam beneath a lid that she covered the skillet with to cook the tops of the four eggs. While she finished up, Noal found a clean pair of jeans and long johns in a dresser in the living room and carried the clothes into the bathroom where the slope of his hot piss steamed until it met the cold stagnant water. He turned and sat on the toilet for a minute but didn't have much success so he flushed, shed the turtleneck, and put on the base layers before pulling on the turtleneck again and the jeans. He rinsed his glasses in the sink under water pushed from pipes that he was relieved hadn't burst during the night. Dried the lenses with some toilet paper and took the roll with him to the potbelly stove, where he dug his pocket knife out of the dirty jeans on the floor and shaved some kindling from a log of firewood piled next to the potbelly. With the poker he dug a hole in the gray ash until he found a shimmer of red coals. Loosened a wad of toilet paper from the roll, built a shelter of firewood above the combustion, and stoked the coals back to life.

The plate Jacqueline brought to him held half a fried tenderloin, two eggs with wobbly yellow yolks dotted with hot sauce, and a slice of toast carrying a soft pat of butter melting into a poured grid of Amish molasses. He told her it looked like a cover of Bon Appetit. He took a bite and said it was as good as it looked and, as he chewed, glanced around the room, his gaze settling again over in the far corner of the cabin, behind the door where the skins of squirrel and rabbit hung from the wall or lay drying and salted on the folding linen drying rack. No sun broke through the clouds outside but in the haze of morning the corner tannery didn't look quite as much like some pagan or Old Testament altar as it had in the firelight the night before.

He pointed at the skins and said, "You ever tried stuffing em?"

"Once," Jacqueline said. "Found some wire hangers in the closet to mold into the shape of a squirrel. It came out pretty grotesque. Horrendous, even. Nightmare fuel. I'm not there yet. I still need to get the tanning down."

"Can I see this deformed squirrel?"

"No," Jacqueline said.

"Why not?"

"I buried it." Jacqueline gestured her fork at him. "Let's talk about when this happened."

"When what happened?"

Jacqueline turned the fork on herself, waving it in a circle that encompassed her face and neck. "This Grizzly Adams–meets–redneck-art-critic thing you've got going on."

"Um. Fashion statement, I guess."

"Where'd you even get a turtleneck?"

Noal gulped some coffee and aimed his gaze downwards. On the chest of the camo shirt, he saw a Carhartt logo, a brand Faxon Feed carried, so he told her there.

"I say keep the beard, lose the turtleneck."

"Maybe when the weather warms up."

"Can you trade the turtleneck for a scarf then?"

"Don't know that they make em in camouflage."

"That's not a bad thing."

One of the logs in the potbelly popped as it released a pocket of hot moisture. Noal's shoulders jumped slightly. The steady moan of the aching, ice-slick woods and the crack of limbs filled the cabin and Noal changed the subject. "I was out here Tuesday morning. Colonel Gardner died hunting out there."

"The man who owned all the land around here?"

Noal nodded, mouth full. "Someone called it in. Found him dead on the edge of the haypatch out there. Just hanging out in his tree stand."

"That's not funny. That's awful. Does he have any family?"

"Widower."

"What about children?" Noal shook his head at her. "Extended family?"

"Not sure."

"Who's going to his funeral then?"

Noal shrugged. "I don't know, Jacqueline. I know that I'm probably not going." He sipped some coffee and had thought that just by mentioning the Colonel she would admit that she had called it in. When she hadn't, he dug the fresh pack of Vantages from his pocket, shook out a smoke from the tight formation of filters, and lit the cigarette. "Did you know about it?"

"Did I know about what?"

"The Colonel being dead out there."

"How would I've known that, Noal?"

He tried a different tactic. "There was a deer about a hundred yards from where the Colonel died. Looked like it had been shot and then some coyotes got hold of it. The Colonel hadn't shot the deer, so the deer might've been shot somewhere else by someone else and whoever shot it didn't dress it clean."

"That's bizarre."

"No shit." He pulled on his coffee that had gone lukewarm now and, taking a deep breath, topped the cup off and continued. "That .22 mag I taught you to shoot with. It ain't got a shit-ton of stopping power. Unless you knew what you was doing, you shoot a deer with it, the deer ain't gonna just drop. Best case scenario it's gonna keep running until it gives out or bleeds out."

Jacqueline furrowed her brow then nodded in acknowledgement.

"You think I shot a deer and followed it to the field where I saw the Colonel in a tree stand."

Noal pointed to her collection of pelts in the corner. "I don't think that's so far out of left field."

It was Jacqueline's turn to laugh at the absurdity of the accusation. "And when he didn't respond to my salutations, I deduced that he had died. And I left without reporting any of it?"

"No. Someone called in anonymously saying they'd seen the body from the road."

Jacqueline gave him a bemused smirk. "Where would I have called from, Noal?"

"I dunno. Walked to a neighbor's or the store or something. Thaxton P.O. is about three miles from here."

Jacqueline forced a laugh. "If you knew just how fucking impossible for me that really was, Noal."

"What're you talking about?"

"Noal. I can't." Jacqueline shook her head. She looked off at a wall of the cabin, one of her hands gripping the side of the table. "I've tried to bring myself to leave this place."

"You could've just come home."

"I know, Noal. I tried."

"How fuckin so, Jacqueline?"

Jacqueline reached across the table for the French press wrapped in a towel and topped off her coffee mug. Then she pointed at the pack of Vantages, which Noal slid down the length of the table. He hadn't seen her smoke since she got pregnant with Dash, a couple days maybe before she met Noal in the stairwell of their apartment unit at dawn, the double lines of the pregnancy test in a Ziploc bag. But she harvested a cigarette from the pack and slid it back down the table like they were enjoying some shuffleboard at a dive bar on the moon. The pregnancy had come near the holidays, and Jacqueline had gotten him the pipe as a Christmas present to help him quit. He obliged her at home but still smoked on patrol to avoid all the Sherlock Holmes jokes, though he hadn't even made detective yet. Noal was about to slide the blue lighter at her, but Jacqueline was already dipping the end of hers into the candle flame.

"I got close, Noal. All the way to our street. Right out in front. I'd taken a Greyhound up from Natchez to Tupelo one afternoon because I didn't want you to be alone at Christmas. I called a taxi to drive me from the station to Bodock. We got to our neighborhood around dusk, after dinner, but as we were passing down our street I saw our neighbors, that older couple, the Tutors, walking their preposterously gargantuan Akita. I'd forgotten or just hadn't thought about them doing that every evening like clockwork and I became afraid they'd see me. I panicked and told the driver to take me back to Tupelo. When we made it there, I got worried I had nowhere to go so I just blurted for him to take me to that Kroger on Main and Gloster, the one with the liquor store next door, and that's when I'd had the idea to go to the cabin and wait for you there. I tried to call the house and let it ring probably thirty times but you weren't answering. I don't know why, it's so stupid, but I was so worried about inconveniencing the fucking taxi driver. So I paid him to wait while I shopped for groceries and two cases of Wild Turkey and had to convince him it was safe to drop me off on a pitch-black road all the way out in Claygardner County. He offered to help me carry my luggage and things but I paid him to go on his way. He insisted I take a flashlight he had in the trunk, which I was grateful for. That was on, like, a Monday, I think. I had enough food to get me to the weekend. You usually came out here on the weekend, even just to check on things, and I definitely thought you might've hunted on

Saturday morning like you usually did on Christmas Eve. But you didn't. Not for three weeks. I ran out of food."

Noal tapped his cigarette ash onto his plate. Thought about her out here alone, that hunger and not knowing what if any day would be the end to that isolation, waiting on him without any idea when or if he would show up.

"So you was right there though," Noal said. "On our street. You could've just waited for the Tutors to pass, right? You could've sprinted up to the door."

"I freaked out," Jacqueline said. "I had a panic attack right there in the taxi. On our street. Cold sweat, chills. Clammy skin. Nausea. Feeling the need to escape but unable to. It was everything I could do not to vomit in the backseat. The driver wanted to take me to the hospital."

"You been having panic attacks?"

"Not out here as much." Jacqueline ashed around the saucer holding the candle and raked a hand through her red curls. "When I saw the Tutors that evening. I realized what it would mean to come back here where people knew me. Even out here the thought of stepping off the property where someone I know or someone who knows me because they know you might see me. The last thing I wanted was to be the recipient of one more person's thoughts or prayers or telephone calls inquiring about how I was holding up, as if you ever find your legs under something like this. All I wanted was for God to fucking give us our child back. And this was the last place Dash was before He took him."

Jacqueline pulled on the Vantage and in the dim light the orb of its coals grew like a bulb receiving a sudden surge of power. A star gearing up to implode and die. "I'm sorry I left you behind. And I'm sorry I didn't think through getting out here and not being able to communicate with you. But once I'd gotten out here, I never thought you'd go to such lengths to avoid me."

"What lengths was those?"

"Ringing that damn bell at random times," Jacqueline said, bracing the saucer with one hand while she stubbed out her cigarette, "so I'd never be at that gate waiting when you got there."

Noal chewed his lip on that and then after a while stood and flicked his cigarette into the potbelly where he crouched and gritted his teeth against his lower back and added a log and stoked the fire. Rearranged the wood so the fire grew, just killing time because it was time.

Then he stood and walked to Jacqueline and took a knee at her chair. "I need to show you something, why I waited so long to come out here."

He peeled the camouflage turtleneck over his head and brushed his beard away from his jaw and pulled the candle on the table closer so she could see his jaw in the dimly lit cabin and waited as her recognition turned to realization and then understanding. Her fist shot to her mouth in shock. Tears glazed her eyes.

"Oh my God, Noal," she said. "You hanged yourself."

"I tried to."

"No, you did. When?"

"Before I knew you was here."

"But after I left you."

Noal shook his head. "It was a long while after you left. After I showed up shitfaced to a crime scene."

Noal told her how he got started drinking early one afternoon and didn't stop until he'd blacked out. Woke up slumped over the dining room table and his badge number being called over the scanner. The call regarded a domestic disturbance, some dude holed up in his laundry room, sitting on the dryer with a shotgun and ranting about how he'd pop off his wife's whole family if they tried to come through the door.

"The call itself was real, but TPD wouldn't have called me over the scanner. Not while I was off-duty. Especially not using my badge number. I mean, they got our phone number. Turned out I was at the end of a dream and the coordinates, the street number, just happened to be the last three numbers of my badge.

"I didn't even know what time it was. It was dark, knew that much. Ended up being closer to morning. I was in a panic and left half-dressed and fighting the urge to take a piss. I lost that battle on the way there. Got a good stream going in a half empty Dr. Pepper bottle. Should've poured it out first cause I filled the bottle up quick. Couldn't shut off the valve once it got started and sprayed piss all over the cab of the truck. Some of it got into the steering wheel and short-circuited the horn so that it wouldn't stop honking even after I pulled up to the crime scene. I popped the hood and yanked the wire from the horn to the battery. Forgot I'd pissed myself so there I was standing in front of—"

Noal waited for Jacqueline to press him, but she withheld questions so he continued. The first morning of his suspension he sat down at the dining room table with the last good bottle of bourbon in their cabinet. The dining room had a sliding glass door that opened up to the patio, and from there Noal could see the old basketball goal looming in the backyard. He went and hunted the only rope they had in the house, a nylon fish stringer that he set on the table, and by the next morning he'd drank himself around to the idea of finally just gathering the will already to slip on off into that long unconscious. Not exist for the rest of forever.

"The nylon dug, like, all its serrated fibers into my neck. But that backboard's all rotted wood, so eventually the rim of the basketball goal broke off. When my legs hit the ground, I blacked out from the jolt of pain that fired straight up my back." Noal lit another Vantage but he was short-breathed and found himself unable to inhale. "A while later Carol dropped by and found me there. It was obvious what'd happened. I'd kicked the patio chair out a few yards away and that busted chunk of gray wood bolted to the orange rim was still anchored to the noose around my neck."

They sat in silence. Only the echoes of the forest breaking on top of itself.

"Does it hurt?" Jacqueline asked. When Noal shook his head, she asked, "Can I touch it?"

Noal nodded and let Jacqueline run her finger tips across the wound still healing into scar tissue. She stifled a gasp and tears gleamed in her eyes.

"I'm so sorry I wasn't there to stop you."

"I dunno that you could've. We both know why I did it."

"I'm sorry I wasn't there to find you then." She sipped from her coffee mug. It was close to noon now. "I don't mean to get hung up on this detail, but were you and Carol—"

Noal shook his head. "She was just dropping off some casseroles."

"And casseroles aren't a euphemism for anything?"

"Just Vicodin," Noal said, and when Jacqueline looked perplexed, he added: "Carol's been supplying me. She only gives me a two-day supply at a time. So I'd see her two or three times a week but only because the doctor wouldn't prescribe any more Percocet." Noal chuckled weakly before he said, "And it ain't like we got insurance now anyway."

A little later, Noal stood nude in the bathroom, only a towel covering him as he watched the cold water drain down the builder's-grade tub he had moved from their house out to the cabin. He had spliced the plumbing from the shared wall of the kitchen to the faucet head when they first moved back to Bodock so they could have a full bathroom whenever they stayed for a weekend. When the level reached about four inches high, he closed the drain again. Jacqueline heard the water stop and pushed through the open bathroom door holding a stew pot of steaming water at both handles with ski gloves. Steam grew into a cloud over the tub as she poured in the boiling water. Noal didn't check the temperature but stepped on in.

"Is that good?"

"Think so," Noal said, easing all the way down into the lukewarm water.

The only light in the room was the kerosene lantern that sat in the sink basin. The mirrored medicine cabinet stretched the short flame so that it lit the small room in dull illumination.

"I'll just be in here then."

"All right."

She left the door ajar. Noal laid his back against the frigid plastic of the tub, his head against the walls of rough-hewn timber. He soaked a bath cloth and wrung some water out before draping the cloth over his face. Listened to the faucet drip from its drooping snout. Earlier, he and Jacqueline had walked to his truck to retrieve the Vicodin he'd left there. He'd taken one immediately and felt better for a while but now he could feel the pain seeping back to the surface like something toxic rising from the ground.

Now that he'd confessed, he realized he was foolish to think that its discovery was anything but inevitable. Of course the revelation would break her heart. But it wouldn't drive her away. And in that truth his fear hadn't disappeared so much as become clearer. He lay in the quickly cooling bath as all the daily, devastating intimacies of sharing a life with someone after such profound loss confronted him. The scar on his neck was just an excuse, a mask he covered the truth with. He would have to be some kind of goddamn audacious to assume he could ever touch another human being he loved, knowing the last person he'd held, a boy with shaggy blonde hair and straight teeth spread even-gapped in his big goofy grin and blue eyes that absorbed the whole world and a curiosity that had driven Noal crazy with love and admiration and interminable questions. Why is the sky blue and Why are trees big and Where do we come from and What is heaven and wind and love. Noal, reckoning his own inadequacies as a parent, had tried to explain things that couldn't be seen to a four-year-old who'd inherited his own stubbornness and Jacqueline's repudiation for bullshit and nonanswers, a growing kid who took Noal's breath away in general and especially when Dash would straddle him, share all his weight on Noal's chest while Noal performed crunches. Everything was a game then. Dash reigning his mare, Noaly, while herding cattle across the Colorado River. Peg-legged Dash steering his pirate vessel, The Noal, through warm Bahamian waters. Dashius Clay pinning Nefarious Noal for the three-count and the WWF Heavyweight belt. Or, as it had been that last night under this roof, Dash Clay, Winston Cup Champion, speeding his Chevy Noal around the last lap at Talladega, two car lengths ahead of the pack. And now how could Noal have ever thought he could return to Jacqueline when the last person he'd embraced had slipped from his grip, cracked the windshield with his beautiful head, and lay between Noal and the steering wheel like only the limp shell of a boy could.

As if waking from a nightmare, Noal jerked the cloth from his face and gasped in terror.

"I'm sorry, Noal," Jacqueline said, swinging a chair into the bathroom. She'd filled a wine glass and sat in the chair at the foot of the tub. "I didn't mean to startle you so badly."

"Wasn't you," Noal said, almost hyperventilating. "I, uh, just jerked awake. I guess I drifted off."

Jacqueline pointed as his throat. "Was this the only time you tried to kill yourself?"

Noal nodded.

"So I don't need to sit in here with you to make sure."

"Make sure what?"

"People slit their wrists in the bathtub."

"I ain't gonna slit my wrists."

"How do I know that?"

"Cause I wouldn't do that on your watch, Jacq."

Jacqueline drank some wine. "Can I sit in here anyway?"

Noal nodded yes and returned the cloth to his face and reached for Jacqueline's hand. They didn't say anything. Outside had become silent, as if the forest had found rest. Noal remembered about the deer and the Colonel and thought to ask Jacqueline once more but decided it was a problem for a world well beyond their present one.

After a little while longer he said, "This is kind of weird. You want to get in at least?"

Jacqueline chuckled sadly. "I need to confess something first."

Noal lifted a corner of the cloth again to see his wife. "All right."

Jacqueline had to gulp half her malbec before the words poured out. "I did hate you after the accident. Even before you told me what really happened. I just couldn't trust a world where events of such magnitude could be so random, where a freak accident could take Dash away. So I blamed you and let you be the reason for—for my resentment."

She had set her wine glass down on the shag rug and the glass tipped red wine onto the purple material when Jacqueline spilled out of the chair to her knees next to the tub. She grabbed Noal in a fierce embrace, wrested him to her, her thick sweater absorbing the wet from his skin. She sobbed then pulled away, cupped Noal's face in her hands, her fingers threading his beard and her thumb rubbing along the length of the scar.

"I almost killed you," she said.

"Jacqueline—"

"Stop. Whatever happened, I don't blame you for it. It was the other car's fault. The other fucking driver and his wife and even God deserves blame and I will spend the rest of my life getting you to understand that if that's what it takes for you not to try, to try, to not try to kill yourself again, Noal. But even when I hated you, I never stopped loving you. Can you tell me you believe that?"

Noal glanced at her big blue eyes which glistened with earnest alarm for her words to be true. For the words to be accepted as truth now, whether they had been or not. And Noal reckoned it didn't matter if the words were or weren't true before this exact moment. Who was he to determine such things. Noal only cared that her words were true now and to acknowledge them as such so that they became truth in this moment. So that the words would become are true even if they'd never been were true.

All he wanted besides what he couldn't have back was to feel forgiven. Short of that, he would take the here and now, his hand in his wife's, safe together while they waited for the world to thaw.

NOTES

"Mistletoe" in *Arkansas Review*
"Fraternal Twins" in *PANK*
"Seasonus Exodus" in *Flash! Writing the Very Short Story (Norton)*
"Bodock, 1816–1834" in *Real South/West*
"The Parable of the Lung" (as "Anglers of the Keep") in *Mississippi Noir* (Akashic)
"Stubborn as a Fence Post" (as "The Agony of Bo Rutherford") in *Stymie*
"Heartworms" in *Hard to Find: An Anthology of New Southern Gothic* (Stephen F. Austin University Press)
"Frison the Bison" in *Sou'wester*
"Twenty Mile" in *Footnote* 4 (Alternating Current Press)
"Offerings" (as "The Bear Wife") in *Cold Mountain Review*

— C. MICHAEL CURTIS —
SHORT STORY BOOK PRIZE

THE C. MICHAEL CURTIS SHORT STORY BOOK PRIZE includes $5000 and book publication. The prize is named in honor of C. Michael Curtis, who has served as an editor of *The Atlantic* since 1963 and as fiction editor since 1982. This prize is made possible by an anonymous contribution from a South Carolina donor. The namesake of the prize, C. Michael Curtis, has discovered or edited some of the finest short story writers of the modern era, including Tobias Wolff, Joyce Carol Oates, John Updike, and Anne Beattie.

RECENT WINNERS

The Great American Everything • Scott Gloden (2023)

We Imagined It Was Rain • Andrew Siegrist (2021)

Sleepovers • Ashleigh Bryant Phillips (2020)

Let Me Out Here • Emily W. Pease (2019)

HUB CITY PRESS

PUBLISHING
New & Extraordinary
VOICES FROM THE
AMERICAN SOUTH

HUB CITY PRESS has emerged as the South's premier independent literary press. Focused on finding and spotlighting new and extraordinary voices from the American South, the press has published over one-hundred high-caliber literary works. Hub City is interested in books with a strong sense of place and is committed to introducing a diverse roster of lesser-heard Southern voices. We are funded by the National Endowment for the Arts, the South Carolina Arts Commission and hundreds of donors across the Carolinas.

RECENT HUB CITY PRESS FICTION

The Crocodile Bride • Ashleigh Bell Petersen

Child in the Valley • Gordy Sauer

The Parted Earth • Anjali Enjeti